THE BIRTH OF A HUMAN

Fox Hotel

Susie Choi

세레나북스
Serena Books

세레나북스
Serena Books

Serena Books

Busan, South Korea

serenabooks@naver.com

This book was created using Verdana, Edwardian Script ITC, Lucida Handwriting, tvN Fun Story fonts.

ISBN 979-11-986635-2-8(43810)

Thanks to: Mom, Dad,

and my editor & illustrator,

for all their help & support.

Contents

Characters

John: [Human] The first human being created by Ron and Ben. Although he is a human, his foxlike long lifespan and mindset made him something of a 'failure' or 'monster' to his creators, who loathe him. He is always questioning his identity, and even after he knows the truth of his creation, he often wishes to feel as a fox would among foxes and as a human would among humans. He likes to find people who are on his side, and enjoys helping people around him. If he thinks something is right, he will never give up on his assertions.

Ron: [Fox →Human] A perfectionist who hates making mistakes. As a fox, he was a scientist, and after he became a human, he became a hotel owner, driving a wedge between foxes and humans and leading wars. He hates foxes, worship humans, and fantasize about the most evolved race. Ironically, Ron's idea of evolution refers to beings with short lifespans and limited ability to communicate with nature. He thinks the 'animals of today' are hardly interested in anything but fitting in, harmony, and working for the whole. He feels this oppresses one's individuality and ambition. He takes pride in his introduction of war, The Virus, and humans. His only mistake, John's creation, is a sort of burden to him, and he hates John immensely.

Ben: [Fox →Human] Once partnered with Ron as a scientist to create humans, but their relationship is not good due to Ron's betrayal. Even after being forced to leave John because of Ron, he uses the Tree of Life to lead John to the Isle of Atonement. As he works with a lot of different people, he's always got doubts and secrets.

Agatha: [Fox] An odd lady who believes in nine religions and a capable civil servant in the Fox Kingdom. In charge of human education at the Human Training Centre, considers John special and always actively helps him. Talented fox that cast the spell on a fox statue, greatly saddened by the changes in humans. Is the discoverer of the creation of humans, and has a huge dislike towards Ron and Ben for breaking the laws of nature. Unlike the other courtiers, she is far from sugarcoating the truth, and is always at odds with the king.

Agatha's Children: [Fox] Naughty Beasts! Knows gossip all around the kingdom, thanks to the fact they're taking peaks through mom's 'classified'. Seems like ordinary kids who like to brag and gossip, but in reality, more confident and braver than anyone. Spends a lot of time alone at home due to busy parents.

Fox Children [Fox] (Autumn, Marina, Midnight, Aurora, Sprout, Dreamer): Some of the children that the Tree of Life has asked for help. Because they are young, they are more curious than prejudiced against humans. Very intelligent, sometimes even more so than the adults. Younger siblings tend to lead the group.

Parents of Fox Children (Storm, Sunshine): [Fox] Polar opposites, so marital quarrels are common, but they've got a thing to be nice to each other occasionally. The children think that they're just lecture machines, but this couple cares about their children more than anyone else. When the children go missing, they quickly cooperate with the humans and take the lead in solving the problems of the fox kingdom.

Human Children (Ethan, Emma, Jackson, Shannon, Alex, Tablo): [Human] Used to the clever foxes in the children's books, so just talking to real foxes makes them feel like they're already the main character of a fairy tale. As smart and mature as fox children, but sometimes have infighting, and their older sisters who have reached puberty are often not as enthusiastic as the younger ones.

Parents of human children (Liam and Wendy): [Human] There's Wendy, a busy woman with a busy life (enjoys saying 'scoop!') And Liam, who seems a bit *too* laid-back, but can handle anything when there's a threat. Grows a whopping 571 kinds of plants. After the children are kidnapped, they meet the foxes, and begin to change the world with Wendy's eloquence and writing skills, as well as Liam's unique simplicity and honesty.

Fox King: [Fox] Hardworking, but a little sensitive, a little incompetent. After his illness, he constantly tires to find the root of his problems, and ends up hypnotized by Ron, who transforms into a trusted servant.

THE BIRTH OF A HUMAN

The Birth of Mankind

1. The Birth of Mankind

On a sunny morning, the king of the fox tribe was sitting down on his favorite chair, looking out the window. What he would call a perfect morning. This was soon interrupted by a careful knock.

"It's about the dogs, your majesty," said one of his soldiers.

The king's face turned into a frown.

"The dog tribe is playing one of their nasty tricks again. They have been attacking a few places. We were able to stop them quickly, but there's only one way we can stop them permanently. You see, the cats have already made a strong kingdom with the tiger as emperor. We should be like them and have you as king! Because we are way wealthier than them and we live 1,000 years while they live only 300 years. Anyways, the dog tribe had been harmful to us for years now," said the soldier.

"This is an important thing."

The soldier said again as he walked away.

The king looked out of the window and saw a big tree covering it, which he had never seen.

He ordered,

"Put that tree away this instant!"

A courtier named Agatha said "Your majesty, you know the legend. If you cut that life tree, it will turn evil."

The king said, "I don't believe in such things! Soldiers, Put that life tree away this instant!"

"Yes, sir." they said.

Soon, the life tree was put away, and everything seemed all right. A few days later, things started happening. The tree turned darker, and the king got sick. Many people were reported dead for no reason at all. People grew angry.

Everybody started to worry, so two scientists named Ron and Ben went to explore.

At first, they focused on its magic powers and how it made the king sick, but soon, they learned that the seed could somehow make a creature's life shorter. This did seem like a reason the king was ill, but it also gave Ron an idea. He said to Ben, "How about we make a new creature?" Ben said "We cannot do that. We do not know how to bring it to life." Ron spoke again. "We can bring it to life! I found out that fox's tails can make creatures come alive. So, what we'll do is put the life seed in and add a little bit of extra-small fox tail. Then..." "Okay." interrupted Ben. "So, what are you going to name the creature?" Ron responded quietly.

"I'm naming it human, and I'll name our first human John."

Ben asked another question. "Why aren't we making him?" Ron said, "I almost forgot! Let's do it right now!"

But since they were overexcited, they messed up on quite a lot of things. They put no seed in at all and a lot of fox tail. They were extremely upset that their very first human was very unsuccessful. And eventually they started to dislike John. I mean, they started to despise John! They thought only about how to not make the other humans 'wrong' like John.

Ben said, "Next time let's put a lot of the life seed in. That will solve the problem." They agreed, and decided to keep on making humans in the same way. But since they put too much seed in at first, a few years later they started to put less and less life seed in, which made them make an awkward sound, which they named "crying."

Then one day, Agatha, the courtier who believed in 9 religions, had a dream that all the Gods that she believed told her to go to a place that was outside fox tribe's territory. Since Agatha was very religious, she decided to go there. And there she saw two mysterious foxes making a creature.

A few days after that, she told one of the soldiers that some people were making a creature. Very soon, she had the soldiers all marching down to the forest, in which they threw the life tree. They discovered Ron and Ben, whom they sent to discover what was making the king sick.

They said, "Stop!"

Just then they remembered that making creatures was illegal. They tried to hide the human babies but they weren't able to hide them. So, Ron ran away and hid. But Ben stayed. He did not want to run away. A few minutes later, Ben realized that they had found him. The soldiers were so angry, surprised, and upset to see that somebody was making a creature. Ben tried to hide the humans but it was no use. They were moving around too much. Of course, the soldiers sent him to jail. After Ben left, everything changed

The humans got to live longer and longer until they got to live for 100 years which made them learn more things, for instance, they started to pollute the earth and polluting the earth made more animals sick. Since anything that hurt the earth was strictly forbidden among animals, this was a very big problem. The humans also used fire which was never used in the animal kingdom (most countries in the animal kingdom knew how to do magic so they did not need to use fire) so all the kingdoms had a very serious meeting and argued over how to deal with the humans.

Most people knew that since the humans were made artificially, they could never cooperate with nature and they only cared for themselves and they felt humans were threatening to them. And their pollution was also a big problem. So, they thought that humans should be taken care of strictly. But not everybody knew this, so nothing was able to be done and they kept on arguing themselves too.

The king of fox tribe then said, "How about constructing a huge building? We'll teach all the humans what to do. The first human has been made differently, so we will take care of him. If the other humans know, then there will be a very severe problem, so somebody's going to hypnotize them so that they will incapable of polluting the earth. Then, after many years, we will do the same with their memory of fire. Hypnotization of the humans will be done by our courtiers. We will have a talk about three hundred years later. Currently, there is something more important. The first human shall not know about this. To handle this problem, we will meet each week. All others thought building an artificial building also seemed wrong, but this seemed to be the only way to resolve the problem, so they agreed. The king got right to work.

He ordered all of his public servants to come and for all the soldiers to build the biggest building that they never had seen or heard of. They got right to work. It took days, then months. Finally, after 2 years it was finished. (Humans would have called it twenty years).

The humans and public servants including

Agatha thought everything was going very smoothly. Agatha thought that if she spread religions to humans then it would be easy to hypnotize humans. She thought it was a good idea, so she decided to teach the humans all about religions. Soon, half the humans had a religion. She was so glad it didn't take long to spread religion to the humans.

And meanwhile, John was walking towards the king's castle. As soon as he arrived there, they put him in a big room with a bathroom connected to it. On the bathroom floor, there was a small wooden door that was locked and covered it with a small mat. John grew and grew every day.

One day he discovered the wooden door hidden under the mat. He got out a dried-up toothbrush and shoved it inside the keyhole. Soon it opened up. It was not big enough for a grown-up but it was just the perfect size for him. He crawled through the door and discovered a tunnel. So, he crawled through it. The tunnel was very damp and dark. Luckily, he had brought a small flashlight.

Suddenly, he came to a stop. Something was blocking his way. It was another door, leading into somewhere. He breathed in, then out. Then, he pushed the door open. Sadly, the door was too small to go down, but just enough to put his face through. He could not see anything other than a long hallway, but he heard weird languages. He quickly slammed the door, and then ran without even looking behind him. He was interested in discovering things like secrets but it was still very frightening.

While this mysterious event took place in John's bedroom, rulers of the animal kingdom were having a meeting. They had a talk about how they would deal with John, the odd creature. Just then, they heard a clicking sound from John's bedroom. One of them went to examine it and saw a small boy. As soon as the king of fox tribe heard of this, he decided to put this to an end.

John however was developing a greater interest in the place under his bedroom. His toothbrush had already snapped in half but he did not care. He managed to squeeze inside the door and crawled through the dark tunnel. Once more trying to remember what he saw. He opened the door slightly, peering inside. He heard the same words but this time he was not afraid. He looked inside this time and saw some foxes with a creature that looked very similar to him.

He actually had thought he had never had anybody like him in the whole universe, since he did not know what had happened at his birth. When he asked, nobody answered. He had also envied others that had parents, so he was happy, because he thought there was a possibility, they could be his parents.

Amazed, he rubbed his eyes once more and looked but he still saw the same thing. If the hole was just a little bigger than he would have been able to crawl down. The wall was very thin. So thin, you could have pushed it over. This gave John an idea. All he had to do now who sneak out at night.

After making his perfect plan, he decided to get out of the tunnel quickly, since John was afraid, they might see him, when they looked up above them. He strode across the tunnel and got back into the castle. He quickly jumped into his comfortable bed and waited until night quietly.

As soon as the old grandfather clock rung twelve times he jumped out of bed and into the soundless tunnel. When he got to the end, John smashed the walls beside the door and jumped on to the highest cupboard that he saw. There was so much dust on the cupboard that he sneezed a few times. He wiped his nose quickly and examined the room once more for a mat to leap down on. Just then, he spied a mat that was coated with rust.

It was not the best place to land on but it was better than nothing. So, he jumped down. There were lots of small rooms in front of him, but since he heard some noises in those rooms, he decided not to go in those rooms. He kept on playing until he saw that it was already 5:00 am.

And when he climbed up the cupboard again, he found out that the cupboard was a little bit hard to climb on top of. He struggled for a while then finally managed to climb up the ridiculously slippery cupboard and back in to the damp tunnel. He did this only for a few times so he still did sneeze a little. Trying to ignore all the dust, John opened up the door as silently as he was able to do. Then, he hopped in bed.

"Aah!" He suddenly woke up sweating all over. Instead of a nice dream about the secret chute, he had had a nightmare about people all pointing at him and saying bad things about him. He tried to get rid of the thought of that dream but it was not easy to do. He tried to think more about his secret adventure and then his eyelids closed.

A few days after that frightful night, he tried to think a lot more about visiting that secret place of his again. He even thought about cleaning the tunnel, so he could go in the morning too. He got out all his cleaning tools for hygiene and blankets and pillows for comfort.

After he finished all the cleaning (which took 3 hours) he was very tired but this was something that made him happy.

It even made him no longer scared of those creatures inside the tunnel. After he was finished, he slowly stepped inside to examine his work for a moment. Actually, he was very happy with his result. He always would watch through the hole he made. He had seen those awkward creatures too much that he was no longer scared of those creatures.

So, when John turned about seven in fox years, John was sent to a school. This seemed late, but this decision was made because he aged slower. (John was homeschooled before for 3 years.) He was 70 in human years.

A week later, John started school. Just as soon as he entered the building some kids started laughing at him and teasing him for not having a tail. John's feelings were badly hurt. His face turned from red to orange. He quickly ran in the classroom and silently wept. He thought school was awful! The next day he told one of the soldiers he did not like school because people always tease him just for looking different! The only thing that got his mind off of that was studying, so that was all he did.

John kept complaining, so when John was sixteen in fox years, they decided to transfer him to a very special school that was used for training spies. He did not like this school either because at 8:00 as soon as they went to school, they would get heavy gear on and train. As soon as he came back home, he asked the soldiers if he can quit school. They all said, "Just try another month and if you still don't like it, then we will try to find a way to get you out of school. But luckily, he was able to learn magic. (Though it was only basic magic that was easier than what other students learned.)

Nobody was greeting John except for the bell. He felt very depressed but he did not know this would be the worst part of his day because during history, the teacher described exactly the tunnel he always had went to, saying things that scared him like "Sneezing is one of the symptoms. If you go too often, it can lead to death."

Just hearing this chilled his blood and made him think that he would never go there again. He was so scared for the whole day that he even bit his nails that when he came back, everybody thought he lost his nails completely! He didn't stop shivering with fear for hours after John thought, "I'm never going to go there!"

But actually, the foxes just wanted John to

stop going in the tunnel. All the things they learnt related to John was not true. Everybody knew that except for John.

Luckily, due to his grades, John was able to graduate at the age of seventeen. Still, even after leaving school, John feared the tunnel, and any others related to it. John was frightened.

Meanwhile, Agatha was teaching people science. But soon, she started to get bored, so she started teaching religion for a few minutes until suddenly, the head public servant came in the room he was ferocious that Agatha was not teaching science and teaching religion. He said, "I'm going to fire you if you do this again!"

Agatha asked, "Do what?" The head of the public servants said, "Religion!!!" Agatha answered "Okay." But as soon as he left, she taught religion again. This was one of the reasons she was the human's favorite teacher. Agatha did not believe that the humans were going to become better with something to attract them.

The humans liked her so much that they made a statue for her called the fox statue. She liked it so much, so she casted good spells that told almost anything and helped almost everything by using all the hope and gratitude the humans generated. Then, she hid it inside a special tube which was extremely long. This tube had stops and other things like seven hundred spells and angry rats. Nothing inside the old building made it look like it had secret things like this. It was connected to a room that was used as a bedroom.

After a couple centuries, these humans that were once trained well started to become horrible in the fox point of view. For the first few years, they went on well without any of the foxes helping or protecting them. Still, the humans forgot the foxes because of a spell the foxes casted on them and this was becoming a large problem.

Meanwhile, off in the distance, Ron had found another plant that looked very similar to the plant he had used for making humans. After years of studying, he realized this strange plant was a plant that made him into any other creature. There was only one thing he disliked about this and that was that he wasn't able to remember what had happened to him when he was a fox after becoming a human. Instead, his memories would change to the memories of a different human that had the plant, only leaving the memories of his name.

He did want to turn into a human because he felt it was hard to try new things when people always put cooperating first and since they lived long, they didn't hurry for things and he felt that it was more of a wrong life. This was one of the hardest decisions of his whole life. It wasn't that he had to choose quickly or something, but he was in a bit of a rush. He finally decided what he would do; he'd just eat it. He had only made this decision because of an old saying that came from the foxes: do not fear before experience. "Why not?" He said to himself as he popped the little plant in his mouth.

He thought it would take a little time to forget, but he was wrong. The time was about 12:45 then, and by 1:00, he had already lost most of his memory. But since his memory was very strong of John, even the plant was not enough to erase all his memory but otherwise he was fully human. Just like how a human would be. Nothing in his mind was different from a human, except for that he somehow still had a strong feeling of what he disliked about John.

Back inside the fox tribe, Agatha was preparing for 3 religion festivals. But just as she went out, she had remembered that she had forgotten to pack all her religion tools. But since she was late, she sped towards her first festival when she found some fruits.

She wanted to give them to all the people at the festival, so she grabbed one. And, at the very same moment, a trap flew on to her head! She fought to get out but instead, some hunters took her. Agatha got angry for two reasons: first was that she had been the entire human's most favorite teacher and now the humans were catching her; the second reason was because she wasn't able to bring anything. And now, the humans were taking her to a place that she heard them calling a "zoo."

Well, whatever this "zoo" thing was, she heard it was something with other crazy animals. It happened to be that the zoo did not just have crazy animals, but it also had humans throwing things at her, no freedom, and so much other horrible things like no privacy and zero respect. She thought of it again but she still wasn't able to understand them. Just 300 years ago, she was there as the most beloved teacher. Now, everybody screams and throws things at her. She shared a 3-foot-wide cage with 20 other foxes, and this was not something that was easy to be fine with. She never got any privacy.

THE BIRTH OF A HUMAN

The Whole New World

2. A Whole New World

While this happened to Agatha, Ron had turned into a middle-aged human man. As he lost his memories of a fox, he instead had become a businessman. Ron was looking around for a place to make into a hotel. He had already thought about building one, but he did not know have to build. He did not have enough money to build a fancy hotel, so he just had to find a good building that was abandoned. Just then he found a building that had some books that was about science and some bushy, orange fur all over the place. He did not see the small sign that said <The Centre for Human Pollution> He quickly scanned the place and decided to take over. After a few months, renovation was finished and Ron started to hire employs.

At fox tribe, John was about to go in that

tunnel again when he got a mission for him to go check on a special thing. He was very sad. He was not available to go to the tunnel and instead just go to a boring place for a statue, but he went anyways because he knew he would get to learn the dog's and human's language for this mission and he liked to learn new languages. He also knew that the statue was needed for the king.

They educated John on what to do, speak, and act for a month, and off he went. When John first set foot on the human's territory, he thought everything was cool. Nobody lived in caves or holes. Castles were not built out of twigs and bushes. Everybody wore 'clothes. John arrived at his destination, a large hotel. On the signs, everything was written in the dog's language. This was weird. It said employs wanted.

That was it! He would become an employ and

37

spy.

That plan might work. He said to himself. It might work. He fixed his hair again to make it look more like his purpose, trying to become an employee. At this moment, he ran into a pack of people who all wanted to become an employee. He also zipped up his pants, and put his belt on, which he never had to wear in the castle. Just then, he read the sign again. Below it said: only 100 people available. They probably needed to take some sort of test. He thought that if there were only 100 people then he could just pass. He looked at the group. It looked like there were at least 500 people waiting to get a job at this hotel. Just then he noticed that everybody else was looking like him. This was very odd, but he knew he had to do this mission, so he stopped thinking about that.

"Hello, everyone!" said a voice behind him. "I

am the owner, Ron Miller." He announced. He said they will do a draw five minutes later. John breathed a huge sigh of relief. He did not know what to do if it was a test, for he had known nothing about hotels. He wasn't usually very lucky but draws were much better than tests. He stepped forwards, took a handful of papers, and then shook all of them out except for one of them. He thought about the words the owner said. It sounded mostly like the dog words.

"Could he be? He then remembered, when he was young, he had seen those people at the tunnel, now, he thought, I might be able to find my parents! Maybe, this mission might not be so boring. Maybe if the things were the creatures he saw at the tunnel, then the language must have changed." He thought, for he felt it sounded similar to the dog's language that he had learned. These thoughts made him think other thoughts. He then started to worry. John did not want to write in dog language. He was not proficient. He just hoped he did not have to type or write at his job.

He sighed and looked off towards the side and saw some guy holding a paper with unusual letters printed on the paper. The man was jumping with joy. This must say that you passed. John thought and looked at his. It had the same letters on it. He did not want to seem unusual, so he screamed what that guy was screaming. He just now had to hope he denied with a job that was not related to paper at the least.

The boss looked at all the people who passed. They were led through dark corridors and given uniforms. John was uncomfortable in his hoodie, so he wondered how he would survive in these clothes. He looked down at the dress pants, dress shirt, and waistcoat he was given. They then arrived at a changing room. As John changed, he also noticed a tie and jacket. The clothes were mostly black, but his shirt was white, and his waistcoat and tie were both grey. John wore everything correctly, thanks to the lessons he took with the foxes, but he tied his tie onto his wrist. John quickly fixed his tie, as soon as he saw how others wore it.

They then all lined up. John tried to say with his body that he could not write, but Ron just gave him a hard stare and scribbled something on his note pad. Ron did realize by John's actions that he was a foreigner, but somehow, Ron felt a strong will to make John suffer.

Ron's voice beamed across the room, telling John he would tell them that they would be told their jobs tomorrow morning and that the money they would earn could be depending on the job they were going to do. John did not care about the second part because he did not know what money meant. However, the first part Ron told him was that he needed a place to stay for the night for today.

Everyone probably had a home to stay in that was close enough but John's castle was far away for he had walked for more than 3 hours and going there and back would take too much time. His bedtime was normally 3:00 p.m. and he woke up at 2:00 a.m. Like all other fox cubs. He looked at his watch and then realized he had only 30 minutes before bed and went behind a tree curling him into a ball as he put leaves over him for more comfort when he slept.

The next morning, John woke up and rushed to the hotel. When he arrived, he saw a new sign. He searched for a person to help him read this sign, but for some reason nobody was out at 2:00 am. John just sat and waited for someone to come and help him.

Finally, at 6:00 after hours of waiting, an old man came along. John asked in a funky accent "Do you know what is written on this sign?" The old man said "Yes." and read: "The hotel opens at 8:00 am." John said "Um... Thanks." The man asked him suddenly if he was from another country. John was not sure what "country" meant but he just said "Yes." As soon as he heard the answer, he said okay, and walked away. John felt he had said the answer, so if anyone ever said anything about his accent, He would say he was from a different country.

He looked at his watch. 7:43, it said on the old watch. (Found from tunnel) So that meant there were still 17 minutes left until he was able to find out his job at the hotel. Then, just as soon as he finished thinking, his clock stroke 8:00 and people started dashing across the grass and into the hotel.

John started running, too, when this happened, for he knew it was warmer inside the hotel. Soon, everybody had joined inside the hotel. Then, after a few minutes, Ron stepped in the room and gazed at everybody and said aloud. "I will announce your jobs." "Okay," said everybody trying to say it at the same time. Ron announced their jobs and John got placed in check-in. He also got a brown nametag with his name on it.

First, he was glad he didn't have to work in the office, where they had to do lots of typing, but as soon as he sat down, he had to pick up nine phone calls, which one of them used words he didn't know well. Plus, a guy came to his table, asking for 7 rooms just for himself and John were not able to handle that. Customers like these came in almost every minute which made him really tired. He also had to type out some things. The other nine people working with him were way better.

Just then, he saw a family, taking a walk. The child seemed hurt. John sighed. He never knew who his parents even were! He then questioned himself, why do I not have parents? The more he questioned himself, the more he got gloomier.

When lunch break started, John took a seat at the table. Handling cutlery was hard, and the food was different. John wanted to see if they had fox food. He also saw something weird; everybody had a dog! They also all had small dogs, no bigger than the size of a human. During work, he kept seeing these things again.

After all this, Ron called him asking him if he was going to stay at the manager's suite. Then, without even thinking about what he was going to say, John asked what a manager's suite was. Ron told him it was something he was able to sleep in. Ron thought John acted in a very odd manner. Then, John said that he wanted to, so Ron led him into a room.

Maybe I should start cleaning. John thought. His room had cupboards, a bed, a bedside table, a mini fridge, and a microwave with a round table and two chairs. And in the corner, there was a bathroom with a small shower booth and a toilet and sink crammed beside it. After this was done, John quickly showered and fell asleep.

The next day, after work, he decided to buy himself a present but since he was not able to get anything because when he went to the store, the person working at the store told him he needed something called money, so instead he decided to just read the book about fox history because he loved reading. The book was something John had spotted in the castle and taken. It had many pages, and it was able to write down everything that had happened in the history of foxes by itself. He read 73 pages, then put a gold bookmark on it and slept.

Though John knew that if he did not go and find it, then the king could possibly die, he did not try to find it until now, so he decided to just focus on finding the statue now. He never went to work on Thursdays, and tried to find the tunnel.

One day when he was about to go looking around the hotel, Ron came in and asked him why he was not attending work on Thursdays, and said they needed him. John felt he may find the statue down at work, so, John said yes, and then he looked at his calendar. Today was Thursday! He changed into his uniform and slipped on his runners. Then, he started to work.

That day, work ended late and he went to bed at 9:30.

Ring! It was 1:37 but John had a reason for waking up early. He walked through the dead of the night. He knew that if he walked for an hour, he was able to go to a shop that opened this early to buy all kinds of things. They were all magic things. He had read in the book that people that look like him were called humans and they did not know that magic existed. He thought that was weird. He got himself a book called <how to do extreme magic> and a wand.

Then, when he arrived back at the hotel, he tried using some magic but many spells blocked him from using that type of magic. He then gave up and just made a glass of lemonade for himself. That was enough for keeping him happy.

Unlike John, who was having a good time,

Agatha was having a gloomy time with the other animals inside the zoo. One day, when she was inside her cage, she saw a creature walk near her. The thing was digging a hole. At first, she thought that it was lucky to live alone but then she got an idea. Holes! That was the easiest way to escape the zoo.

She started to calculate. She thought about using magic that time, but she thought she may get caught, so she continued her calculation. From her cage to the door would be meters, so since she could dig 1.1 meters in a minute it would take her 11 minutes to go. She took a bundle of her food, and started digging. When she got half way, she had to go back to get some moss for her bed. She was not able to go out in the crowd though, because they would probably put her back inside the zoo.

She was an expert at humans, so she knew

around 3:00~3:30 was the best time to get out. So, at 2:45 she woke up. She then realized that she was very close to fox tribe and when she arrived near fox tribe, she saw a hotel with shadows of humans inside! When she saw that the hotel was the same building as the human training centre, she was quite surprised.

She decided to spend the night outside and put the moss down on the ground and slept. When she woke up, she went straight to the castle. The king was so surprised to see her. He said "What happened to you?" Agatha told him the story and he got mad that they were treating foxes like that. Then, Agatha told him about how the dogs got such good care from the humans.

The king suddenly rose from his chair and said, "I wonder if John is doing well. If he gets the statue, we can fight the dogs."

John was not doing well that day. He had a very bad cold and a harsh day with the customers. The next morning, he searched for the statue but he was not able to find it. Still, he was determined to find it and started searching as soon as it got bright again. Just then, he found a tunnel. It had to be the statue. He was delighted, but also wanted some rest, so he told the foxes he had found the location of the tunnel (he used magic to do this) and said to himself that he would explore it soon, and went to sleep.

The next day was a Sunday, so John decided to go on a walk to the forest. On his walk, he started to feel tired and his eyelids got drowsy, but at the same time a feeling came over him that brought shivers up his spine. For some reason he was scared to death and was horrified by an unknown cause. He decided to go back home. When he got there, he was not able to get rid of the thought of that forest because it somehow made him have a misty and drowsy feeling. He knew he was able to go there any day but a strong feeling came over him each time he tried to do that. It was a feeling that he could not ignore. He felt that strong feeling again and again every day.

The next day, he decided he would talk to someone about this, and went to Ron's office. When John told him how he felt, Ron casually smiled and told John

"It is not like there is something is over there. There is no reason you can't or should not go in there."

John then said,

"I'm too scared to do that. Something is warning me over and over not to go in there."

Ron laughed, and spoke.

"Come on. If you are so scared, then I would be glad to go with you. It's going to be okay."

"Are you sure?"

John asked again, but Ron had no answer that time.

"I just can't seem to be sure about never going there until these feelings stop. Nobody can find out why I'm having this kind of feeling or how long it will last. It's not easy...

Ron smiled at John and gave him a pat on the back.

"Thanks" said John, and walked away to his room.

Perhaps what Ron said was right. He knew that it was not any kind of feeling that made him really 'sure' but he had just trusted that feeling. He gazed at the window, and then sighed. He did not understand why they had made him go on such an important mission when he was too scared to go on a walk. John also felt sorry for Ron having to listen to him.

Just then, he got an idea. He knew Ron liked

poetry, so he got him a small book of poetry and a newspaper. While he walked back, John read the newspaper.

There, he saw on the headlines: <Murder reported in nearby forest >.

He realized now that he needed to trust that feeling. He wanted Ron to know too. If he didn't, Ron would go in the forest. He dropped off the book and the newspaper at his office.

Ron walked down the hall to his office after checking the halls and saw something. It was a gift from John. Ron put the book on top of his desk and started to read the newspaper. He dropped the paper five seconds later and moaned. "How... he could not had known... It's not possible." Ron was in shock, and tried to calm down. This wasn't difficult, since knew nobody could know. His victims all killed each other after being hypnotized by him.

Meanwhile, in the dungeon of fox tribe, Ben was thinking about a good way to escape this old dungeon. He wished that there was at least a window in this dreaded dungeon. This thing could work. He knew he needed to wait for "the day" when they all got to go out of the dungeon for a day.

He knew after a week it would be the day and he could escape. Nobody dared to escape though, because of the harsh consequences. Ben wanted to prove that was not true. Finally, he went outside. He saw a wedding going on so he hid in there. Soon, he found out that Agatha and her husband were having a wedding. Shortly after that wedding, he started planning how to get moving without being caught. He felt danger. Some cops seemed to be chasing him. He quickly ducked under a bush and hid there until he saw they were gone.

Ben was very happy, though he knew he had to stay hidden for a year, a decade, or even forever.

He did not bring a single drop of water and he was more worried than ever. He tried to remember where the sea is. He knew how to gather water from the sea, and he knew he was able to find clams and fish so all he had to do was find out where the sea was. Then, he set off for the sea, hoping that by noon he could get to the sea.

Anyways, while Ben was going towards the sea, John was packing some lunch for a picnic. He put a sandwich inside the basket and a bottle of lemonade. He whistled and went off to the seaside. He walked for about a kilometer then came to a stop. Fresh air touched his cheeks, making them red. Then, he started to walk around the sea.

After such a long walk, he went towards a bench and took a sip of lemonade. The seaside was very quiet. Just then, a fox appeared. He just stared at him, and ran away before he could say something. After the picnic, John still was not able to get rid of that feeling. Nothing seemed normal. He thought of that fox again. He seemed as if he knew John.

Meanwhile, back at the sea, Ben was thinking about John. He knew it was John, the creature he made. The thing made "wrong." He had a feeling he did not like John, and that was true. He didn't like him at all because he wrecked him. He loathed him.

He then started wondering where Ron is. He remembered only that he ran away. He must be somewhere around here. He thought as he picked up the clams that washed up on to the seashore. He then put a tree trunk over another and put the clams under them. This would last him only about a week, so he needed to gather more.

While he did that, he also tried to turn his mind away from where Ron went and of course all the anger about John. All these things that worried him seemed better when he collected the clams. As soon as he felt he needed to stop, the feeling came over him again. He felt as if he could do anything to get rid of this tiring feeling that comes over him. Well, maybe not anything.

He then grabbed a stone and grinded it a few times to make a small knife. After that, he took a small piece of wood and emptied the inside of it with the knife to use as a cup. At last, he started putting in the finishing touches. He dug a hole and put the cup inside. This way, the clean water like rain could fill his cup.

And after he did this, he tried lighting fire. This job was very tough. He tried mashing rocks together and by rubbing two sticks together, but it barely made any sparks.

While Ben was doing this, John was at work at the counter. Work was getting tough. At first, he only worked at the counter. He worked on documents and calls, and sometimes helped people with check-in. After a week, John worked at the counter until lunch, then for his last two hours of work. The rest of his time was mostly spent in the main halls, which he cleaned. He also cleaned the elevators. John also spent half an hour in the kitchen, washing the dishes and mopping the floors. The good foods were never used for the workers, and the best food yet was macaroni that was left out, so he often ate by going to a restaurant.

The hotel itself was a very good place though. This 20-story building was divided in two areas. The first 5 floors were used for staff, and the other floors were for customers. Each suite looked the same, but the rooms did not. They looked almost the same except that they each had a different picture on the walls, and the last room of each floor was used as a swimming pool, fitness centre, playroom, or kinds of things like those. The restaurant in the building for customers was a good place with expensive food. All the expensive food they bought was also the reason why the workers got bad food, John thought.

The only problem was that there were only 30 workers in this building now, (a few left) so he had to do most of the work. This was making him very tired. After work, he felt so tired that he went to sleep right away.

Meanwhile, Ben was trying to build a house. He gathered logs from the creek and linked it together with dangly vines to use as the floor. He then put a roof on top, once again linking it with the vines.

After a month of work like this, a house 6 feet wide with a wooden bed, table, and chair was made. The bathroom was just a deep hole with leaves used as tissue, but he felt proud he built it on his own.

One day, while he was sitting on his chair, he got a good idea. Barely anybody knows this place but it is wonderful. Maybe if I go to another place far away from here then I won't have to be hiding from people anymore and plus, it will be easier to survive. And so, that day he made a huge water tank and a food tank along with a huge raft about twice the size of the house and slid it under the house. And on the extra space, he put the food and water tank. Then, he made a sail by sewing leaves and bendy wood. He looked at the raft, which was now a boat.

He felt a little bit weird that he was leaving this place, but he was also glad that he was not being chased. He slowly pushed the boat and set sail. Just then, he started to get worried. What if the sea was stormy? What if his boat broke into pieces? I'll just have to hope for the best, Ben thought, as he hopped onto the boat and set sail.

He went out into the sea and touched the water. It was such a pleasant day. The clouds were floating towards him, dancing a jig as they flowed in the blue sky. Everything was just perfect. After looking at the sky for a few minutes, he started getting a little bit hungry, so he grabbed a snack and then went inside his house on top of his boat he built.

Ben thought he should fall asleep to prepare himself for the long trip, but he could not fall asleep. After counting the 100th sheep, he finally fell asleep. However, he did not sleep long, because a storm flipped the boat upside down. He was flipped and tossed all around the boat. Luckily, after a few minutes, the storm stopped.

Back at fox tribe, Agatha was talking to her husband.

"I think that I should go back to the zoo I was trapped in. If I find out more about the human culture, then maybe we could find some of the things that could improve fox tribe. Plus, maybe find out some other things."

Her husband then said in a worried face.

"I can't send you to that dangerous place. You can just think about ways to improve the country here."

Agatha said to him, "I also have another reason. Everything is too well-going, and I am getting too bored of this. And who knows? Maybe I can find another cure instead of the statue for the king."

"But..."

Agatha said, "If you do not want me to go, it's like not wanting the king to get better, the country to improve and me to get happy. "

"All right," groaned her husband and spoke.

"You have to use a little magic to talk to me twice a day. You know we need some contact. Also do this if it is an emergency. Okay?"

"I will. You have to drop the kids off at their grandparents' house because you don't know how to take care of them."

"Well, when are you going?"

Agatha said, "Tomorrow."

Her husband said, "Sure. I'll go drop the kids off!" trying his best not to look concerned at all.

The next day, Agatha woke up early and took a shower under the rain. Then she skipped off to the place she got caught last time. As soon as she walked under the trap, it flung over her head. The people had a short talk and then moved her to the zoo she was in before.

As she entered, the smell of rotten meet and muddy cabbage greeted her once again. She thought it was horrible but she knew that she could find good things somewhere in here.

She listened to the talk of the zookeepers. It sounded like they were going to change the floor to block her from escaping. This meant that she could never escape even when she completed her mission. She knew that was not really important because she came here just an hour ago. Her main purpose was to see what they could from the human culture, so she needed to listen to their talk. They usually talked inside a building near her cage so whenever they had an open window while talking. She could hear all the talks of them.

The first day, the zookeepers did not have any kind of special talk which was a shame for Agatha. But the next day, they talked more about what the humans' rules and other things are. Then Agatha thought there was not too much difference in most rules except that how people think of money. In fox tribe, nobody used money. The humans did this with everything. She thought this was pretty interesting, so she listened again.

This time they said things about war! Agatha thought once again. One of the zookeepers said that bombs could surely help them win in wars but the other one said because of them if another war breaks out nothing is going to be able to exist. Agatha did not know what a bomb was but by their talk it was probably something very dangerous. Maybe they should try making new rules, Agatha thought. She then thought once again because she knew it would be hard to fix so many rules that are wrong. She felt that she was a little tired so she went to sleep.

That night, she thought, "Humans are animals that like creating things no matter what it is from wonderful statues to deadly tools for wars. Maybe, if they just switch a little bit of their rules with some other countries, they won't need to think of new rules." After Agatha thought of that, she was quite pleased with her idea, and thought that she should go back to fox tribe and organize her ideas and present them.

So, at night Agatha dug a deep hole and

crawled through it. She went deeper and deeper until she hit something. She touched it again and found out that the zookeepers had installed an electric pad in the ground.

Now I have another problem, Agatha thought. She could use magic and fly but she knew humans were moving around at night and she looked nothing like a bird so all the humans would notice and it might turn into a huge problem. She could teleport, but she was not that good at it because that was an extremely hard thing and it was way too dangerous for her.

This was a real emergency. By using magic, Agatha quickly contacted her husband and talked to him. Agatha told him she finished her mission but she was trapped in the zoo. Her husband then said that he would try to think of a way to rescue her but he said he could not think of an idea.

But actually, at that time, he was just skiing with his friends and chatting. Her husband said to his friends, "I have a problem. My wife is trapped in a place called the zoo. Can you rescue her?" His friends, simple minded and loyal, immediately said yes and off they went.

At that time, John was taking a walk near the zoo Agatha was in. When he saw Agatha, he was so glad he saw a fox, so at once he bought the ticket to go in to the zoo, and went straight to the fox cage and said to Agatha. "Why are you here?" So, Agatha told him how she came here and that she quickly needed to get out. John then said to her. "You could escape only if the hotel I work in buys this place. So, I will try to get my boss to buy this, and we will stay in close contact. Could you help me find the statue?"

Agatha asked "What statue do you mean?"

John said "I can't tell you unless you tell me something. How come the human and dog languages are switched up?"

Agatha hesitated for a moment, and started her story.

"The dogs had a time when they were weak, so they held a meeting. "

****

"We must befriend the humans." The Dogs said. "Humans like cute animals. Now, look in the mirror. Do we look cute? The answer is <No.> we need someone to make us cute!"

Then, another courtier said foxes can all do magic but the public servants are the best!

"They can do almost any kind of magic in the world. So, the adult foxes wake up at 4:00 and sleep at 6:00. I'm not sure about the kids, but their routine is probably the same. If we go while they are sleeping, we can catch them."

Everyone agreed with that decision, so on that very night, as soon as the clock stroke six, they crept inside the fox tribe and saw some things that looked like sparks of magic. When it was 1:39 they had got to the place where magic sparks were coming from. Soon, they saw plenty of people in the building, wearing uniforms. They took one of the lightest ones because they were all sleeping and they had to carry them to dog tribe. And while doing this, time had passed. It was 2:00 now. And just as they headed out, a little fox cub spied them and said that the dogs were here.

And soon, everybody was awake, chasing after them. Then, these dogs all rushed back to dog tribe with the public servant. When they got back, they asked the public servant to make them cute, and threatened to kill him if he failed to. He felt he needed to live so this public servant made them the cutest creatures of all the animals and ran off.

Then, impressed at their looks, all these dogs started to study how to make cute poses and lovely faces. Now they just needed to go to the human world. Luckily, one of them knew the way to the human world. They then realized that they were in the human world because there were humans everywhere all the streets. Then, they got in action and started to try out their cute poses.

And after a few years of this, they started befriending the dogs. Throughout time humans started using dog language and dogs spoke in human language

****

John then told her. "I need the fox statue, the statue to cure the king." Agatha nodded, and told him he mustn't loiter. She said "Didn't you say you had to convince the owner to buy the zoo?"

So, John quickly ran away to tell Ron what he thought about buying the zoo. Ron hesitated for a moment but then got an idea and told John that John had to take care of it. John said yes and went to Agatha again to tell her the plan. John explained. "So, since I take care of the zoo, I will take the key to your cage and let you out. Then, you need to duck behind me and we will leave this night. OK?"

And shortly after that, John left. Thinking about how he could tell Ron about going out at the middle of the night. Then, John thought, "If I pretend to go on a walk then I would not be suspected at all."

That night, John brought Agatha out of her cage and went to fox tribe. When they were about half way, there they saw two foxes. Agatha moved and then saw they were her husband's friends. They said they were trying to rescue Agatha and asked why John was here. After all the talk, John went back to the hotel.

While he was resting, he thought everything happening was odd. The foxes had given him many missions other than finding the statue such as recording the human's behavior or learning their culture. Because of this, he was always busy collecting rocks and buying things. When he was at fox tribe, the people would always go out. And they always tried to be careful in front of him. They also always hid the infinity-page book from him. As he thought about that, he fell asleep.

The next day, when John woke up and looked at the clock, it was 10:00, two hours past time he was supposed to go to work. He quickly ran down the halls. While moving, he scolded himself for not waking up at the right time.

After work when everybody was gone, Ron looked at John. He thought "Why did he come so late to work? And why is he acting like that? There's something odd. Something suspicious. I wonder what he's up to these days. What if he is planning to do something to the hotel? Maybe all the robbers and weird customers are because of him too. They have to be." Ron thought that from now on, he should start keeping an eye on John.

Meanwhile, John was thinking. "I may have to start going into the tunnel. I almost forgot about the king. He relies on only me. I need to do it quick. He said to himself and added. I will prepare for a week, and go away to the tunnel. I need to pack, and read about the tunnel in my book."

While this was happening, Ron was preparing to go to John's room. When he arrived, he crouched down and peered through the door. John seemed to be saying something. Ron felt more suspicious.

The day before the grand operation, John started to pack. He had attempted to read about the tunnel, but he was not able to find it in the huge book. So today, he concentrated on packing. He took a toothbrush and toothpaste, enough food and water to last him three months, all his clothes, his pillow and blanket, cutlery, the book and all the other books he owned, and a notebook along with stationery. John was preparing to go down the tunnel. He had already prepared and packed, by dividing everything into two large suitcases, and he even packed a pair of dress shoes. He took the things and put them into a thick leather sack, and put it all in the bathroom.

The next day, Ron was walking down the hall checking the rooms. He opened the door to John's room and saw John, sitting in the washroom. Ron asked, "Why are you in the bathroom like that?" John answered, "Um, so I, I was going to take a shower. Yeah, I'm not lying!" Ron looked at John and said "Okay." But he knew John was trying to hide something from him. He just did not want John to get suspicious.

Back at John's room, John was thinking. "I was almost caught. Good thing he did not ask me about more things. But why is he asking me? He usually would not. I feel he knows everything about me. Maybe I should just go into the tunnel another day. John thought and said to himself quietly and slowly. He kind of sometimes acts like a fox.

Back at the office, Ron was thinking. "I should go out again today to John's room. He said he was taking a shower and was not even holding a towel. He is so weird these days." And so, Ron went to John's room and once again peered through the doors. This time, he was reading a book that seemed surprisingly old. As Ron was about to see the title of the book, John put it away.

Ron then went back to his office and thought. "What is John trying to hide from me? What if he is going to do something bad to not just the hotel but also me?" Ron then started to feel like he should try to follow John to the places he goes.

Just then, Ron saw John going out of the

doors and followed. At that point, John was going for a walk. After taking the walk John spotted a coat. So, he and quickly ran towards the hotel. While he ran, he saw Ron and thought. "Why is he out here? What if he is following me?"

Just then, he remembered the coat was brown, the same colour as Ron's. I guess he could. He thought as he walked to the hotel. At that point, he said to himself quietly. "I probably should go into the tunnel right now." It should take a while for him to come back.

At that time Ron was looking for John. He thought that if he comes in suddenly, then he could get all of the secret information from John. He opened the door when John was about to go into the tunnel.

At that moment, John's mind started to spin fast. He thought that if he said he saw Ron outside, he would be able to talk about something else so he said, "Oh, I saw you outside when I was going on a walk!" Ron thought in his mind, "How does he know that I was following him?" then said "Yeah, I was about to say hello to you! Why did you go away when you saw me?" John said "I was in a hurry to use the bathroom, so I did not really have time to say hello." Ron said "Okay. Anyways, why were you out so far away?" John replied, "Well... It is because I wanted to go on a long walk today." Ron said, "Yeah. Anyways, I need to go now. Bye!"

That night, Ron thought. "Why is John acting like he is trying to hide something?"

Meanwhile, Ben had just arrived at a place. After the storm, he lost half his food so he had to gather them again. He got all the food that he knew was edible and the things that looked like it was edible.

First, he ate the things he was sure it was edible but unlike the sea where he was at, there was not much food so he had to eat food which he was unsure of. Most of them seemed all right but one of the plants had a funny glimmer. He thought "I am not too hungry now, so I think I will not have to eat this right now." Ben thought again. "I wonder if Ron is all right. I know it is better not to think of him but I really wonder where he is."

But Ben did not know that the plant he was holding was actually what turned Ron into a human. In fact, he did not even know that Ron had become a human. Ben then sighed and lay down in the wet grass. He thought, "I am not so sure about eating this plant. It took a little weird and I don't even know what is going to happen to me. I will have to eat it though. So, I guess I can take a little bite now."

He then said to him before he took a bite. I feel like time is flying. I still remember making humans with him. But maybe, Ben wondered, wouldn't it be better if I was a human? Perhaps I'd be better off as a human. And as he said the last word, he bit the plant he was holding, and in a few minutes, he turned into a young human aged fourteen. He then later was found by an orphanage across from the hotel John was from.

THE BIRTH OF A HUMAN

The Meeting

3. The Meeting

Back at the hotel, John was having a gloomy time. When he wasn't working or doing a mission, he always thought about himself. John was lonely and felt sad all the time. He thought about what he could do then contacted Agatha. Agatha said "While being in the zoo, a learnt that there was a place here called the orphanage." Then, she told him about it. John was deeply interested, so he went to the adoption centre across the street.

As soon as he went in there, he saw a little boy. He asked him his name but he did not answer. He tried again and again but he did not say anything.

Finally, after the ninth try, the little boy said quietly to John "I'm Ben." And when Ben said that, he felt weird. A strong feeling of hate came over him. He felt he could not like John. While Ben was thinking John went to talk with the other kids but each time he went to the other kids, someone seemed to say, go to Ben! He then said to himself, weird. I feel like I want to rely on Ben, even though he is a little kid. As he went out, he said to himself later at home, next time I think I should talk more to Ben.

Just then, Ron walked behind him. He asked, "What are you thinking about so seriously?" John answered "I went to the orphanage just to see the kids and one of them just gave me a weird feeling." "So? That's the only reason about you being so serious?" "Yeah, I guess so." "Well then, bye!" Ron said to John but in his mind, he felt suspicious. Then he walked around the halls and went into his office to rest.

Just then, John got an idea. He could go

down the tunnel! The time was just about right and all his things were in the bathroom. John showered, and wore grey trousers and a black hoodie on top of an indigo polo shirt, the darkest clothes he had. On his back, he wore the sack twice the size of him. The sack was red, but he made a black cover for it, so he could blend into the darkness.

He was about to go down, but then remembered the people of fox tribe told him to ask Agatha about the tunnel. So, by using magic he asked Agatha to send the map of the tunnel and where to go and by using magic she quickly sent it to him.

John thanked her and then lifted the mat off the wooden trapdoor and went into the tunnel. It was pitch black and was made of smooth wood. Just then, he got an idea. "I put all my items in a very thick sack and the tunnel is quite steep.

Shouldn't I glide down it?" He thought and went on to his back.

He said to himself again, "This was a terrific idea." He then slid down the tunnel quickly using his sack. The tunnel was truly a marvelous and long thing, with many sharp twists and turns and traps. John only allowed himself to sleep after checking that there were no traps on the map nearby.

Meanwhile, Agatha was taking a walk near her house with her kids and husband telling stories to her kids about her adventure in the human world. Later, when the kids fell asleep, she contacted John and said to him, "How far have you gone?" John looked at the map and said "Not far." Agatha then said "Okay." She felt like she wanted to help John find the statue.

The next days, she contacted John again and

asked if he wanted help, but John refused. He said he wanted to succeed his first mission given to him, and that he wanted to be responsible. Just then, she got an idea. Her husband's friends could help her. She contacted them and told them to turn John's mind from doing his mission alone.

So, her husband's friends went to the hotel, but they could not find where the tunnel was by pretending to be customers. They were trying to find John, but it did not work. Plus, because of their bushy fur, they had to wear clothes specially made that made them look like humans and they were not able to move well with them on. Suddenly, they remembered that John was not a customer and was a worker so they had to search the manager's suite but they knew customers could not go inside so they had to just sneak into the manager's suite at night.

And while Agatha's husband's friends were making a plan, Ron was thinking. "John has not been at work for a week. He clearly has a plan. I should go to his room this night."

Meanwhile, inside the tunnel, John was thinking "Now, it has been pretty long since I have been in here and I'm not even half way down. I think I'm starting to lose my patience. He then stood up and opened the sack. He looked inside to find some food and got a banana. John was trying to save his food in the long, dark tunnel. The only thing that made the tunnel a wee bit brighter was his two flashlights strapped on to his sack.

Back at Agatha's house, Agatha was talking to her husband's friends using magic.

"Have you found John yet?"

"No. We can't seem to find where he lives."

"It's fine if you did not find him yet. But

please tell me if you find him! Oh, and also, it's the room with the tunnel in the bathroom."

"Okay. Thanks for telling us."

Agatha's husband's friends then waited until night and creeped into a room that looked empty. And Agatha said when they stepped into the bathroom, there was a tunnel. They carefully stepped inside and walked through the tunnel. They then saw a track that looked like something was dragged across the tunnel.

When they came to the end of it, they saw John in the distance. They ran towards him and said, "May we talk to you?" John then turned across and looked at them. He said, "Sure. But first can you tell me why you guys are here?" So, they told him about why they came here and that Agatha wanted to help. Then John said, "Well. I want to kind of do the mission on my own and I'm almost done."

"She just wants to give a little help."

"I think I'm fine for now. But if I need help, I'll call her right away."

"Okay, bye!"

"Wait. I think you know that you guys came too far to go back. How long did it take you guys to come here?"

"About one week?"

"I'm not sure if you would like to travel another week."

"Well, if we go with you, it will take longer to go back."

"Bye."

As they left, John thought. "I do not really have anything to do. I will start to organize." John stopped and sewed his bedspread and blankets together, then sewed them onto the sack to make a sleeping bag. He made a food compartment, a clothes compartment, and another compartment with other things and books. He moved his flashlight towards the front and sewed a pillow onto the sack.

He was still bored, so he opened his book. John was on chapter 7. He was reading about the part where the tree was removed, and John kept reading. It introduced two scientists, and John wanted to know what happened to them, so he continued reading.

John suddenly froze.

It was about how he was born and what happened. The picture showed two foxes, using their fur to create a creature. *Him*. He thought about school. He now understood why they bullied him. He also understood why everyone hid so many things from him. In the book, it told him that he was not born, and made by two foxes. He had been protected from the truth.

But when he saw their names, he thought one of the names seemed familiar. In the book it said "Ron" and "Ben" had made him. He thought Ron sounded a lot like his boss' name. But then he thought there are thousands of people with the name "Ron." And besides, those guys are foxes!

He then turned to where the picture was. In the picture, there was a fox that looked unbelievably similar to Ron, but he did not notice for he was too shocked with the news about how he was born. He then started to cry a bit. He wept and wept, then fell asleep, not even noticing that a page fell out of the book.

Meanwhile down at the office, Ron was thinking, John has not been here for a long time. I was going to go that night but I was too tired, I must do it now. So, Ron walked and he arrived at John's room. When he opened the door, there was nobody inside. He then went into the bathroom, and found the carpet thrown over to one side and found a tunnel hidden under the carpet.

Ron thought, John must be in here but I cannot go right away. The tunnel looks very long, so I should at least pack some things. So, he grabbed some food from the booth the customers were using, all his other belongings, and he grabbed a long piece of wood and attached wheels to it, then ran across the halls up the staircase, and into the tunnel.

While he was moving, he saw a piece of paper that looked like it had fallen out from a book. This seemed to be something John had left behind, so he carefully put it into his pocket. He then discovered a trail that looked like something was dragged across the tunnel. He then thought,

John must have been here, and looked at it.

While following the trail, he started to get hungry, so he grabbed a snack. The trail then seemed to end which was replaced by footprints. He then saw something else. Fox fur. Ron started to get more suspicious about John, and this time, there was even footprint of a fox. Ron thought weird. None of the foxes have disappeared from the zoo. What is he trying to do here now? All this is giving me a headache. Maybe I should rest for just a moment right now. I feel really tired. And after he said that, he went straight to sleep.

Meanwhile, John was still sliding towards the statue. He looked at the map and sighed. I still have to go like this for a month! He said to himself as he popped a slice of apple in his mouth and thought. I need to get the statue. The king can't live longer without this. I need to speed up, he thought. Another part of him said he should stop here. After all, the king had fooled him. What was the point of saving him? After some thinking, John decided this was still something that was important, far more important than his anger, so he looked at the map. There were two paths. According to the map, it said to go to the right, so he turned right.

The tunnel started to get damper and damper and he quietly said to himself, this feels like when I was young. That tunnel was also damp like this. Suddenly he thought 'What if this is the same tunnel? No, it can't. It was not this long.' As he ran, he thought the name 'Ron' kept him concerned just a little. Plus, the shock from the secrets of his birth was not small, so, this made him be unsure. And suddenly, he thought, would there be a reason to put all this important stuff in such a normal place. "I guess nobody would suspect it that way" he said. But as soon as he stopped thinking about its other stressful thoughts filled his head again. He couldn't stop thinking about them.

Back then, Ron was following the trail. There weren't many things left for him to use as a clue, so he pulled the piece of paper out of his pocket. He carefully examined each word with care. For a second, a devilish glare seemed to appear around him. Ron's face slowly darkened, then lightened up again. He smiled, and muttered "I've got it! I remember it… very vividly."

At that time, Ben was lying down in bed. He felt excited. He was going to escape and go somewhere. The orphanage was so small and dirty, and the rules were far too strict for a little boy. He did go to school, but it wasn't very good and he had to stay in the orphanage and work on Fridays. Of course, he had a plan. He was going to stay in the hotel across the street for a day, then leave the place and go far, far away. He had saved up his allowance for a year already.

The next day, he went outside and went across the street. It felt cold. Ben was wearing only his plaid shirt that was given to all the kids at the orphanage. Ben went into the hotel and hid in a food tray. He was pushed up to a room. He opened the bathroom door and saw a tunnel. He went in and soon saw a man staring at a paper. He took a glimpse at the paper and saw his name on it. He looked at it more closely and realized that it was something about him, and his biggest mistake. He read it but still only remembered John being created, nothing else.

He wondered why that man was holding the paper when the man looked up. He asked Ben why he was here. For Ben, the man seemed familiar. The man asked him if he knew about this paper. He answered him. He asked his name. It seemed like he knew him. He asked the man.

Why are you asking me this? The man said nothing.

Ron wanted to hear everything, so he quickly introduced himself. The boy was young, but he was Ben. Ron was absolutely sure, but he did not know what to tell Ben. Ron finally said quietly, "Are you the man I worked with on the project with?"

Ben was greatly puzzled by this man's behavior and did not know what he meant quite yet, but Ben said yes because he assumed it was about the creation. Ron responded "Very well. You will follow me and obey me." Then, Ron whispered "You want to get rid of him. Don't you?" Ben said "Who?" Ron said "You see, John." Ben nodded this time. Ron then continued "You will also help me on other things. You know, just to get the foxes in order." "I... I just want to know the rest of the story. I don't remember much other than the creation." Ben said. Ron said "Sure you will. Now just follow me! We have no time to waste!" Ben agreed and they went down the tunnel.

They went on the wheeled vehicle and zipped away. It was very fast, but it was also quite wobbly, and Ron seldom stopped, and Ben almost fell off. Ben said "Can we stop?" Ron shook his head. Ben then said "We've got to. I'm famished and I need to eat." Ron ignored him.

Suddenly, John heard footsteps behind him. He looked behind him and saw two silhouettes. John felt staying here would not do any good so he took off. No one was supposed to come in the tunnel. Who was it? And why were they here? He felt like the people he saw were following him. Why would they? He then continued sliding.

Just then he got a call from Agatha. He said

"Hello?" Agatha told him that she needed to do things quickly then asked him how far he had gone. He checked the map. "Um... About two weeks left." Then Agatha said "Okay. I am busy, so I'll have to hang up. Bye!" "Bye!"

John then thought that he should eat lunch. He peered in the sack and saw only a bag of lettuce. Now, this was a problem. He thought about asking the fox tribe for food but he knew they did not have time to send him food. Just then, he got an idea. He had read in the book that the fox statue can do almost anything. So, maybe when he arrives, he can get some food to eat. For now, he had to rely on just water and lettuce. He now had two reasons to get the fox statue, so he ran quickly towards the statue.

Meanwhile, Ron and Ben were searching for John. They had not seen John yet and Ben started to get tired. Ben started to feel drowsy now and asked Ron if they could take a break. Ron disagreed. He said "We can rest later, right? So, let's go." Ben continued riding, but felt an odd urge to disobey. He didn't know why he even had to always agree with what everyone said. He wanted to share his ideas.

While that was happening, Agatha was going home when she got a call from John. He said to Agatha, "Are you busy?" Agatha sarcastically answered "No." John then said "I have a problem." "What is it?" "I ran out of food." "We can't send you food right now. The king is sick and looks like they are preparing for a battle and that means we need to use a lot of food. Don't you know it takes a lot of power to send enough food for you to eat! We're in danger."

Agatha paused then said "Oh, I forgot to tell you something." "What is it?" "After you find the statue, you will see a wiggly wall. If you push it and open the left door, you'll see a horse soon and you will be able to come back to fox tribe. And don't open the right door. That was part of my trap." "Bye."

Meanwhile, John was wondering about the right door. He checked the map. It told him he had a couple days less than two weeks until he got to the statue. He was concerned about a lot but at least, this was going smooth enough for him to handle.

Just then, a thought popped into his head. Who were the people that I saw? I've never seen them before. Once again, he heard the sound. He kept on sliding. This time, he caught a glimpse of a boy. John wanted to know what was going on but continued sliding. Soon, he could not hear the noise.

Meanwhile, Ron and Ben were taking a break.

They had almost caught up to John but he ran away and they almost ran into a wall. They got up again and started looking or John again. Ron said "We almost caught him. We were pretty close." He ran away to get him. "If we go now, we could find him." They walked for a long time (the wheels fell off the vehicle) when suddenly they heard a sound from down the tunnel. They went to examine it and they saw John but John was sliding at a tremendous speed and they could not catch up to him at the moment.

Meanwhile, John was trying to find food. He had already gobbled up the lettuce so knew his bag did not have any food but he checked his bag anyway. He knew the only way to get food was to find the statue and he ran his hardest he could to get there in a week.

Just then, he got a call from Agatha. "Hi, John" "Hi" "There is a big problem" "Oh no. What is it?" "You know how I told you that the dogs looked like they were going to fight?" "Yeah" "They started to attack and about 2 humans were fighting with them. It's getting crazy and you need to quickly come back!" "Actually, to find the statue, I need food." "Okay. But since we are busy, I can only send you a little bit of food because sending you a lot of food will take more time." "That's fine." "I will send the food soon. Bye!"

Soon, the food arrived and John started eating. It was a plant that grew in fox tribe called Kibosh. Now he couldn't go very fast. The hill became uphill. He felt tired. He heard footsteps again and ran away. As soon as the footsteps stopped, he stopped running too. He felt dizzy.

Just then, he saw a glimmer. He instantly ran towards it but he could not find out where it was coming from, but he kept running towards it. He did not ever know why he was running. All he knew was that he wanted to see where the glimmer was coming from.

Suddenly, he stopped running.

A step away from him, there was the glorious fox statue. It looked as if someone had sprayed gold over it and had a mystical colour. It looked like a fox, but John felt happy after finding the statue. This was the time of his life and he felt amazingly happy for the first time. He started to weep. The goal of his life was accomplished and he felt like he had the world. Then, he gazed at the statue for a moment and quickly grabbed it. He pushed the wall and opened the door. He then came across the horse. John hopped on and the horse instantly started moving.

Soon, the horse came to a stop. He realized that where it had stopped was in front of

Agatha's house. John opened the front door and said hello to Agatha. She said to John "Hello, how have you been?" "I'm good. Oh! And here is the fox statue." "Isn't it mystical? The king will be better in no time."

Agatha then caught a nice chicken and gave it to him. Agatha said "Will you please bring the statue to the king?" John said "Well, I still have to go back and complete some missions. After that, I think I might want to come back here. Agatha said "Well, the government said that you should start a career by being my apprentice. Then, you can work for the government in some sort of way. While your apprentice, we've got to work together to clear up things about war and prevent it from happening." John said "So, as soon as I finish the missions, I can come back?" Agatha said "No, they say you should still be a spy while you're my apprentice. After all, you've got the training." John said "Anyway, you should bring the statue to the king." "All right. I can do that."

After he left the house, John thought, I want to see what's behind the right door. So, after a long talk about the statue, he said that he needed to complete another mission and went back on the horse. He opened the right door. First, John saw a room appearing to be a classroom. Another space was filled with books and documents labeled 'top secret'. John thought for a moment, then took all of them and put them in his bag in the same order it was on the shelves and explored farther. Then he saw a tiny machine. He clicked a button and suddenly the ground collapsed, revealing a ladder. He climbed down it and put another book into his sack.

Ron and Ben were at the end of the tunnel. Ben said "I am so confused. Shouldn't someone be here?" Ron said "John has to be somewhere.

Now help me look for him." "Okay." Ron then said, "Hey, I found an entrance to somewhere! Come in." Ben said "There are two doors. Where should we go?" "Let's go to the left. I have a feeling John will be there." "Okay. Wait. Isn't that a horse?" "Let's try it." So, they went on the horse and arrived at Agatha's house. Ron thought "Weird. I thought John would be here."

Suddenly, they saw Agatha entering her house. They couldn't recognize her because she went straight in the house but it still gave them a strange feeling. It also made them wonder why there were so many foxes. Ron said "This must be fox tribe. We have to be careful that we are not caught." Ben said "Can't we just go back to the tunnel? You can also explain about fox tribe" Ron said "That would be safer I guess." Ben said "Then let's go back. Maybe somebody will be in there." Ron said "Okay". So, they went back to the tunnel. Ron said "Ben, don't you feel like we should go to the other way this time?" "What are you talking about?" "I mean we should go to the right door." "Okay"

Then, as they went on the horse, Ben asked, "Could you tell me about John's creation?" Ron said, "Oh, you were kind of being pathetic, so I suggested we created a creature, but you messed it up." Ben was about to say something, but they arrived and went in the right door. "Where is this place?" "I don't know. Wait, I hear a sound." "What is it?" Ron muttered "Sounds like a person. Maybe it's John. Let's go investigate it." "Wait. Is that John?" "Yes, it is." Meanwhile, John was investigating the rooms. He thought "It's so peaceful in here. What a good place to be. Suddenly, he heard footsteps. It sounded like the footsteps he heard in the tunnel. He thought, "Oh my, what's happening?" Just then, he saw a door and tried to open it but before he opened it, Ron and Ben came dashing into the room. However, John didn't see them because he opened the door and escaped. John quickly ran back to his room.

As Ron rushed him towards the door, Ben thought everything happening was odd. He was currently doing something he did not want to do and clearly displayed injustice. Ben also hated hearing all those negative remarks that were given. He did have a strong feeling of hatred for John, but Ben felt he was headed for a different direction with Ron. He felt guilty but decided to help Ron. He then started to wonder about the house he saw when he went out of the tunnel. The person coming out of that house gave him a strange feeling for some reason. It made him want to go inside.

THE BIRTH OF A HUMAN

An Encounter with the Truth

4. An Encounter with the Truth

Ben slipped away back to fox tribe. He went out and knocked on the front door. There was no answer, but he went in. There were three kids. They said in fox "Why, isn't that a human?" He asked "Where are your parents?" in English since he did not know how to speak fox. Of course, none of the foxes understood and the oldest one said in fox, "What are you saying?" Ben then felt something strange and familiar and understood that language and tried to speak it. He said in fox "I am ……. to ask where your parents are." One then said "It's trying to. Anyways, she's always at work because some dogs attacked and now, she comes back at midnight. Our dad is a professor. After that school got so famous, we almost never saw him. Anyways, who are you?" He said "I'm Ben."

Suddenly the kids' faces froze. They said. "We aren't talking with you. You were related to that crazy thing!" Ben asked "What crazy thing? Why don't you want to talk to me?" The oldest child said "The whole human incident. You know, it's pretty much all your fault. The humans got out of control and..." "How do you guys know so much about this?" They replied, "Because we are Agatha's children." Ben now realized why he felt that strange woman gave him a special and weird feeling.

He then said to the children "I only remember a little of that time. Could you tell me?" He had actually said this because the kids seem lonely but also because what Ron told him did not seem like the truth. The kids accepted because they were very bored. They asked him "You know this is fox tribe, right?" Ben said, "Yes, I know."

"A long time ago, before we were born, the King moved a tree because it was covering the window. Ben asked, "Why didn't he just cut.... tree?" the kids said "It's against the law of every country except for the humans to damage any living things. I did not know that when you turn into a human, how you think about things change too." Ben said, "What do you mean? How do foxes think?" The kids said "we are more caring for nature. We also are better than any other creature. Anyways, back to the story.

So, the King put the tree in a forest. But suddenly, he gets sick, so you and Ron go to the forest where the tree is, and try to figure out why the King got sick. First, you concentrated but you soon found something called the life seed which makes life shorter and your tail to make something called "Human."

Your first human did not turn out how you

wanted it to be for you guys because you guys did not put in any life seed and put in too much fox tail. As a result, that human got to live forever and thought like a fox. The only thing that was human was his looks. That human's name was John. You guys thought he was made wrong. You guys did not like him. Anyways, the other humans were made how you wanted them to be like.

Then, our mother saw someone there and reported what you were doing because it's illegal to make creatures here. However, the police came and Ron ran away. Ron ran away and you stayed. As a result, you got arrested, and the humans started polluting the earth for some reason. You can't blame them, though. You were there and you made them with your very paws.

Anyways, the pollution made the King even sicker. We came up with an idea to train them to stop polluting the earth. So, we pretended to be humans and wore something that made us look like humans. They easily got fooled and followed us into a place called the human training centre which is now the hotel Ron owns." Ben was very surprised. He wondered if Ron knew that it used to be the centre.

Just then the kids started to talk again. Our mother taught some humans there and taught them how to restore nature and to stop polluting the earth. Eventually things started to get better and the pollution reduced. Still, the king's sickness did not seem to get better. They actually had been holding meetings in the animal kingdom though, and the king had gone there but his sickness stopped him from going and without him the meeting was not able to go on. So, our mother started brainstorming some idea like using "the book"

Ben asked, "what is the book?" The kids answered, "The book is a book that writes down everything in history. It takes a lot of power to make because it writes down everything by itself and also has special secrets and magic but it is very fragile. If you rip a page, you cannot restore it ever. Our mother thought that would help us figure out how to deal with this situation and it did." Ben asked "How?"

The kids answered, "Uh, we don't know. Then, Ben asked, "How do you know all of these things?" The kids said, "We read the book out mother keeps. There is only four in the world now because one disappeared." Also, your grammar is quite odd. Don't you think?" Ben then replied, "Well... Yes."

Actually, Ben wasn't paying much attention to the question. He had thought about something. He was going to betray Ron. Ben had joined him because he seemed bold. But in truth, he was overtly deceitful and did not let Ben think or do anything independently. Ben sometimes even felt in an odd way that he could not explain as if he were being filtered out. He also repressed him a lot. Ben decided he would try to fight John alone and ran towards the human world.

Meanwhile, Ron was thinking of a plan. A plan to make his desires comes true. He thought about what was wrong. He needed wipe it out of the world to create a utopia. He did not like foxes and how they thought. Ron said "The fox, snobby and hypocritical, uses whatever method to get to their goal. They shall be changed into something more agreeable, such as a human. John is an even bigger problem. He is a horrid creation and mistake, and not unlike a misspelt word. When you spell something wrong, you erase it. Therefore, John must be erased from this world. I must create a plan to accomplish this."

After he finished his plan, he thought what if the foxes recognize me? How will I turn foxes into humans? Will the humans believe me and other things? But he knew that first he had to go to fox tribe to get a fox to hypnotize and to fool the foxes. But he did not know how to get to fox tribe, so he put on fox paw gloves and shoes, and wore a cloak covering his entire body and face, only slightly showing his eyes. He put on red lenses to seem more mysterious.

Ron kept walking around until he found a fox wandering around wearing a wreath and leaf coat. He thought this must be fox tribe and followed that fox. Then, some foxes crowded around him and brought him to an old fox, saying they brought anyone to the castle to see if the king would be cured. He looked very sick. Ron then suddenly remembered who the old fox was: he was the king. He thought this is a great change to fool everyone by telling them about John.

Ron lifted up his head to show his glowing red eyes and said with a beaming voice (he remembered fox and was fluent) "I see all of you have been making erroneous assumptions. You do not know what the disease is caused by, though I am certain you will be able to cure the king, so please listen. You must all find John, for he is the one causing the disease with his evil mind. He has partnered with the humans. Peace can only come after John vanishes."

Most of the foxes seemed convinced, saying things like "I knew the dirty beast had to be planning a plot!" "The man's right! It's all plain mischief when John's around!" Just then, a fox dressed in odd things and religious items flew into the room. She shouted "John's got the statue! Look at this!" as she held up a small, glowing statue.

All eyes were on Agatha now, as she handed it to the king. She also handed the king a paper that has the spell to cure diseases.

The king read out loud in a trembling voice, the paper shaking. Ron was shaking just as much as the paper. He was trembling with fear. When the king read the last verse out loud, everybody held their breath and waited.

They waited,

And waited,

And waited, but...

Nothing happened. The king let out a cough. Now all eyes were fixed on Agatha again, but this time they were angry eyes. They pushed her to the side and looked at Ron. Ron said, "Just try to rid John! He's the one causing all the trouble. It was all fine before his birth!"

Agatha interrupted "Excuse me, but the king was sick before John was born! A couple centuries ago, he cut that blessed tree and…" A courtier snapped back "Shut up! How dare you mention the subject!" Ron said "I suppose all you courtiers would know better than to disagree with an idea that will save the king, and all of us. Everything did start from John!" He then glanced at Agatha, watching her face beginning to get red.

Ron then thought "I have very little time. I better finish quickly." Ron thought. He said he needed to go and went back to the human world. He returned to the hotel and got ready. He took off the cloak and changed. Just when he was about to go outside, Ron remembered that he had forgotten to bring a hypnotized fox, so he got out a fox costume he made and went back to fox tribe and tried to find a fox.

Just then, he heard talking inside a house and went in. In there, he saw two fox cubs and Ben. Ron thought, "Why is Ben here?" He asked Ben to come outside and said to him. "Why are you here?" Ben answered, "I was um…Just investigating some things." Ron said, "Why did you not tell me?" Ben answered, "Sorry, I forgot. What were you doing?" Ron said "Just some things. You don't need to know." Ben then asked Ron, "Can I do some more investigation? I am trying to find something out." Ron couldn't trust him but said he was fine with it, because he was planning to do some special things.

After checking that Ben got back into the house, Ron went to get a fox to hypnotize. He found a fox and tried to hypnotize him but Ron was not able to hypnotize the fox and the fox then tried to sue him.

After hours of searching and running away,

he found a fox he was able to hypnotize. He carried the hypnotized fox along with him. Ron went over to the human's side and changed into his uniform. Then, he wore his brown coat and put a hat on.

Ron went up on a podium and tried to show he had an announcement to make. Everybody looked at him, because they saw many cameras taking pictures of him and reporters trying to ask questions. (He had bribed them) Ron said John, the zookeeper of the hotel, had been training the foxes from not only the zoo, but also from all around the forests and had been planning to harm the town. He showed them the hypnotized fox, which was trying to attack the humans and added that John had also been murdering innocent residents taking a walk in the forest.

Half of the people did not believe him and half of them got fooled. Then, he said, "The foxes have actually established a society under John called fox tribe and they are using John as a spy. They are going to attack soon, so we need to attack before they attack us. You see, it won't be hard to do." The audience clapped and cheered this time.

Just then, Ron saw John and said "That's him! It's John!"

As soon as Ron said that, they all ran towards John. John was quite puzzled and asked what was happening. The townspeople didn't answer and instead started to ask him questions. They asked about fox tribe, and John did not have a choice but to lie. Luckily, the people believed him. They then took him to Ron.

John was still very puzzled, but when Ron looked at him, John suddenly felt shivers down his spine. Ron was the person that created him, even though John had no idea how he was a human. This all made sense since the book also said something about his creators hating him. Ron looked at him again and started to mutter some odd words. John tried to resist it. He looked deeper into Ron's eyes and tried to fight it, but it seemed so strong, and it was hard to fight. John started to get tired. Finally, when he was about to give up, he saw a silhouette of a boy.

Ben dashed towards John and pulled him away. John didn't know what was happening now. John still felt dizzy and limped over to the ground. Ron also seemed a bit startled, so Ben dragged John through the door. John told Ben where he lived, and Ben carried him up.

Ron said, "As you have just seen, John has many followers. It is our duty to stop John. To do this, I'll tell you where all the foxes are. They are all out there, across the forest, and the foxes live in their holes and caves. We have to get them before they get us. We will form an army, and we will need thousands of people. I will provide weapons and proper gear."

THE BIRTH OF A HUMAN

The Beginning of a Split

5. The Beginning of a Split

After saying that, Ron said he needed to go and left. He quickly dashed to the harbor and boarded a boat. The boat went to an island, and from there Ron used a plank to float to the other one. There, he started to search frantically. He was trying to trace his memories back to where he found the life tree. After hours of searching, found the life tree. It was only about as big as a flowerpot. He took only a single life seed, but Ron thought it was enough to make someone ill. If it shortened their lives, that meant it made them ill! He then took the tree and put it into a grocery bag.

Ron then went back to the hotel and told his workers they were having a 'health checkup', and that they needed to sneeze into a cup and give it to him. After collecting all the samples, He started to extract viruses from the samples and mix it into the seed. He wanted a perfect mixture, so nobody gets too ill, but still sick enough to be scared of the virus. It also had to be something that did not harm the foxes, because the humans would suspect him if the foxes also got sick from the virus. He also put in some other things he needed to put like a special medicine he could try making which would make people angry and aggressive so that they could get in war with the foxes faster.

Soon, he was able to get the mixture he wanted, so he made a different mixture, this one to cure the disease. After he finished this, Ron went back, and called his friend who owned the restaurant down the road and offered to advertise his food for him at the hotel. Ron went to the restaurant and went inside the kitchen. It happened to be Sunday, so there was only Ron and his friend in the store.

They talked for a while and discussed the budget they needed. When his friend left to use the washroom, Ron dropped the virus into all the foods he saw. Then he had a longer talk about how to display the sign that would advertise the food, and Ron left. He also called a friend of his, who made signs, and told him that he needed to make a sign for the local restaurant and asked him to go there and design the sign. Ron did this so that they wouldn't suspect him when the virus started spreading.

Meanwhile, John was talking with Ben. John had already thanked him a million times, while Ben stayed calm and looked at John in the most unfriendly way a person could imagine. Ben only was helping John to get rid of Ron. He then would also betray John and start making his own moves. However, John was still not taking the slightest notice of that and thanking him.

John said "When I wanted to give up, you magically appeared! I realized it was you! I'll do anything for you! How on earth did you even get here anyway?" Ben said "I left." John continued "I am so thankful, and I promise you that you're going to be home in the orphanage soon, safe and happy! Don't worry!" This was the worst thing Ben had heard.

Ben said "I thought you were going to do anything for me." John said "True!" Ben asked "Well, I despised the orphanage, and I don't wish to return." John said "Young fella, you have to go back where you're safe and happy!" Ben said "Where I was is somewhere that makes me unhappy. It's also not very safe, considering the fact there's a family of rats living in there and that you get beat."

John stared at Ben. Ben said "Could you

consider adoption?" John said "Well... I see it isn't all that pleasant there, but it's hard for me to adopt you. Still, I think we can try." So, they went to the orphanage and John was able to adopt Ben, so John took Ben back to the hotel.

John wanted to do more for Ben, so John asked Ben what he wanted. Without hesitation, Ben said he wanted to go to school. John nodded. Ben said that he wanted to go to school. He had told John this because he wanted to learn more things and develop his advantages so that he could start again better and protect himself from getting into worse situations.

John agreed and then realized that to send Ben to school he would need a lot of things and to get those things he would need a lot of money. As soon as he got back to the hotel he asked if he could work every day. After that John asked Ben which school he wanted to go to. Ben wanted to go to a private school but because Ben saved John and John wanted to help him, John signed Ben up. He then went to the store and bought some things that Ben would need for school.

After he came back from the store John fell asleep. He was so tired that day. First, he was captured by some people, then he met Ben, then he had to go to the store. And so, he fell asleep right away.

The next day, John went to work. Ron was not there. John was quite glad, because He knew that it wouldn't be very pleasant to see him after all that's happened.

After work was finished John still could not find out where Ron went, so he went to get some more of Ben's school supplies. He was not able to find anything for Ben, but he got an idea that could help him a lot. He walked back to the house and took out his wand. He thought that Ben might think he was weird if Ben saw he was doing magic so he went into the bathroom and took a look at the list. John made all the things on the list but some of them came out wrong. He made a fountain pen, but it didn't have ink, the pencil case was as big as the tub, and the textbooks were typed in fox.

John asked Ben to find the pictures for his school supplies list. Ben wondered why John had asked him to get those pictures. John quickly made a computer and a printer and gave it to Ben telling him to copy the pictures off of the computer. He then added, "That computer is yours now." The computer was useless to John. Ben printed the pictures off then gave them to John. John packed all of the things he made in a brown backpack with leather straps and put it on a hook. He said softly to Ben, "You have school tomorrow, okay?" Ben did not like John treating him like a six-year-old, but he thought that this was the only way for now, so he went to bed and stopped thinking.

The next day, when Ben went to school, everyone was looking at him. John had made some minor mistakes on three or four items even after the second try, and everyone was staring at Ben because of his weird equipment. Ben had decided not to care what others thought, so that didn't affect him a lot. He was too concentrated in the lesson. He needed to learn more if he wanted to outsmart his opponents.

Still, almost everything felt easy for him, because he used to be a scientist. Everything he learnt in science and math was unbelievably easy, and he couldn't understand why his classmates were struggling. Everything else was still interesting enough to learn, though it was all fairly easy. Ben only struggled in English classes.

When Ben came back home, John asked him how school was. Ben said "Fine." John got a bowlful of meat, mashed potatoes, and broccoli and gave it to Ben. Ben felt weird. He could not find out why John was acting so nice to him. Barely anybody would act like that to him. He also felt weird about having to act like a kid to John. He felt a good and bad feeling he could not describe with words.

The next day, when Ben came from school, John asked him how school was again. Ben had a hard time fitting in, so he said "Difficult." Though Ben didn't feel as awful as John thought he did, John suddenly felt a sense of belonging. He was able to relate to how Ben felt. He was happy to have someone he could relate with. After the short talk, Ben fell asleep. John felt good, and he thought about when he was little. Fitting in was hard after two long years of homeschooling, and looking different was a big problem. He always wanted someone to talk to. John assumed that Ben was going through a time like that, and John wanted to help him. After all, Ben was only a child that didn't know much other than the things little people like to think about.

Meanwhile, Ron was going to the hotel. He was trying to figure out a plan to make more of the virus for he did not know where to go to find more of it. He also needed to revise his plan, and get some things loaded up. Ron knew that in order to do this, he needed a space of his own.

Suddenly, he got an idea. He could attach an even bigger tunnel that went all the way to fox tribe. That way it would be easier to do his plan and to do all his experiments. He started to think about how the tunnel would look like. He would make the tunnel clear just in case he found something interesting outside. It needed to also have a lot of rooms and lab tools along with a transportation he could use inside the tunnel. He also wanted to have a room to store military weapons, he wanted a transportation cart, and a big office, and a place to put the hypnotized fox.

After making the plan he went to the store and got all his things, and ordered large glass tubes. He then connected all of them and placed a track on top of it. After, he got some old vehicles and made them into a whole new transportation. After he was done placing all the lab tools in the rooms, Ron got some lights and screwed them in.

He looked at his work and decided to test the vehicles. It was not a very comfy thing to ride on, but it was certainly fast. It was similar to a car, but it did not move along as smoothly, it was extremely fast, and it was made out of old vehicles so it was rusty, even though he had painted it. After testing it out, Ron was so tired that he fell asleep.

The next day, Ben was walking back home from school, holding on to his long, charcoal-coloured coat so it didn't drag across the grass (John had made the uniform larger than the actual size) and staring into the sky. He was too busy thinking about things to bother looking down, but soon, he tripped on something. He uncovered it and looked at it. It was very shiny, and very hard. Ben stepped back and looked at it.

It didn't seem to be dangerous, so he uncovered it a little more, enough to see the other parts. Ben saw clear glass, and the glass was shaped like a tube, connected with strong, iron cables. The insides showed a rickety vehicle that was a mixture of black and purple, a bucket of paint beside the vehicle, and several doors that were closed, with weird steam lurking outside. Ben looked at it. He felt weird. Just then, the door opened up, revealing a silhouette of a man. Ben turned to look, but quickly moved towards the side after noticing the person look upwards. Ben noticed who the person was.

Ben dashed to the hotel as fast as he could and brushed the dust off his favorite coat that was now not very clean. He was a bit worried. He wanted to call John, but did not want everybody downstairs to notice. Ben made up his mind, changed into his pajamas and put his coat back on. He snuck down the staircase and pulled John to the side. John pushed Ben away and said "You can't interrupt me when I'm working here, all right? Now, let's get to bed." Ben thought for a moment, and said to himself that he would take a risk. He pulled John over again and whispered to him in fox "It's an emergency."

John went over to him and gasped. Ben said in fox "If you busy, come later. I not interrupt." John told Ben to wait just five minutes, and John soon came back. John was astounded that Ben could speak fox, though it wasn't fluent, and could not focus on his work.

When they were all settled in their room, John asked "How are you a human?" Ben told him. John thought about how ironical the situation was. While his creator was Ben, John was his legal guardian. Ben seemed to notice that too, and tried to act like a grown-up. John then said, "Why were you in such a hurry? You don't even speak to me much." Ben said "Well, I have something important to tell you." John asked "What do you want to tell me?" Ben said "Today, when I was walking back from school, I tripped on something. It was so hard and shiny, and it felt bumpy. I was curious, so I uncovered it, and there was a glass tunnel that had some sort of laboratory inside. There were many doors, with steam lurking out, and I saw someone coming out one of the doors."

John asked "Who was it?" Ben hesitated for a moment, and said "It was Ron." As he said that, Ben was slowly able to see the colour drain out of John's face. John said, trembling "Oh no... I think I know what's going to happen, but I don't want to say." Ben said "Nothing could happen if you say it. I'll just tell you all the facts I know. Ron detests you with every ounce of his heart. It appears he would like to put an end to you. You see, you are made wrong, and we shall have to erase you."

John shouted "I'm perfectly fine!" However, Ben continued. "It appears that Ron wants to change the world in his own ways." John asked "Did Ron tell you about your lives before? Like I mean non-human?" Ben said "Yes, but he exaggerated some parts." John said "So he does know what happened before?" Ben nodded. John said "I guess if Ron knows both fox and human sides well, he could make them fight. You see… The day you saved me, as soon as Ron told everyone to get me, they were running like crazy towards me." Ben said "The way I see it, the solution to this problem, which is mostly you, is most likely you. You've got to do some things."

John felt like he was blacked out. It felt like too much to do. John knew he needed to think of a plan and that there was no time to think about his feelings now. He asked Ben what they needed to do but Ben said he had not thought about it and that John needed to figure it out.

Meanwhile, Agatha's husbands' friends were taking a walk near the human world. After a while, they were starting to get bored until suddenly, one of them came up with an idea. He suggested going to the human world. Everyone agreed so they went to their houses, wore their human suit, and went to the human world. One of them remembered that they needed a place to stay so they went into the nearest house and were kicked out within a minute. They did not know why they had been kicked out so they tried over and over again but the results were the same, so they decided to go to the hotel they had went.

They needed the paper they used in the human world so they went all the way back to fox tribe and asked for the green paper Agatha called money they had used to Agatha. Agatha gave them a sack full of it and they headed back to the human world. They got a room in the hotel and then went outside to explore. When they went into one of the buildings, they saw a screen as small as the human's front paws. It was something humans made magic with called a phone. They went to all the shops that sold them and bought every single one. They wanted to show the king those amazing things so they went back to fox tribe and went to the king, showing him and the servants how to work it, what it does, and what you can create, but not everyone was interested.

However, they left most of them there and they brought some of them to Agatha. They taught her the same things they taught the king and Agatha gladly accepted them. Agatha decided she would convince the government to use these things. She also thought that it would be nice if she gave some to John so she put the things in a box and went to sleep. The next day, she was very busy. She had no time to send it.

Meanwhile, Ron was preparing to move on to his next plan. He went to the nearest phone store to buy a phone but they were all sold out.

He asked one of the staff what happened and he told him two men with a sack full of money bought all of the phones in the store and left. He went to another store but they said the same thing. Ron started to wonder who the two people were and asked the phone store staff how they looked and what they looked like they were doing but he could not get any clues or a hint. Ron now needed to find out a way to do his plan with only one phone.

Meanwhile, Agatha was sending four phones to John. John was amazed, because Agatha had a phone when all of them were sold out. John asked Agatha where she got it and Agatha told him that her husband's friends gave it to her. Agatha told him that the government had it too and they have a secret website which she had created and she told him also that he could use her ID to join the website.

He told Ben about it, and Ben said that he would try to think of a plan. Ben first divided up the phones so they each had two, and said one would be for sharing information and using the website, and the other would be private. John nodded. They went on to the website, recorded past events of fox tribe, and shared them. Ben didn't have any trouble doing this, but John was having a hard time after knowing what the foxes thought of him. However, they managed to finish this.

Meanwhile, Ron was walking around the halls of the hotel, inspecting the halls. When he got to the fifth floor, He took the key and opened the door a little bit.

It seemed like John was already sleeping. He was holding two phones and was fast asleep. John's orange and brown hair was tangled and sprawled all over the bed, tangled into someone else's. Ron opened the door a bit more. It revealed the pale face of Ben. Ron closed the door. Ron mumbled "So it was him that saved John. Funny... I thought he hated John more than me." He quietly walked back to his room.

While Ron was doing this, Agatha was coming back from work and returning home. She was happy to see her husband and children because she had worked for 3 days and nights. But for some reason she was starting to head towards the human world. She then arrived at the hotel. Suddenly, she saw a dark figure approaching. He was heading in to the hotel. Agatha wasn't following because she didn't have her human costume, but she still wanted to find out who it was.

The next day, Agatha wore her human costume and went to the hotel. She wasn't able to find anyone but found a big tunnel covered with dirt. The tunnel was made out of glass and had metal cables that attached the glass tubes. There were rooms all along the tunnel which had tools or bottles with liquids. As she kept following the tunnel, she walked back in to fox tribe. When she reached the end of the tunnel, she saw a small door and climbed inside.

She wanted to see what the liquids, were so she took some of the flasks and adventured farther into the tunnel. She saw a thing that had handles and lights so she climbed on. It bumped all around the tunnel but managed to stay on the tracks. It was also way faster than a car and blew all the fur off her.

She then climbed off and opened another door which led her in to another tunnel. It was very steep so it was hard to climb up but she kept climbing. After a while, she got tired, so she used her magic and climbed up, which took only a minute.

Then, she saw another door. It was bigger than the last one and had a rusty handle. Just then she realized that this was the place she put her fox statue. Agatha still did not know what the glass tunnel was. She then stopped thinking and opened the door.

Agatha saw John in the corner with a boy up to his chin. She went up to John and asked him what was happening. At first, John did not answer her but then he told her his plan and said that he was stuck. Agatha handed him the bottles and told him it might help. Then she asked about the kid and John told her that it was Ben and about what he was doing here. Agatha ordered John to stop Ben from using the phones and to leave him. Agatha quickly left and went back to fox tribe. When she returned home, it was already dark outside.

Meanwhile, Ron was going to the tunnel he had built. But when he entered the tunnel, he knew something was wrong. There were fox footprints everywhere and some of the bottles were gone. Some fox had ruined his tunnel completely!

Ron was not very happy with what had happened and he was determined to succeed his plan now. He thought that it would be better if he went to fox tribe and checked what their weapons were so he headed to people that did not need to see fox tribe after dressing up like a fox and wearing a fox costume he made in his lab by using special chemicals. When he asked to see the weapons, they refused to show him and asked why he wanted to see them.

Ron said he was sent from the government to check it but they still refused because they did not want to show the tools to other people that were not related to the weapons so Ron said that he was a new army general that came here to check the tools.

As soon as he said that they led him into a room stalked with rocks. Ron wondered why only rocks were there, but he decided not to ask because they would notice he was a human, but curiosity got the best of him and he asked them. They thought he was joking so they told him it was because it was very important to not be unnatural and use something that was not from nature, so they used rocks. This made Ron very glad, for his plan would work out even better this way. As he happily headed back to the human world he started to skip. His plans were working out amazingly.

Meanwhile, Agatha was looking at the web site. Suddenly, she started getting ten texts that were all about how she had so many IDs. Agatha told all of them that she had a lot of backup ids because she forgets a lot so that was why. Then, she started exploring the website and checking if there were any more updates.

As Agatha was enjoying her rest, John and Ben were studding the virus in the bottle Agatha had given them so that they could find a vaccine for it and stop Ron's plans. At that time, Ben was thinking of an idea. He thought that John needed to learn some magic. He thought that John already knew most magic so he decided to teach John how to do complicated magic. Ben knew that if the foxes found out, they would definitely get into a bad situation, but he thought it was worth doing, so he decided to talk to John about that later.

A couple hours after getting to bed, John woke up because of a light coming from the back of the room so he silently crept towards it. He found out that the light was coming from the bottle with the virus inside of it. He put it on the counter to show Ben later and then went back to sleep.

Meanwhile, Agatha was walking near her house with her family but she was still thinking about the miraculous adventures that she had in the human world and she could not concentrate on the walk. Besides, she had nothing to do and adventure was calling her more than ever. She knew she could not go but she told her family that she had to go somewhere and quickly left. Running through the cold, dark woods Agatha went towards the human world.

She heard human sounds so she hid in a bush and waited. A man was climbing out on to the stage and dozens of people were following behind. Because it was so dark outside, Agatha could not see who was on the stage, but he seemed very familiar to her. Suddenly, chills went down her spine. The person on the stage was talking about the foxes starting a war and trying to take over. Agatha knew that the humans might start a war but he did not know who, or what was behind all of it.

She knew she had to tell John. The man continued to speak. "We should attack soon so the foxes are not going to win. They have special war tools and we need to attack them quickly. Then, Agatha heard shouts and cheers. She knew that the war was about to start. She was scared but she knew that she did not have time for that and she was determent to find a way out of this war. First, she let John know and asked him to think about what they could do. John was a little bit stressed.

Suddenly, he had run in to a bunch of big

problems. He was not sure what wars were but he heard that it was a scary thing. He thought that Ben could help him so he went to Ben and asked him if he could do anything. Ben thought that war was not going to be dangerous.

Meanwhile Ron was thinking about war plans. He could use his tunnel also as a food transportation and war tools transportation. He knew he could make a lot of money with that business and control the war. He was very excited. Ron called an arms dealer he knew, and told him about John and his army trying to start the war. The arms dealer thought this was a joke at first, but Ron showed him the headlines that the bribed reporters wrote. Ron was easily able to get many weapons, enough to give each to everyone in the country. Ron thanked his friend and went back to the tunnel. He left the weapons at his tunnel, but he took a box full. Ron now wore his fox costume and cape, and put on his lenses. He headed for fox tribe.

THE BIRTH OF A HUMAN

The Prelude to War

6. The Prelude to War

At fox tribe, the king had just gotten the news that the humans were going to invade their land. He knew that the humans had better tools and that this was going to be the biggest war in fox history. His magic was weak and not many people could use magic good enough to make the humans go back. He immediately contacted all the courtiers and ordered them to find out a way to make the humans go away. Agatha thought if the humans were coming then she could use her magic to fly them back to the human's world, but that plan would use up most of her energy.

The castle was full of arguments and angry courtiers. Suddenly, the door swung open, and a man dressed in a black cape entered. Ron looked around and said "I see we have a problem here."

The king said "Very true. We can't let the humans come to our kingdom, and nobody has a decent idea." Ron said "I have a good plan. The humans are armed with amazing weapons and they can make this kingdom disappear in a matter of hours. I think we also shall be armed. That is the only way to drive them out of the land. Here I have some fine guns…"

Agatha said "If we are armed, we will be acting in a very unnatural way! We can't possibly do that!" Ron said "Oh, well, the humans will kill every one of us with their 'unnatural' weapons, and the kingdom will come to an end. All animals naturally have to be ruthless to survive." This seemed quite right to the foxes, and the king clapped. Ron tossed them the box and left.

He knew one box was not enough to fight the humans, but this was quite significant, as the foxes had given up their important value to get the humans off their land.

Agatha thought. "I will need to ask John to find a way so that I can figure out a way with him." She quickly said to John, we need to find a way to stop the war. We cannot let the thing happen, especially with the new weapons being used. John thought that he needed to ask Ben for some help. He told Ben about what they needed to do and how they were going to do it.

Soon, they decided that they could spilt the work in half by one person working on the war things such as how to stop the war with the other person working on the virus which was about the bottle and the vaccine (the virus was spreading rapidly and Ben found out that there was a relationship between the virus and the tunnel). Since the work they had to do was related to each other, they could help each other out. Ben decided to do the vaccine and John wanted to work on things about the war. They also tried to figure out more about fox tribe and Ron's plans.

John knew that they needed to ask Agatha for help with things like the war and sent a mail asking for help. John asked Ben if he needed any help. Ben said "From whom?" John said "A lady that works with me at fox tribe. She's kind of like my boss." Ben said "So is she a fox?" "Yes. She's the one that gave us her ID." Ben asked "What's her name?" John said "Agatha. She's a very talented woman."

Ben shrieked. "You don't mean I've been working with her all along, right?" John said "Well, she's helped us from the start!" Ben panicked "Does she know about this? With me working with you and all that..." John said "She does! For some reason, she doesn't like it. I have no idea why, but she told me not to share all my information with you." Ben said "Don't you know what happened?" John said "What happening?" Ben told John the whole story, and John said he wouldn't mention the subject anymore. Ben told John he hoped that didn't happen.

Ben said, "I don't need any help. If you would like to help me, could you learn just one thing from me? For us to foil Ron's plans, it would be better if you learned more magic." John said, "I know a lot of magic! I can call, send things, make things move, and though it is not very good, I can even copy things off paper and make them 3-D! Most of your school supplies are by me!" John then showed Ben all the magic he knew.

He then saw a big frown on Ben's face. John asked why he was frowning and Ben answered "Well, all the things you've shown me are not much different from what a first-grade student knows." John did sometimes feel that the magic was too easy but he never knew that the foxes were even hiding that from him. Did the foxes even trust him? Ben started to speak again. "We are going to start to learn more right now."

And so, they started to learn some magic. They first studied how to copy things properly, and do everything without moving. Then they tried floating and moving things by using magic. They tried some harder magic like blocking serious attacks and creation of things like a needle or pencil. Ben then went out on a walk.

Meanwhile, Ron was asking people to gather around the town square. More people from different places had also joined. He said "The foxes snuck here yesterday and took some of our weapons. They are now fully armed and ready to battle. We now have no choice but to attack! I have prepared a plan for us. The foxes are up early, so we've got to do this at midnight. That's when most of them are asleep, and even the ones that are up should be very, very tired. We will dig a hole there, and we will attack! They probably have no more than a couple of boxes, so they shall be defeated easily." All the humans agreed and the people started to get armed.

At that time, Agatha was checking her texts when she realized that John sent a text to her. It said that she needed to teach him some magic. She said that she would do that as soon as she got enough time to do it and read their ideas about the war.

She thought those ideas were good and decided to tell them to the king because she could not think of any of her own ideas. She wrote them down on a piece of paper. After sending in the ideas for the war to the king, Agatha went to bed. It was too late to go home, so she had to sleep in the castle.

Just then, Ron was going to the weapon storage and pulling out all the weapons they had. Conventional weapons, counter weapons, any kind he could find. All the townspeople had already been sent back home, it was night and he was disguised, but Ron was worried that someone would find him. After taking all of the weapons, Ron placed it inside his tunnel along with the food they needed for war which he had gotten from the humans that gave him it and from the food storage.

Ron planned to start a small battle over in the field by tomorrow, and then expand the battlefield so it covers half the city and a quarter of the fox tribe (that was about the same size) He called the citizens to the town square and told them to prepare for the war. He showed them the weapons and gave them flak jackets.

Ron then said "I plan to attack tomorrow. It will only be a small battle in an area that will not affect our daily lives, but to get there, we will have to dig a tunnel, leading up to a corner of the forest. There, we will attack the foxes. It will be easy to win, and our tunnel will start near the forest, so we won't have to dig too long. Please come here again tomorrow at nine."

As Ron left, all the townspeople started to talk about the war. Some were worried, but most of them thought this would be easy. However, because they were all talking, they didn't notice a boy amongst them.

Ben was trying to see what was happening, and why the war was starting. Ben now knew what happened, and rushed back to the hotel. He didn't expect that they could stop Ron before the war happens, but he may be able to stop it before it gets even worse. When he returned, he told John about what he saw.

John said "Perhaps we can stop them by creating a fence around the whole forest with our magic." Ben said "It won't be easy for just us to create a fence, and even if we do it, they will dig underground." John nodded. Ben said "We better think of a way to make the war end as quick as possible, or we can't stop Ron." John said "Then let's start planning."

John called Agatha and asked to speak with her. Ben hid in the washroom, not wanting to be seen by Agatha. Agatha quickly started to walk to the hotel in her human costume. She was quite worried about what had happened and rushed to the hotel. She dashed out of the forest, crossed the street not knowing the light was red, and nearly got run over by a car. Everybody stared at her, but she showed no interest. She looked at the hotel and ran inside, sweating and panting. She was so tired she put her front paws down when she entered the hotel.

When she arrived, John said that there was some bad news. When Agatha asked what it was, he said "Ben saw Ron and a herd of his followers. They're going to attack tomorrow, just a small battle is what I've heard, but it sounds pretty serious. Ron managed to get his hands on some weapons." Agatha looked at John and said "I've told you not to trust Ben. It doesn't sound right. He isn't someone you should be listening to, especially since he's talking about Ron. They're a nasty lot... They were making trouble centuries ago. I bet they're still partnered up, tricking poor you."

John said "What's going to happen if you prepare for the world that's good for them?" Agatha said "It's us suffering to protect our world.

That's how the minds of the evil work. You are special. I want you to stay good. I can't let this happen to you." John said "It's still going to be worth it. I'll contact the king." Agatha then left, sad of what John had become. John told the king, who told some his generals to try and use their magic to protect fox tribe, though the magic was not very strong.

Meanwhile, Ron was giving out some food, water, weapons, and the rest of their armor to the townspeople in the forest. After he was done, he ordered them to dig a hole towards fox tribe. Though it was very hard to dig, the people kept going towards fox tribe. It soon became quite far enough for them to start digging up, and they slowly climbed out of the tunnel.

The place seemed odd, and was coved with moss. However, looked around, the realized this was a mixture of twigs and rocks. It was also small, and was only about the size of a closet. Ron, who was leading told the townspeople to all go back down and prepare their weapons. Ron took his own gun and loaded it up.

He ordered the townspeople (or rather solders) to be quiet and told them this was the fox's castle, and that they were in a storage room. As soon as Ron opened the door, it revealed a corridor, with rock walls, roof and floor. The floor was carpeted with moss. Ron told the solders to come through the door and silently walked down the hallways, except for occasional clonks that somebody's boots made from hitting the stone wall.

Ron then walked into a room that was full of hay. It was a little bit larger than the closet that they had come out of. Ron told some of them to stay with him, and for the rest of them to go downstairs and hide in a different room, until he ordered them to get out and attack. Ron and a few of his solders peeked through the door, and saw a fox trotting through, with his bushy tail sprouting out of his body. It was mostly orange, but it also had a lot of white parts. The fox approached closer to the room.

Ron held his breath. The fox opened the closet next to them and walked back. Ron had brought a camera, and he took several pictures of the fox as it walked by through the little crack in the twig door. When the fox left, Ron started to walk around the castle and take pictures. The human solders were surprised to see that a creature like a fox had such a big castle. They then went downstairs, and a fox wearing a wreath nearly saw them, but they ran into a room. They then called to the people in the downstairs rooms, and they all went together into a huge room with ten foxes.

The terrified foxes let out a yelp. The humans shot their guns at a fox, but missed. Instead, it hit the rock wall and made a dent. A fox tried to use magic, but for some reason, it was not very strong, and he could not shoot sparks at the humans. The humans all started firing their guns, and shot a few. Most of the foxes ran into another room. Ron rapidly led the solders out into the field, knowing that the foxes would follow to get revenge. The fox that had dodged the first bullet came out armed with a small pistol and started to shoot. The fox had a horrible aim, but managed to hit one human's leg. The human started to scream, and the fox was shot. Another fox peeked outside but went back in. Ron told the rest of his troop to stay and went into the castle, but hid under a stack of hay that was in the big room. Ron made a hole to peek out of, and started to listen.

The fox that went in said "Humans are

attacking! We've got to defend ourselves!" To the few courtiers that were trying to finish their work. The others said "Nonsense! We would have known if they were coming to the castle!" The fox that had just witnessed the humans said "Well, you can go look outside and see for yourselves. Every ounce of what I said is true." Most of the foxes laughed and just stood there, but a couple of very curious foxes took a peek out the door and started to scream "Humans!"

Now the other foxes got curious and went to the door, though they still thought that they couldn't possibly have come here. The foxes all gasped, and started to run upstairs. They needed to report this to the king. They had difficulty explaining to the guards at the door of the king's bedroom why they wanted to see the king, but they got in. The fox that had told all the other foxes about the humans stepped towards the king and asked his to come downstairs.

The king said "Nonsense! I am trying to relax in my room and you come bursting through! Why, I don't even know how you got through the guards!" The fox then said to the king "Your majesty, it's urgent. The humans are all there right outside the castle doors. All of us have seen them with our very eyes and they are armed." The king stood up and walked downstairs with trembling legs, panting because it was difficult to breathe. As soon as he looked out the window, he started to cough and ordered all his courtiers to come to the castle immediately due to a serious emergency. They quickly came, wondering why they had been asked to come to the castle at a time this late.

Agatha was also rushing to the castle, throwing on her wreath. She was about to enter the doors, but saw people waiting outside. Human were waiting outside the castle and

Agatha thought she knew why they had all been summoned to the castle. Agatha thought for a moment, the climbed up the wall and through a window. She would have flown, but for some reason the magic inside her had been fading.

When she got to the room, she saw her fellow courtiers wearing a solemn look. She whispered to a fox beside her "Is it anything about those humans outside the castle?" The fox beside Agatha nodded, and whispered "Well, the humans are going to attack, and they are armed. It's only a matter of time until they come crashing through the door. Agatha said "Then you should not have called everybody here then. I suppose the humans are going to attack us when the room's full of foxes, so that they can attack more efficiently!"

As soon as she said that, Agatha marched up the hall to the king and said "Your majesty, please send us back to our homes. The humans are waiting until the room fills up with foxes to attack, and by inviting more of us, the humans will be able to attack more foxes!" The king said "Do you have any evidence?" Agatha said "No, but..." The king said "Then please return to your seat."

Soon the confused courtiers arrived, and the king briefly explained what had happened. Though the king tried to stop her, Agatha took no notice of that and told the others her theory of the humans attacking. Not everyone agreed, but the foxes decided it would be much safer for them divide into two groups.

One group would stay, and the other group would hide in one of the offices located in the castle. The small number of weapons they possessed had been given to all the courtiers, and they decided to communicate by magic.

Agatha was in the second group, and hid in the office. She disapproved of using human-made murderous weapons and had given her gun to another fox whose gun had broken apart. A fox in the office said "What can we do? We will never be able to fight with only these, especially when our magic is so weak." Another said "We need to use our guns. There aren't many, but we ought to count on them"

Another fox was simply bored, and was duplicating his tails until they filled up the whole room. The fox that was leading the rest said "Phillis, don't be so foolish, you're supposed to concentrate on this!" Phillis tried to create a convincing theory and said "I was thinking about a solution to our problem" The other fox made a stern face and said "Perhaps you thought you might contribute to the meeting by duplicating your tails?" "Um... You see, I thought tails, I mean duplicating, could be the answer. Perhaps duplicate the guns?" "Brilliant!" The other foxes chanted when they heard the answer.

They immediately reported this to the others, who were very happy with the idea. They immediately made many copies of their guns, and all the weapons they had were now transported into the big room. The courtiers started to go back to the big room, but they froze. A deafening noise was heard from the big room, and the sound of something shattering was also heard.

It was new to the foxes, but it was something that still brought fear into their hearts. The humans burst through the castle, and some of the foxes that did not fall behind narrowly dodged the bullets. They did not know how to use the gun. The foxes that were able to hide found out a way to work the guns and tried firing it at a human. The human looked towards them, and fell.

The foxes were quite confused, but this clearly startled the humans, so the repeated, and repeated, and repeated. More of the humans fell down, and they felt that they were winning this thing. It clearly was a scary and exiting thing, but eventually a human burst through the storage and some foxes fell to the ground. Others broke through the wall with their guns and ran back to their homes.

Agatha was one of the foxes that narrowly escaped the human's attack. She didn't look back, ran straight back home, and dashed into her bedroom. Her husband was back from work. He looked at her and said "What's the matter? Why are you here so late?" Agatha just crouched onto the ground and rolled over in the dirt and mud that was covering the floor. Agatha groaned "The battle started, it's just as I thought it would be. I narrowly escaped the attack."

Her husband said "It's what you expected. Didn't you say it was a matter of time before the castle got taken over by humans?" "That's how it already is now. I don't even know whether anybody else is safe. Anyway, I have no plan of going to work whatsoever tomorrow. It's too dangerous to risk." "So, you can look after the kids since you aren't working, right? I'm exhausted. I ran around the house for an hour." Agatha nodded and went to sleep.

That night, the human solders cleared out of the castle. They had looked around, but did not see anything essential near the big room. Instead, they tricked the fox guards and solders into coming outside and started to battle in the middle of the forest. The middle of the forest was just a large field with a swamp in the middle.

Ron and the humans expected the foxes to come without weapons, but to their surprise, all of them were carrying a weapon. Even some courtiers that had followed to see what was happening were fully armed. Ron was quite confused, but pretended to be calm and started the battle.

It started to rain, and both the humans and foxes had lost some of their solders. The foxes retuned to the castle and the humans went towards the human's area and set up their tents in a large circle shape. Ron also built a hut to use as the storage. Ron handed out food and built a fire in the middle of the circle because of the cold wind and rain that was blowing towards them. Ron asked all of the humans to sleep and looked at the sky.

At that time, the foxes were having a

meeting in the castle. The king's illness had gotten worse, and many foxes were injured or dead. The foxes had never experienced a situation like this, and were panicking. They knew that they needed to do something to defeat the humans. They argued for hours, and finally concluded that they needed to recruit more solders to fight, and that they needed to use their magic to move the humans away from their land. So that night, the foxes marched around the kingdom and advertised that they were recruiting. A couple other foxes used their magic to move the tents away from the kingdom.

The next morning, when the humans woke up, they realized that they were at the town. For a second, they thought it was a dream, but then they found out that they had somehow been moved away from the battlefield. They then quickly moved back to the battlefield and fought. This time there were more foxes, and the foxes all shot bullets across the sky unlike last time, when most of them didn't even know how to shoot a gun.

After coming back to their tents, the humans realized they needed to form a plan. Ron called attention to them all and said "I have found out that more foxes have been tricked into John's monstrous plan. We do not have many weapons and yet they have managed to get an endless supply. We cannot just go out into the field and attack. I will have some of you go behind the foxes and strike, while the rest attack the foxes in the field." The humans nodded.

Meanwhile, John was setting up a session with Agatha to practice magic. John informed Agatha that Ben was also present, and Agatha refused to do it. However, John had persuaded her to try one session. When John told Ben his plan, Ben said "No, not with her! Did she even agree?" John said "It's for me! She didn't want to do it at first, but I told her to try it just this time! Can't you do that too?" Ben groaned and nodded his head.

John started to call Agatha. Agatha also groaned. John said 'Well, aren't you going to teach me?" Agatha said "Don't you barely know anything? I shouldn't be teaching you right now!" Ben told Agatha what John had learnt while pretending to talk to John. Agatha gave John some spells to practice. John did it. Quite impressed, Agatha asked him to do some harder things. John did it without much difficulty. Ben was also impressed this time.

They taught his how to do blocking spells and attacking spells. This time, John did not succeed. After half an hour, John was able to do both with ease. "Wow, that's great!" Agatha said. "It usually takes months to learn that." Ben then asked John to do a much more advanced spell. Agatha tried to stop him, because of how dangerous it was.

Finally, after blowing up the sink and breaking the whole mirror, John made some progress. Agatha wasn't very happy that he destroyed half the bathroom, and told them to hang up. John still wanted to continue the lesson, but Ben just turned the phone off, scowling at John.

Both the humans and foxes now ran to the battlefield. The humans attacked in both directions and took most of the foxes down. The surviving foxes shot at the humans. Many humans got hit. The battlefield was full of blood as the solders rushed away to their places. The humans went to the tents, and the foxes went back to the castle.

Meanwhile, Ron was looking at the war. He was very happy with how things were going. He felt that the word turned into a much better place when everyone was against each other. He said to himself he would come back soon and ran to the hotel.

Ron opened the door to the hotel and walked along the corridors, moving slowly towards John's room. When he peeked through the door, he saw John and Ben together, working on something. John had a slight smile upon his face, but Ben was simply staring off into space. It didn't seem so friendly, but still Ron wanted to erase that image from his head. He wanted Ben to make a better choice. Ron knew to show that, he needed to come up with a trickier and cleverer plan. He needed to start winning them.

At fox tribe, they were trying to make some plans. They had also realized that the foxes that went to the battle had stated acting differently. The shock that had come from the war was significant; many soldiers had been injured. However, many foxes were unaware of this, and simply accepted it as a new way of war. They continued to duplicate the guns and weapons, yet they advertised it as a wicked human creation, and encouraged more foxes to go against the humans and join the war with various items. This worked quite well, and many foxes that were convinced registered.

Soldiers who joined the battle that was happening in the field and in the human area of the forest were all given weapons and protective gear along with clothes. Most foxes were not used to wearing clothes, but as the humans attacked, they soon realized that the clothes were their only hope to make the small chance of being safe a bit bigger. The clothes they wore were not necessarily clothes in the human's point of view, but to the foxes the long, thin light brown piece of fabric they wore were considered the military uniform.

These 'clothes' were taken from long lines that went across the trees that humans hung their blankets on, and were trimmed so that there was a hood that covered their head, a collar that protected their necks, and holes for their legs. The rest covered their tails and dragged across the ground. These were taken by soldiers that had been trained to take the 'clothes' off the clotheslines. Because of this, the humans were having a hard time replacing their blankets.

That day, ten foxes were running into the castle. They were all close friends and wanted to join the army. They went in through small doors which revealed a room full of foxes. They were not courtiers, but newly hired workers that did nothing but register young foxes that wanted to join into the army.

The ten foxes asked to join the army, gave the workers their information, and went off to the creek. The creek was what split the fox tribe and the battlefield. Another fox was waiting for them to lead them to the battlefield and give them their gear. The fox gave them their weapons, showed them how they were used, and lead them across the creek. They did not have to swim, because a dead tree had been placed over to use as a bridge. The gently flowing water sometimes got on their tails, which bothered them. After crossing the bridge, they were taught how to wear clothes, and were given the brown piece of clothing.

They were able to hear the grass rustle. The soldiers stopped and looked ahead. There were now tents built out of sticks and covered with leaves all over the fox area of the battlefield. They were sent into one of the tents, and realized that they were way bigger than what they seemed to be. Like many fox homes, instead of the ground, there had been a long tunnel leading underground. The underground tunnel revealed several burrows, which all had signs on them. They went into the burrow they were asked to go inside, and saw several beds made of twigs, leaves and moss.

A great number of other foxes saw them and waved with their front paws. They were also wearing the green clothes. Some foxes that helped them adjust into the camps took them into the training burrows where they learnt to clean and use weapons. After they were given the pamphlet about humans, the other foxes started to train them, and they stayed inside the burrows that day.

That night, they stood guard outside the tents and endured a sleepless night with other foxes standing there. The foxes standing guard were mostly new soldiers that had not been in the army for more than a week. The next day, they got dressed at five, and went inside the tents. A single rabbit was given for them to share, but they were excited. The second day was the first day they could fight the humans. They reviewed how to use the weapons, and marched out into the battlefield.

The humans also came out, holding the guns. The young foxes shot the gun once at the humans, but the human swiftly dodged it and shot at them. They ducked down, but one got hit and was carried back to the tents to be cared for. Many of them got killed or badly hurt that day, and the foxes fell into despair. The humans had a nice plan.

The human troops that continued to march towards the foxes were happy with how the battle was going, and continued to shoot at the foxes. It was odd having to battle four-legged creatures, but that made the battle easier. They did have a hard time however, because the foxes outnumbered them and they had much more supplies left. Anyway, they wanted to go back home after winning.

Meanwhile, at fox tribe, they were starting to talk about something else. The captured humans mentioned something about a human named Ron. The tried to find it in the book, but when they came to the page that should have described Ron, it had disappeared. A courtier said "One of the people handling the book must've ripped a page. It's a pity the page disappears on every book when it's damaged on one book." A courtier said. Many foxes had ideas on what Ron was.

Agatha thought that the captain of the humans was Ron. Not many foxes agreed with that idea, since it seemed pretty reasonable. Still, many foxes disagreed was because Ron was a fox, not a human. They then asked the humans how Ron looked like. They refused to tell. The foxes let them go. Everyone was thinking about how Ron could turn into a human. Most people thought he simply used his magic to turn into a human, but Ron could not have done that. It was not possible.

Meanwhile, John and Ben were enjoying a nice cup of tea on the terrace. It was Sunday, and they wanted to have a happy Sunday. They had only just changed, and it felt peaceful in an odd way. They could see the forest and see the battlefield far away. Looking like a green blob with a brown patch in the middle of it. The distance was so far even the biggest trees seemed to be the size of a speck.

Ben spoke about the war. "I heard it's getting bigger. I assume the foxes put some kind of magic on the guns. They could not still be fighting if it wasn't for that." John nodded, but he seemed a little perky. John was constantly twitching his head left and right for some reason. Ben felt John was being odd.

As soon as Ben finished his sentence, John pulled him outside and started to run. Ben could not understand why John would have done that in the middle of a meeting, but Ben had an idea. John just trusted his feelings, and Ben thought he wanted to start the project. He dashed across the valleys and right in to the battlefield. There, he saw Ron and a huge army behind him that seemed like it could make another war.

Now, he thought was the perfect time to use what he had learned from studying the virus. He stepped back and thought about what he had learned. He then took a small bottle out of his pockets. It was what he had been studying for this moment.

The reason they had studied the virus was to find the cure for it and to use its power to stop the war. They had not yet found the cure for the virus but they did know how to stop the war with it. To use its power, they had to cast a spell that reverses the power of the virus and makes it go the opposite way. Then, they programmed a small chip that made its power bigger and made it resist any evil powers, and to solve the biggest problem for a short period. Then again used magic to melt it into the virus.

John opened the cork of the bottle and watched it as the liquid moved slowly spreading on the ground. Suddenly, the liquid on the floor lit up and shot into the air. The sky became covered in dust as a strong push moved both armies' away from each other and slowly calm down. After a few seconds, the sky cleared off and the field was back to normal but nobody was moving on the battlefield. Something too great had happened for them to get back up on their feet, and everyone was petrified.

The magic did not last for a long time and it eventually wore off, but while all this was happening, Ron was inside and the magic was too weak to get to him, so he was very surprised to see that only half the soldiers were still fighting. He did not know what happened except for that someone had used their powers to do that because it was impossible to do without using any kind of strong magic.

At that time, John and Ben were running back to the hotel. Because they ran as soon as the magic started to work, they did not get to see how much effect it had until they saw some solders walking back to the town, gasping. They saw that their idea had succeeded and smiled as they ran to the hotel because they were too tired to talk but inside, they were filled with joy.

When they got back to the hotel, they told each other about how amazing it was. Ben thought that John needed to practice his magic so he asked for John to do all the magic he learnt so far and John showed amazing skills. Then, Ben said that when the war gets worse, that they will need to use their magic for two reasons. One was because he needed to use magic like this when he needed it and the second was because they used magic recently and if they do it now, they will already be ready to stop the magic from coming in.

Besides, John needed to train more to do the magic perfectly. Ben then thought to himself that was good and realized that was the reason other people did not get very concerned when John did some things very rapidly and said to John that he could take a little rest, when suddenly, they heard the ground rumbling and shaking as the saw flames shooting up into the sky and hitting the houses along with people spilling out into the mucky road.

Back at the battlefield, the foxes that did not get out of the battlefield had a plan. They got the materials to create a landmine on the human's side and made it much bigger with magic. The human that stepped on it ran away, and it blasted. It was mostly human soldiers that were injured, but part of it exploded right in the town that John and Ben were staying.

The people in the town mostly ran away, but some people did not have enough time to escape, and it hit them. Luckily, the hotel was a little away from the place the bomb exploded so everyone that was in the hotel did not get hit including John and Ben. But they saw the explosion and what it did to the people and felt terrible, though they were thankful that they were not hit when it happened.

This made them once again realize that anything could happen, even after great efforts. But the most surprising thing was that the foxes were using pyro techniques.

[Foxes broke the law of nature!]

They were so surprised none of them had noticed that. They got up and looked out the window.

Everything was burnt and messy and the sky was a reddish colour. Shortly after most of the humans that lived in the city were back at where their homes were and settled down but nothing seemed the same. Everyone was still frozen and too scared to speak. Ben and John were terrified and could not think of a thing. But this did let them know that they needed to start thinking of a new plan to stop the war, for they could barely see anyone on the streets.

Meanwhile, Agatha was wondering what had happened after hearing some bangs in the battlefield which was awfully close to her home. She tried sending a text to John, but he did not answer. Agatha started to wonder what was going on at the human's side. She very punctually changed into her human costume and walked into the streets of the human world.

Everything was silent and she could see people crying on the streets beside their burnt homes. Now that she really knew that something was wrong, she wanted to try fixing the problem together with John and even Ben, so she went to the hotel which she once knew as the human training centre. She snuck upstairs using the elevator, and walked into John and Ben's room.

It was not a weekday, but both were dressed quite well, and they looked as if they too, had been outside for quite a long time. John briefly explained what had happened, and told her they were concerned about the events that had been happening as well. John also told Agatha they had heard it was the foxes who had created the landmine. Agatha said "After some recent changes, I have been quite left out, but I have overheard talk of using human technology to defeat the humans. Why don't they know the humans are no good at all? There isn't one good bit in them!" John looked slightly offended, but simply continued on with the conversation. Ben told the others about other things he discovered and went away to the terrace. Agatha then talked to John about some more problems, and then left.

Later that night, John got out of bed and woke Ben up. He said that he felt a strong feeling and that they should move to fox tribe and make a plan there. Ben felt weird. He did not know if he should trust John or not because fox tribe was defiantly not a safe place for him but Ben decided to follow John's instructions and leave, but he said that they should leave after at least a month.

John allowed that, and they agreed to leave in a month. Just then, when they arrived at the hotel, John started to pack his things. When Ben asked why, John said that he felt like something was coming and that they need to leave tonight and told Ben to pack his things too. John then took his book and also put that in his bag and then put both of their bags in a big sack which he used when he explored the tunnel and put that in the corner of the room.

Meanwhile, in the battlefield, Ron was thinking of a plan. A plan to get rid of John for once and for all and to turn Ben back into his side. He was going to go to the hotel and get to Johns room, then kill him right away. He planned on doing it that night, at 12, when John would be asleep. After making that plan, he quickly got ready for the act and started packing any tools he could use at the hotel while getting at him. As soon as he was ready, he set off for the hotel at 11:00 so that he could arrive in time.

When he went to the hotel, he took a quick look at the rooms and walked inside the hotel so that he could get to John's room. The hallway was full of workers, so Ron hoped John was asleep, inside his room. At that time, John was walking out of his room and walking into the halls when suddenly, he saw Ron!

THE BIRTH OF A HUMAN

Something Strange Happens

7. Something Strange Happens

Ron was moving towards him quickly and That made his heart beat like crazy because he felt like Ron knew all about their plans and if he did, John knew that nothing good was going to be happening. But trying to be calm, John asked why he was still awake at night and Ron said he had some work, starting to turn red. John then walked away, but could not erase the thought that Ron was planning to do something that night. Ben said he did feel suspicious about what happened but said they should have stayed inside that day.

Meanwhile, Ron was walking back to the battlefield and thinking about what had happened that night and started to wonder why John suddenly asked that and started to wonder why John was still awake at that time because he knew John normally was asleep hours before that and he felt like John was up to something very strange. He decided to watch what he was doing.

John packed all the things in his room in to a sack and then opened the window and tossed a rope down. Then, turning off the light, he climbed down with another person which Ron recognized as Ben and ran. As soon as Ron saw what they were doing, he went into the room and climbed down the rope, then ran at them. Ron could not see anything, and so he went back to the hotel.

Meanwhile, Ben and John were running through the woods. They ran until they were too tired to run, and they knew they came too far to go back so they decided to spend the night there. They gathered some twigs and added leaves on top, then pulled out an old, blue blanket and a green blanket to sleep on. But as soon as they finished the shelter the twigs flew away. This time, Ben, who had experienced a similar situation tried building a house.

The house was very sturdy, and was large. After building the house, they put the sack in the bedroom and created a bed, a table, and a food storage. Then, Ben made a big panel and slid it under the house so that water would not leak even if it rained so that he did not have to build the house all over again and John helped. Then, when they were finished, they went inside the house and went to sleep.

At that time, Ron was at the hotel, hanging his coat, thinking about why John escaped from the hotel. Then, he slowly walked towards John's room. The room was empty and all that was left was the old wooden table. As he looked around the room, he thought about how to find John. He thought for a moment, then got an idea.

Since many people had the virus, he was going to make that into an issue and then use his hotel to isolate the people and foxes (though people and foxes will be staying in a different part of the hotel so that they do not share their culture), then use that to get the money he needs to find John.

Even while making it in to an issue and isolating the people, keep sending hypnotized foxes and humans to get information where John is and if possible, kill him. He hoped that people would have forgot about what happened in the forest so that he could go on with his plans.

He started his plan right away. He went to the battlefield, and went to the humans. The humans saluted, and looked at him. Ron told them "The foxes have a plan to take all the humans crossing the border to hold them hostage. They also seem to be trying to send diseased people here. I believe we shall develop a system so that if any of us must go to the fox's place, they will be kept in the hotel, to reduce the risk of disease and to keep them safe." The humans nodded and started to send soldiers to the border. Ron wore his fox suit and told the foxes the same thing, that the humans were planning to hold them hostage.

Then, he returned to the town and turned on the television. It told him that there were 876 confirmed cases, saying that this virus was impacting everybody. Ron thought that this was the right time to start his plan and went to the town square saying that the virus is a very scary thing and that he, to prevent it will make his hotel into an isolating hotel for people who have crossed the border and added that it may cost a 'little' bit of money but it is needed. He then went to the fox's side and put up a poster saying that any foxes that have crossed the border should stay in the hotel.

All seemed to go well. However, Ron was not dumb. He had already divided the fox's area and the human's area and even made separate doors, so the humans knew nothing of the foxes that stayed here, and the foxes knew nothing either.

The next day, a human family with six children Eden and Emma, Jackson and Shannon, Alex and Tablo came to the hotel and asked for the biggest room to stay. Ron got a quarter of a floor for them to stay with a big terrace that had some shaky bricks between the other side. The Mom, Wendy looked at the rooms and then started to move the things. "This will be our home for at least a month. I want to make it feel like our house."

She looked at her husband, Liam which was

sitting on the couch and said, "Can you help me clean the rooms?" he said in an annoyed voice "I'm busy." Wendy yelled, "How are you busy when you are sitting on the couch sipping coffee? We have a lot to do, so clean up this room!" as she vacuumed the floors. After she cleaned up all the rooms and set up the furniture, she looked at her husband. He had shoved in all his plants in the closet, and was watching TV. Wendy sighed and sat in front of her computer.

She was a journalist, and needed to know more about these strange foxes, and the virus. That was the reason they had come. She opened up her computer, and started to work. (Wi-Fi worked *here*?) After about two hours, she looked at the bored kids. She decided that they needed to do something and said that they should pick a room to sleep in. Eden and Emma, twins in middle school chose the room farthest from the door. The twins entering school next year, Jane and Jackson chose the room beside their parents, and Alex and Tablo who were both three, slept with their parents.

Then, she realized that there was no place for the kids to do their schoolwork, and looked at the room where her computer is. It was small even for three of four people, but since they did not bring a desk and that room had a couple desks which were actually low shelves, she decide they would use that room. She took the file that contained their schoolwork and put them on top of their 'desks'.

The kids looked tired, and it was quite late, so she told the kids to brush up and shower. After they were done, she washed the baby twins and sent all the kids to bed. Then, she looked at her husband, who was a gardener. He had brought all his 571 plants and was still watering them. After an hour, when he was done, they went in to their room and went to sleep.

The next day, when she woke up, the kids were already awake. When she looked at the time, it was 9:45 am. She quickly made breakfast and woke her snoring husband. She yelled at him, but he did not seem to wake up. She sighed and decided to wake him up after a few minutes, and walked out of the room.

Just as she was about to wake him, she heard her husband rustling under the sheets. When she stepped into the room, he was changing out of his ugly striped pajamas. She pointed at the clock and said, "Don't you even know what time it is?" and then told him to come eat breakfast. While Liam ate breakfast, Wendy told the kids to do their schoolwork as she washed the dishes.

When the kids stepped in to the room, they

were shocked by the room's size. They thought that there must be a better option and walked through the halls when they came across a room with plenty of desks. They sat down and started to study. Jackson asked, "Should we tell our parents?" Emma said that they should keep this a secret. Everyone else agreed. "We could form a special room in here!" Jackson said. They all ignored him. After they were done studying, they noticed that the room happened to be right beside their parent's room but connected through a different hallway.

They showed their work to their parent's and then was about to go to their rooms when they heard the doorbell ringing. They saw somebody drop something on the floor, so they picked it up and gave it to their parents. Their dad did not seem to know a thing about it, but their mom did. She said that it was a meal kit that you have to cook. She said everything was already prepared and that she ordered this.

Speaking of meals, they were quite hungry. Breakfast was just some food that was left over and they did not have any snacks. Soon, lunch was ready. It was not tasting that great, but it was better than nothing, so they had it. The baby's must have been hungry because they started to cry. Their mom started to feed them and told Eden to wash the dishes.

Just then, some people knocked on their door saying that they needed to close the blinds because of security reasons. They closed the blinds, wondering what had happened. At that time, some foxes were going into the hotel. They found it strange that half of the hotel had their curtains down but just walked in.

They were a big family so they got quarter of a floor. After all, they did have six kids. Their names were Autumn, Midnight, Marina, Aurora, Sprout, and Dreamer. When they first came in to the hotel, they noticed the huge terrace cut in half with a tall, shaky brick wall. The mom, Sunshine told the kids and her husband, Storm to not touch the bricks because if it broke, they will have to fix it. Then, they unpacked and got into their rooms. It did seem pretty messy so she cleaned it up and then told the kids to go out and play in the terrace.

The youngest kids, Sprout and Dreamer went to play but the older kids like Midnight and Marina went to hang out in their rooms while kids in the middle like Autumn and Aurora ran across the room. Sunshine reminded them to be careful so that nobody gets hurt. Suddenly, she heard Sprout whining. His hand was stuck in between the bricks. Sunshine carefully pulled Sprout's hand from the bricks but two of the bricks fell down and she was not able to put the bricks back in place because then the other ones would all fall down. Then, she left and sat on the table.

Meanwhile, Sprout and Dreamer was looking through the hole when they saw some weird creatures that were looking at them. They were about the same size as them but they had absolutely no fur at all and did not have a tail. They also sometimes tried to stand up and then fell but the strangest thing of all was that when they babbled and mumbled, they were not using the same baby language. They tried to communicate, but they could not understand a thing that they were saying. They tried communicating by their facial expressions, but that did not work either. Just then, their moms scooped them up and brought them inside.

Meanwhile, Aurora, Autumn, and Marina were doing their homework. For about an hour, they were able to concentrate but then, they started to get bored. That was when they started to hear a strange noise. It sounded like talking, but they could not understand a word. It also seemed like some animals groaning, but it had a very different accent then the dog tribe or any other animal. Since they could not concentrate on their schoolwork, they went to their parents and said they were done. Luckily, they had done a lot of homework for the first hour, so they were able to play.

But a few minutes later, their mom called them, asking why they did not clean up because there was flying objects, things made by the kids. She then yelled, "Put these things back in the box!" The kids quickly put their things in a small box. Then, they went out of the room. But as they stepped into the hallway, their mom grabbed their bushy tails and yelled at them, saying that they should be more careful.

Then, after her speech which seemed like an hour ended, the kids went in to their rooms. They had barely anything in the room to entertain themselves with, so they went in to the balcony. They tried playing with their siblings' toys, but soon they got bored again. Just then, they saw that there was a hole in the wall. Aurora tried putting the bricks back on, but then some more bricks went on to the ground which made the hole big enough for Sprout and Dreamer to crawl in and out if they wanted to.

Aurora said, "We can't tell mom. She is going to get so mad at us." Everyone agreed with that because they knew that things were going to get ugly if she found out. Just then, they heard their mom telling them that they did not unpack some of their luggage. Just then, they remembered that most of the things they could have fun with were in there so they ran inside.

Back at the other side of the hotel, Wendy was doing some work on her computer. There were many things she needed to deal with. When she finished, it was night and the kids had already gone to bed. Then, when she was about to go to bed too, she saw that her husband was taking up almost all of their bed. She sighed and laid down on the tip of their bed.

The next morning, she woke the kids up, and then gave them their breakfast and told them to do their homework. Then, she checked what they did and told them they could play though Eden and Emma stayed inside their rooms. As soon as they stepped on to the balcony, they saw Alex and Tablo trying to say something to the wall.

They wondered what they were doing, so they went behind them. That was when they saw two little baby foxes trying to communicate with their little brothers. They thought that they had crawled up from the forest nearby and tried to get them away from their brothers but even their brothers were interested in them and they did not know what to do because they were so close together. Jackson said that he was going to snatch Alex and Tablo as he went close up.

Bang! Suddenly, they heard a sound. It was coming from the forest. The building shook a little bit as a small tree fell on the ground. They quickly ran inside and told their parents what they heard. Wendy and Liam thought that it was probably something about the war because they were the only ones that watched television. But still, they did not want to tell that to the children because they knew that they would have nightmares. They said that it was just the wind and told them they could stay inside.

Meanwhile, John and Ben were thinking

about a way to get back to the hotel. They could not stay here forever, and everything was only getting worse while they were away from the hotel. Plus, the cabin was not good enough for a place to live in. John wanted to go back to the hotel but he did not know what to say to Ron. Ben said that it was only going to worse if they kept staying here and said that it was also dangerous because it was not very far from the battlefield.

Soon, they packed their things and set off towards the hotel. Ben said that summer break was almost over and that he needed to get back to school. John said that he had all of his things for school prepared and that he just needed to check the schedules. They both were a little bit worried about settling back here but they had many things to do so they were not too worried yet. When they had unpacked and brushed up, they heard a big noise upstairs. They were a bit annoyed that they were being so loud, but they knew that the hotel was always like this.

Meanwhile, at the battlefield, some solders were walking towards the fox tribe. They went around most houses and put a small, round thing right beside each house. Then, they went back and went to sleep. The next day, at dawn, the foxes woke up and started to shoot at the humans when suddenly, they heard a big sound coming from their town. Many houses were turned in to ashes. Some foxes threw their weapons on the ground and rushed back to see what had happened while most continued shooting for they knew that the humans did this because they had attacked recently. They could not understand the soldiers that ran away to see their family risking getting burnt or shot. The battlefield was probably safer.

Meanwhile, Ron was looking down at the

scene. He thought that now was the perfect time to start his next plan at the hotel. He slowly walked out of the battlefield and headed towards the hotel slowly. He went around the hotel to see if his plan was working out. He checked all the hallways in the human department and the fox department. He also checked if the employs knew anything about it. He was the only one working in the fox department though he planned to hypnotize a couple foxes. When he saw a few foxes come in Ron took them to his office. He hypnotized them, but it did not last very long so he had to put them in the zoo. Well, it used to be the zoo, but since John left it had not been cleaned and they had sold all of the animals. Ron had cleaned a small part of it and locked them in there. Then, he hypnotized them so they did not remember. Their work was very secretive. As he thought of this, he went in to the for department again and went out of the hotel. He sat on the bench and thought of his plan again.

Ron had noticed that the humans in town were not affected by war and had not fallen into despair or had become a prisoner of foolishness. He decided that they need to be trained. It would be just like school. He would only teach the mother and father of each family. Then, they would teach their children. Once they had completed the basics, then they would learn harder things. If they were pretty good, then he would teach their kids and perhaps even make a real school for their children.

He was going to clean the rest of the zoo and use it. Also, there was a huge attic which was empty. He was going to use that too. He also was going to do the same training for the foxes, though he would have to do it separately because if they had any contact, it would be very dangerous for him because he would lose his trust and the foxes and humans might get close.

After he made his plan, he walked slowly into the battleground. He had found the soldiers easier to hypnotize because other foxes would not get hypnotized and try to block themselves. He was lucky that nobody had known who he was because he was always dressed like a fox. He even was right now. As he thought of this, a young fox looked at him. Ron thought he would be the perfect guy to hypnotize. He looked at the fox and pulled him to the side. Ron silently walked towards him and stared at him. He thought of what he wanted the fox to do in his head then started to mumble slowly. Flames started to dance in his eyes. The fox's eyes were starting to shake. Soon, he seemed that his mind was completely controlled by Ron. Ron took him to the zoo and put him in a different cage apart from all others. This was because he planned to use the fox for a different purpose then all the others and did not want him to have any contact with them. He was going to be one of the mind-trainers for the foxes. At first, he thought that he could just hypnotize them all, but that would be too tiring and even if you tried hard, it wore off in a month. For most of them, it would wear out in a day or two.

Meanwhile, in the hotel, Sunshine was cleaning the rooms of her six children while they were doing their homework. This time she had given them a reminder not to forget to clean the room after they were done. Just then, she heard the announcements on the speaker saying that from now on, all the full-grown men and women were going to have to go upstairs every week on Tuesday, to have a health check, and to make sure that they were crossing the border for a reason both safe and acceptable.

Sunshine was confused. They were not

allowed to go out of their rooms. They were isolating. So, she called the front desk and asked to explain. Then, a man explained that they were going to go one family at a time and that they needed to go at 1:00 pm. Sunshine still did not get how they were allowed to just wander off upstairs, but she decided to follow the instructions. Then she looked up at the calendar. It was Monday! She was so surprised. She instantly looked around the rooms to find Storm, but he was not there. Gladly, she soon found out he was in the bathroom, because she heard him singing in the shower.

At that time Ron was sitting at the front desk, answering calls from all the floors of the fox department. Almost nobody was able to work in here, so he had to be here. He was so busy from all the phone calls asking about how it was possible to go out of their rooms. Soon, there was less phone calls coming and he got to have a short break. He thought about how he was going to lure them. He knew that he could not just ask about how they were feeling bad and start telling them it was because of how they were not being treated fairly in the community and turn them away from society. That would be too silly. He started to feel funny in his stomach.

Meanwhile, on the other side of the hotel, John and Ben were talking. They were starting to wonder why Ron had not been doing anything for such a long time. Ben said that Ron probably had another mysterious plan up his sleeve and added that when he was with Ron, that Ron had told him that he was going to start another plan and that what he was doing right now seemed a lot like it. Then, John said that now that he had started a huge war, He was going to start effecting the townspeople. Just then, it was time to go to work for John so he waved and headed out the door as Ben got ready for school.

Summer break had ended. The supplies were similar and he had made the new supplies last night. He was very excited for his new school year.

At that time, Ron was getting ready and going in to the human department. He waved to John and then ordered him to come to his office. As soon as he arrived, John asked why the hotel was divided. Ron said that He wanted to talk about that and said that because of a very dangerous spreading virus, He had turned the hotel in to an isolation hotel and that he did that so that the community would be safer in this dangerous war situation. Then he quickly said to John that he was going to work in this department. He then looked at John. He seemed to have understood all the things, but also thinking about something else. Ron tapped him on the shoulder and then said, "Today you also have to work at the kitchen and help make the food." John then nodded.

He went to the front desk, worked, then walked towards the kitchen. It was quite big, so it was divided into many parts for slicing, cooking, baking, and washing the dishes. Most of the kitchen was extremely clean, but where they washed the dishes, were not very clean, and there was always some kind of ooze coming out the sink and dishwasher. That was also the reason why nobody volunteered so he had to work there. As soon as he arrived, he was asked to rinse all of the plates and put them in the dishwasher. He knew that this was a never-ending job because as soon as he loaded the dishwasher there was always a second load coming on. After two hours of doing that, he had to go to the front desk and work until it was time to go home. He knew that it did not mean that he was allowed to go home. He had to clean up and unload the dishes all by himself.

When he got back to have a talk with Ben, he had already finished dinner. John heated up some leftover soup from lunch he had brought and sat down. He asked Ben how school was ('It's different, but it's all right.') and then said that there was something very peculiar. He said that Ron had turned the hotel into an isolation hotel and that he felt like Ron was planning something. John said that he could feel something coming. Ben said, "He probably wants to do something to the people in here." He said that they should investigate what is going on.

THE BIRTH OF A HUMAN

Short Resistance

237

8. Short Resistance

Meanwhile, on the other side of the hotel, the foxes were all sitting down near the fireplace, reading a bedtime story when suddenly, they heard a soft voice saying something. It seemed like a foreign language, except that it did not seem to take the form of the language of the animals. A sound that seemed to be a beast's growl! The children were frightened, but the mother had already noticed what that language was.

It was the language of the HUMANS. She knew this because she was a cop. She knew something must be wrong, but what? She could not understand what happened. Just then, the voice stopped. Then, the children came out and asked what had happened. She said that it was just a lady reading and that it had sounded weird because it was on the other side and it made it sound different. She then told the kids that it was bedtime and sat on the couch.

She knew that this was the territory of the humans, so she thought that the other side might be being used as a different facility for the humans but she could not get rid of the thought that something was going to happen. Perhaps the announcements were related to that too. She said to herself that she was worrying too much but a voice inside her was telling her to investigate about this problem and that this was important and that this was going to be the biggest event in her life.

She shook her head and looked at the clock. It was 8:00. Way too late to be sitting in the living room. They went to Bed at 4 or 5 and their children went to bed at 3. Plus, there was a big day ahead of her. But even as she was getting prepared for bed, the thought about this secret kept on telling her to think more seriously about this situation. She ignored the thought and plopped on to the bed, hoping to fall asleep.

Soon, 2 hours after she fell asleep, she heard Dreamer whining. When she got to her room, she heard Dreamer say something. Surprisingly, he was still asleep. But just as Sunshine turned around to get back to bed, she heard a sharp yelp from behind her. It was Dreamer. Sunshine figured that he was having a nightmare so she carried him to her bed, and put her down in between her and Storm, which was snoring loudly. For some reason, she felt that all this was happening to give her a warning.

Meanwhile, Ron was sitting in his chair. It was very late but he couldn't fall asleep. He was way too worried about what he was going to do tomorrow. He wanted to cancel this meeting, but he knew that was impossible. He had thought about this while he was working, while he ate, and even while he was talking to others. But still, he was not able to find a good plan. He did not even know what to say as soon as they came in. He did have an idea though. He could say that they were needing to have a conversation about how long they were going to isolate, and then talk about what they were going to do after they were done, and ask them what happens there. Then wrap up the meeting so that he could really start talking about the important things. This plan made him way more relieved, and he was able to stop thinking about it and go to sleep.

Meanwhile, at the battlefield, the human solders were getting prepared to go over to the other side and attack them at night. They knew this could be dangerous because of the night watchmen, but they knew that if they were quick, they would be able to shoot a couple of them.

They quickly proceeded into the tent and looked around, trying to blend in with the shadows as much as possible. The foxes were still sound asleep, not noticing a single thing, but one of the night watchmen were coming in to the tent and had spotted them. He quickly woke up the others and the humans were held hostage in another tent, made with bars along the outside. So, on that day, nobody was allowed to sleep in case there was going to be another attack.

Luckily, nothing else happened, and they were able to go back to sleep at 6:00 am after it was clear there was going to be no more attacks. When it was time to wake up, they were all very tired and did not even want to move a muscle. But they knew that if they did not fight, the humans would come in the tent, so they moved their sleepy, tired bodies off of the cots. But when they got outside, nobody was there. They thought of this as some sort of plan so they cautiously moved into the battlefield. After a while, some of them were allowed to go back inside the tent and rest. The reason why they could not all go inside was because they knew that it was still dangerous to let everybody return to the tents. When the lucky few entered the tent, they breathed out a sigh of relief. All of these tents were suddenly filled with tired solders.

Each solder had a wooden shelf beside their cot which was used to put their belongings on top of. They put their hats there and plopped on top of the cot. This shelf had three spaces and the solders belongings were placed like this: first part: hat, clothes and boots. Second part: instruction sheets that they learned a long time ago for polishing their guns. Third part: books and pictures of their family. As soon as they looked at these pictures, they felt like they wanted to go back to their family. This attracted them and lured them towards their home and friends. This also made them feel like they were doing this war for nothing at all.

They weren't fighting for land, or for money. They were fighting for nothing, and yet they were so strangely enthusiastic for it. They were fighting, but when the war had started out, it was to find out about how the humans were trying to do something to them. So far nothing at all had happened and they were getting tired of it. Just then, one of the humans rushed in and started going towards the tent where the hostages were held. Until then, there was only two people guarding it. The hostages must have sent a secret message to the others so that they could escape. They put on all their gear and went to the gun storage to get their guns and started to run towards the tent while the foxes that were already outside started to fight with the humans. But it was too late. They had already escaped. As soon as the foxes noticed this, they rushed to join the rest of the group.

Meanwhile, at the hotel, Sunshine and Storm were getting ready to go upstairs. They entered a huge room, and a middle-aged fox was sitting at the end of the room. He said that he was one of the workers here and that the owner was unavailable to see them at the moment, but that they needed to start to talk about how long they were going to stay. He took a sip of water and continued. "You guys have stayed here for 2 weeks. You are going to stay here for at least 3 months. You see, the virus is extremely dangerous. We are planning to give you a test. It is to check how long you will need to stay. You will go through some paperwork and then answer some questions and do some physical checking too. It's pretty simple. Oh, you also need to bring your children this time" Storm whispered to sunshine. "That does not seem simple at all!" But then the fox ordered them to go back until next week. They quickly did what they were told and went downstairs, then sat down on the couch.

At that time, John was working at the top floor, cleaning the plaza when he suddenly heard a noise. It was a familiar language. A language he had not been daring to use. He listened again to make sure. It was the fox's language, and John was very surprised that he was hearing it. Just then, he felt exactly what it was. He did not even take the elevator. He just ran down all of the steep steps and flung into the room and started writing down each and every idea in a neat sentence and rushed back to work. This time he took the elevator so that he could catch his breath and take a break.

Then, he cleaned the rest of the plaza, the windows, the halls, and the carpet. He knew that He now had to get back to working at the front desk. For five minutes there was complete silence, except for the sounds of flipping paper and writing. Then the telephone started to ring madly. He picked it up. Suddenly, he heard a voice. It said in fox "say this: as you know, we are here to discuss the problems of your stay... And then read your script.!" Then the man hung up. John slid his notebook out of his pocket and wrote down every single word he said. He was very confused for this call did not seem like a normal call he would get in the hotel. He flipped through his notebook again but was not able to understand it.

Just then, the phone started to ring again. It was a family asking if they could book up a room and John told them the answer. After that, there were a bunch of similar calls that he needed to answer until it was closing time. When he entered his room, he said to Ben that he needed to listen. John took out his notebook and said that there were many peculiar things going on.

He first showed him what had happened to him when he was out in the plaza and Ben did not say anything for a very long time then said "Something must be going on at the other side of the hotel. John, have you ever gone to the other side?" John thought for a moment then said "No. I have never gone there. In fact, nobody on this side is allowed to go to the other side. It's forbidden because it is not our work area. Ben tapped his fingers on the table and then said "Have you ever seen anybody go in there that is not staff that works on this side of the building? "No." John said. "Even if somebody went there, we would not have seen them if they went during some dangerous times where you have to close the curtains. Other than that, I haven't seen anyone except for my boss. Ben stared at John and said "Ugh. Shouldn't you know what's going on by now? Ron's got a plan. A dangerous one too. We will need to find out more about this." Just then, John remembered that he had to tell

Ben about the strange phone call too.

He said "And also there was a strange phone call telling me to say something. I wrote it all down." He then showed him the notebook. Ben gasped and rubbed his eyes, then looked at the paper again. He then said to John "If all this is true, then I know exactly what Ron is up to. He must have some foxes on the other side. This has to be true because if you heard the fox language from the other side, and you are forbidden to go there, then Ron must be planning to do something with the foxes. Now, the only way to find out how to stop him might also be related to the virus because he turned it into an isolation hotel for the virus. He is using the virus but pretending to protect the people from it! To find out how to do this, someone needs to go to the other side of the hotel. But still, that might be risky, and I will be at school and you will be at work so this plan is impossible."

John said "We can go on the weekends. But if what you're saying is true, the other side will be filled with foxes and they will notice because we are the only humans among them. But if we be clever, we can actually use this to distract them. You will pretend to be a confused boy, and go into the hotel to distract them for as long as you can after they find you. If you do not get caught, then spy on the inside of the building. While you are doing that, I will climb up all the way to the top floor and peer through the window." Ben gave John a confused look and said "How are you going to climb up that high building?" John said, "Well, I happen to be a very fast climber. Still, I do need a safety guard." Ben then said, "well, it sure is a nasty drop from the top floor, and you are going to get a broken bone or two at the very least unless you put a rope down there, and if you do, then the inspectors will see it right away. John looked at Ben and smiled. Then, he said, "You know how you taught me how to do magic? Well, if I can make the rope invisible, then I can easily climb up that thing. Ben said "Not bad." John replied, "Let's go fetch a good climbing rope from the store nearby right now! And also, I feel famished. I haven't had anything for dinner and we ran out of food already."

Ben nodded and grabbed his coat off of the hook. Neither of them was willing to go on the subway, and the taxis were hard to catch, so they decided to just walk. First, they stopped by the convenience store to get some food, and then they went to a climbing centre and asked to borrow a very long rope. The people asked how long they wanted it to be, and they said at least 15 meters. Soon, one of the staff came back holding a very thick and long rope, tied together in a knot. Then, they said that it still would cost some money to borrow, and pointed at a board that read: PRICES. John gave them some of the money and left as Ben walked along. When they arrived, they put the rope away and sat down at the table to make some plans.

Meanwhile, Wendy was checking the homework that her kids did. After checking, she told them that they were allowed to go outside. Now they were pretty used to having the hole in the wall and were able to keep Alex and Tablo away from it. But they were looking over the railing and not paying attention, and that's when they ran to the wall and sat down. They wanted to go there so much because of those creatures. They were the only playmates that understood how their life was like, and they were starting to learn what the weird words meant, and now they were able to find out some of what they were talking about.

After a couple minutes of waiting, the creatures showed up. Alex and Tablo said that they wanted to know what their names were, and it seemed the creature had understood. They said that they were a fox, and that they were named Dreamer and Sprout. Alex and Tablo introduced themselves too and asked Sprout to teach them how to speak their language. Sprout tried his best, but they could not say anything. Dreamer and Sprout were able to understand English and Alex and Tablo could understand fox, but they could not speak each other's language.

Just then, Dreamer said "Why don't we mix up the languages so that we still use some of the language we are comfortable with?" They all agreed and started mixing up each letter they had, and tried speaking it, surprisingly, this worked way better than all the other ideas. Because when they spoke their own language and tried to understand the other one, it was harder. The new language was still difficult and hard to learn, but it was working out very well and it was also fun too. But after a while, it started to seem a little dark out, and Alex and Tablo knew that at about this time their moms were going to grab them any second so they said that they would meet again at playtime tomorrow because they still needed some time to themselves so they could rest. Then they waddled back to their siblings and lay down so that they could get some attention and rest until it was time to go inside.

Just then, the door slid open and it was time for them to change, brush up, and go to bed. They were actually glad that it was time for them to go inside because it was getting very cold.

Meanwhile, on the other side of the hotel, Sprout and Dreamer were still thinking about the new language they had just discovered. They tried to talk in it whenever they were alone but never when their parents were around because they would not understand anything. They did sometimes do it when their siblings were around though, because they secretly hoped that one day, they could have their own secret community. But still, some of their siblings were nearly as clueless as their parents, and it was hard to give them clues.

While this was happening, Marina was studying. She had an exam after a week which she would take with her class by magic and it counted for quite a lot of the grades, and she needed to keep up her grades while she was not at school. For her and her twin, they only were expected to study for 4 hours a day when they had important tests, but she still was worried about it because she had a very good grade average at school.

Just then, her sister Midnight came in. She asked if Marina would go and play magic board games with her, but Marina said she was fine. They were twins, but they were so different. Midnight was athletic and playful, but she was quiet. Also, Midnight was the tallest kid in the class from first grade but she was smaller than all of the others that were two years younger. Actually, she thought that Autumn was way more like her. She also thought that Midnight was more similar to Aurora. After starting to think of all these things, she could not concentrate so she decided to go play a board game with Midnight instead but when she arrived, it was not just Midnight, but all the other girls were there too. They were in the middle of a round. Marina could tell because the board game was hovering high in the air. It always did that automatically and lit up. But that was the only thing that she knew about the board game because she had only watched other people play.

Meanwhile, on the other side of the hotel,

Ben and John were sitting on their beds and still planning what to do to climb up that rope. The biggest issue was how to climb up the rope after it became invisible. They thought about only making it invisible when anybody came, but if it was hanging along the side of the wall anyone could spot it very easily. Besides, it would take too long to cast the spell if they see anybody even coming. It was also very likely they would not be able to spot anyone all the way up there or inside the building. After an hour of silence, Ben came up with an idea. He said "We could buy a harness that stays very close to the rope. Then you can feel and see the harness on your hips and the rope connected to it. Also, even if you want it to disappear, it would not take long and you would still be feeling it though it may be a little harder. I do wish that you could turn invisible. Then things could be so much easier. But with magic, you can't really turn living things invisible."

Ben then frowned. He said "Do you know how to get the rope up?" John replied "I think that if we borrow a tall ladder, we can do it. And since we do not want to get noticed we will do it at night. Of course, no ladder is as tall as the building, and even the construction ladders are not that tall. They still are about a meter or two smaller but if we aim carefully, we can hook it on to one of the tall polls on the roof. And then we could bring the harness up too, and hook that on to the rope then make the rope invisible. Then, if you let go of the harness, it will drop on the ground and will be ready for the next day!" Ben then said, "where are we going to get ladders that big? We can't go to a construction company to borrow a ladder." John said, "Well, paint stores have huge ladders and they have tons of unused ones. We could at least ask for them. By the way, if we are going to go, we will go early in the morning tomorrow, so you won't miss school.

When they open. We have no time to waste. Tomorrow is Friday and we shall go on Saturday night, but we will be busy getting things on Friday. All the things like ladders, harnesses, and perhaps even binoculars too. So, I feel that since we have a big day ahead of us, we should get to sleep right now." Ben agreed and turned off the lights.

The next day, they set off to the shop and bought all the things they needed. (Ben left in the middle to go to school) but after visiting the very last shop, John had gone quite far away from the hotel and were tired, so he decided to call a taxi. But when he looked up, a taxi was driving along, almost as if it was following them. He signaled for it to stop as it came around the corner and hopped on. The driver had a plaid hat on that nearly covered his eyes and did not speak very much, and the leather part of the seat had mostly come off, but John knew that it was the best way to get back home. Soon, they were back at the hotel and were arranging their things.

Meanwhile, Alex and Tablo were getting on to the porch. They were very excited because they got about an hour before anyone else came and they were wanting to continue on the language that they were creating. They knocked on the brick, which was a sign they had made up that meant to come. Soon they heard them whining to come outside and Both Sprout and Dreamer were on the terrace. Alex and Tablo said, "We still need to work on our language We got the talking part over with but I think we need something to write in later when we let our siblings join. Don't you think?" Sprout said "Great idea!" and looked at Dreamer to ask him what he thought. But just then, Dreamer said, "We barely know how to write, so how can we even recognize out writing when we settle it?

Also, we don't even know how many letters we are going to use!"

Then Alex said, "You don't need to be like that. We can think of all that now and choose what to do. First, let's figure out what kind of message we should put in to the letters." Sprout said "What do you mean by putting a message into the letters?" Alex answered "Every language used some sort of special meaning in creating all the letters. All of them have one identical meaning but inside of them, each letter gets a different message. The other messages are very important too, but the one identical meaning is the most important one. After choosing that, the rest of the meanings will naturally come to us and depending on how many of them come and what meanings they have, we can choose how many letters we will have. So first, let's vote on the one special meaning. Who has an idea?"

Right away, Dreamer and Sprout put their hands up. Dreamer spoke first. "How about something like being helpful?" Sure, Alex said and wrote it on his hand with a marker rolling around. Then he said "Sprout, your turn. What do you want to say?" Sprout said "I feel that we can also do something like taking care of each other." Alex said "That's kind of like Dreamer's idea. But it is a good idea. Any more suggestions?"

Just then, Tablo put his hand up. He said, you know how we are communicating and connecting, and it's also how we made this language, so I feel like it should be communication. That would include all kinds of feelings, actions, and words while communicating." Alex also wrote that one down with his extremely messy writing.

Alex said, "Now we will conduct a silent vote.

We will put our heads down and vote by putting their hands up. But still, you are not allowed to vote yourself. I will count the votes and the three of you will vote, then someone else will count the votes while two others vote. Ok?" They all agreed and put their heads down, so Alex said for them to put their heads down and counted the votes. Then he wrote it down on a piece of paper that was flying by. Then, he tapped Sprout's shoulder and he got to count the votes so they voted again. Then, they announced the chosen idea.

Alex said "For the first vote, Sprout earned zero votes, Dreamer earned one, and Tablo earned one." Then Sprout announced, for the second vote, me and Dreamer earned none, and Tablo earned two votes. Dreamer got a total of one vote, none for me, and Tablo three. This makes Tablo's great idea the message for the words in our language. Now, how will we make it so that it can go for each letter?"

Just then, Alex said "I can explain that. First, we will symbolize the idea into a simple shape. ('like what?') Then, we will make all the others like that, but with only a piece of the main shape. So, if the shape was #*) Then the other letters would each have something close to it, even though the letter I just wrote is not very simple. Also, the main letter will also be the first letter. Tablo, could you tell us what you think the shape should be?"

Tablo said "I think that it should be something like many small shapes with one big shape connecting it because it seems pretty clear what it means. Still, I do not know how to draw it. Do any of you have ideas?" Sprout put his hand up. He said "I have an idea. You can draw a circle in the middle with seven rectangles surrounding it." Just then, Dreamer said, "Why seven rectangles?" Sprout answered "I don't know." So, dreamer said "That's a lot of rectangles and rectangles are super hard to draw. Why don't you do something like four circles surrounding one big circle since circles are easy to draw and there are four of us?" Sprout then looked at dreamer and said to him, "Four circles look sort of weird. How about three circles instead of four circles surrounding the one big circle to represent four of us still, because even if three circles are surrounding one big one, it would still be four." Tablo looked at him and said, "That's a good idea! Now, we need to think about what shape the other letters should be."

Just then, Dreamer looked at him and said "How come only you guys get to think and plan the ideas?" Then, Sprout said "Yeah. It's only the humans that get to do it." Tablo said "That's true. But we still need leaders. How about we have an election to choose one person from you guys and one from us so that later, when we get some more people, we can still have the elected people to lead and help out." Sprout then said, "Let's vote right now. Then he peered out of the metal railings and said, it looks like it's 3:45, by checking the sky." Alex said "How do you know that?" Sprout said, "Humans are so unwise! We all know it. But we have no time! Let's vote." But just then, their mother's hands gently scooped them up and carried them inside the house, because for Dreamer and Sprout it was bedtime, and for Alex and Tablo it was dinnertime.

Meanwhile, John and Ben were planning what to do. John checked when it was going to get dark outside on his phone and Ben made plans for how to do everything that they needed to do. They leaned the ladder against the wall and grabbed a rope. John decided to climb up the ladder while Ben held it. Just then, a man walking on the streets spotted them and asked what they were doing so John said, "We are repainting the hotel, so I'm getting the ladder ready." The man said "Is that your little brother?" Pointing to Ben. John replied "Yes. He is here to watch me." Then the man walked away. John sighed and said coming down the ladder "That was close. We almost got caught! We should have made a plan for what to do."

Then he tried casting a spell to the rope to make it invisible. Nothing happened. Ben said, "You haven't practiced for a while so it might take some time to make it invisible. I can try." Then, he casted the spell. It worked right away for him and only the harness was showing. He asked John "Are we all set now?" John said "Yes. Now we will come back this evening."

Later, when it got dark, they came out again to do their plan. It had gotten darker way earlier then they had expected so they went outside earlier than when they expected to go. That day, it was dark because of all the grey clouds covering up the sky and raining. John looked at the sky and said to Ben "Wow, it looks like all of the clouds are crying." Ben answered "It is perfect weather for us because not a lot of people come out on rainy, dark nights. I will go in whenever I see a family going into the human's side so that it looks like I am a confused boy even if I get caught. Then the people will get confused and I can look around the hotel for a couple minutes if I get lucky and while I do, you will climb up the ladder and go upstairs to see what is happening."

Then Ben added "Now you never seem sleepy after four or five. You must be getting used to this time. Wait, but if Ron is training the foxes for something, then they must be asleep at this time. So, this plan can't work." John said "Well, we can try." While they were talking, time had already passed very quickly and it was about seven thirty. It was still raining hard and making everyone's shoes get wet. There was also a family going along the streets and the curtains were all slowly closing on the fox's side. Ben had quickly noticed that, and had already started to walk towards the fox's door. He also nudged John over to the place where the harness was. John started to put the harness on. The harness felt strange without the rope showing. He put the harness on. He could see the white colour of the harness and feel the harness around his hips. Then he started to climb the rope. It was just a plain rope, but he tried to remember what he learnt when he was in spy training school. He knew it would be the same opening his eyes or closing them since the rope was invisible.

Oddly, he felt like the rope became visible as soon as he closed his eyes. He could see the outline slightly and grab onto them. Suddenly, he could not think of anything else. He saw the rope more clearly in his head. He did not feel any emotions but he felt the fiery power building in his body and moving him. It all seemed like a dream. Suddenly, he could see the pole and feel the end. He grabbed on to it hard and opened his eyes. As soon as he did, he seemed to feel all of the confidence slowly back away from his body and melt like ice cream into the cold night sky. He saw the ground, so far away from him. John hoisted his body onto the roof and hooked his harness onto the tip of the pole.

Then, he saw the windows. He could not open the curtains nor open the window lock, but he could hear the soft whispers of a female fox. He heard the language that made him feel comfortable. But over all the voices, he could hear a clear, loud voice. He felt someone walking towards the windows and walked to the top of the roof. The voice was hard to hear because of the distance, but John heard the word 'stay' 'time' and 'program'. Then, it all got very quiet and he could not hear anything. He then noticed a paw pull the curtains away. John kept quiet.

He prepared to go down and closed his eyes once again. This time, the power built up very slowly and very gradually, but the power was larger. He was able to see as if he was completely opening his eyes and the rope was not invisible. It surely was an incredible power that he was able to handle. Now, he saw his feet about a meter away from the ground and he pushed off the wall, swiftly landing on the ground and crouching down, blending into the shadows.

Meanwhile, Ben was slowly walking across the halls and moving along. He was trying to stay in the building for as long as he could without getting caught. John was spying in the most suspicious and secretive space, but Ben knew his most important job was not distraction. It was finding out about the hotel. He hid behind elegant stone blockings that were covering the wall. They seemed just to be there for a decoration. They had tiny gaps in the patterns, so he could see through. He saw an empty hallway for a minute or two, but then a litter of young foxes scurried through, following their mother and father. They all seemed very busy.

Ben decided to follow them. Then he noticed that the hotel seemed a little bit odd. Most of it seemed renovated in a human style, but some pieces reminded him of the fox's architecture such as the round doors and the tips of the floor hiding moss under it. But still he tried to keep up with the family scurrying along. Then, suddenly, the blockings seemed to get very narrow, so Ben looked above him.

Now, the blocking had turned into a railing.

There was a tube at the top, and his part was just holding it up. There were also bumpy parts that he could use as grips now. He moved very quickly. Then, he noticed that the blocking seemed to get way larger again. The grips went away too. Then, it completely ended. He still needed to follow the family that was going up though, so he hid behind a row of cabinets. Then, the family stopped. There was a large wooden door with golden handles on each side. The family knocked on the door.

Ben went up right behind a small cabinet. Then, the door opened. The family went in. At that time, Ron had just been getting ready for another meeting. He was in his fox suit, and attaching his ears. He did everything just in time before the next family came in for the meeting. He accidently dropped a pencil though when he went to open the door.

Just then, Ben had spotted a yellow pencil with tooth marks in it. He thought it might be a good clue, so he held it and walked behind the family. But just then, one of them looked back. Luckily, Ben dodged back and went behind one of the cabinets at the corridor.

Meanwhile, John was getting the ladder out and leaning it against the wall. He held on to his harness and closed his eyes once again to climb up the ladder. He reached the top of the ladder soon, and then put his harness on. This was because it was difficult to take it back off after it was tightened and the ladder was a little too short to jump up and clench the pole to take the rope off. John climbed up to the roof of the building again. He took the hook that was holding the rope onto the pole off. Then, he wrapped the long rope onto his wrist and looked at the ladder.

It was quite a jump and the ladder was not stable. John could not touch even the very tip of the ladder. He then got an idea. He linked the hoop of the rope onto the very end of the ladder by throwing it down. He then held onto it and went down. The rope was unraveled again. John quickly went down the ladder. He then took the rope off from the ladder and wrapped the rope around his wrist again. After that, he put away the ladder and went to the hotel to look for Ben.

At that time, Ben was at the end of all the obstacles but still hiding in the blocking surrounding the wall. He then saw a dark silhouette approaching very carefully from behind the building and gently pushing the door open. He backed up towards the railings. Then, it came in. Ben didn't dare to look up still. But then, he heard a very familiar voice. It was from John. He opened his eyes and looked at John. Ben said to him "We need to get out quickly. Open the door and let's go outside." So, they went out of the building and quickly went to their room.

As soon as they sat down on the bed, John said to Ben, "I was not able to do anything because all the windows were closed. I did hear a faint voice of some foxes talking, but that was all. Did you see anything?" Ben answered "Yes. I found out many interesting things. Let me explain them to you. First, I hid behind a metal blocking, and followed a fox family going up the stairs. But while I was following them, I saw some odd things in the way the building was built. It was very similar to the fox's architecture." Just then, John interrupted and said "I think I read that somewhere. I think it was something about this place and how it was used as a place to train humans for some reason and named it the human training centre... But I do not remember what page it was." Then rushed to his backpack in the corner of the room.

He said, "Do you remember when you were about to tell me how I was born and I told you that I read it in a book? Well, that book tells me nearly everything, and you can look up everything in it. It is also where I read the facts about this building before. Perhaps we should flip through the book and search for that." Then, he pulled out a thick book. Ben gasped. The book was at least as thick as the mattress on the bed and the cover was all worn out. He had only seen John put it in to the bags but he had never seen it that close like right now. John carefully set it on the bed and said "Should we look for traditional architecture? Or should we look for human training centre on the index?" Ben replied, "Search human training centre. So, John then flipped the pages of the book and said to Ben, "I can't find it because the index is too long and confusing. It keeps changing order somehow."

John then asked Ben "How about we ask Agatha?" Ben frowned, but before he could answer, John had already called Agatha. But before he could say anything, Agatha spoke up first. She said "We have a lot of important things to discuss. Do you remember the statue that you gave me? Well, we were going to move it to the castle and then use it to make him feel better, but for a moment, he seemed to be completely cured which I forgot to tell you at the time since that was a day before the war started. And then the war started up. And ever since, he has been feeling worse. So, we tried using the fox statue, but now it does not work. There are other things too still. The war seems like it won't stop which I know you are working your hardest to solve, but also, the virus that you worked on seems to be spreading more and more. Now, could you tell me what your problem is?"

John said, "Now Ron is running an isolation

centre for the virus and we found out that they have foxes on the other side and that he is telling them odd things. But then, we also thought that this building might have been here for ages! But not just that, it also seems like the foxes have built it too."

Just then, John was going to tell Agatha about the human training centre and the big book, but he stopped himself because he thought that Agatha might not be very happy if she knew that he just grabbed the book off of a table, so he told Agatha that he wanted to talk more about the isolation hotel. Agatha said "That seems very interesting. So, I know that you guys are working on the vaccine, and trying to find out the purpose of the hotel, which I am quite interested in. But what I am most concerned about is that Ron is doing some odd things to the foxes. I think that they may be disguised. Also, Ron must have found out how to make a fox suit!

That has to be how he is communicating with the foxes."

John said, "What you are saying does sound right but we have some more things to add. So, a couple days ago we made a plan to find out what Ron was doing so Ben was following some foxes going up stairs, and he saw them going in to a large attic. So that might be the place where he is teaching them odd things."

Then, Ben said "They seem to be starting something up again. This has to be Ron's new plan. I have found out about Ron doing some virus-related things while being near him and I know that this is what he was talking about. So, we need to start studying more about this problem." John responded "I had also noticed that because while I was at the hotel working, I heard someone commanding me to say something about the hotel and virus. So, it might be that Ron uses foxes to tell things to other people sometimes."

Agatha said "That is possible, at what you are saying is truly a very difficult and important issue, but I also think that as for a different subject such as Ron's plans, I am quite certain that he has not gone very far. And so, to prevent it getting worse, we shall develop a plan. I think that you should try actually contacting with a fox on the other side of the building. Then, once you guys get a little bit closer, you can maybe call me. Of course, you would want to start by using fox suits." John and Ben agreed then said to Agatha "We should contact often to share what is going on. Ok?" Then they hung up.

Meanwhile, the foxes on the other side of the hotel were sitting down on the couch. The foxes were gazing at the sun. But just then, they heard a knocking sound. And as soon as they heard it,

Sprout and Dreamer started to whine and scratch at the door. So, Sunshine let them out. As soon as they were let out, they looked at the other side. They knew Alex and Tablo had sent a signal. And as soon as they looked, they saw Alex.

Alex said to them in the language they had made up and told them, "Tablo is sick. He caught the flu going around. Anyways, I called you to talk about our words and language. Actually, I have been practicing." As soon as Sprout and Dreamer heard this, they were surprised because they had done the same thing.

Alex told them that he had also invented all the letters for the language and showed them it and showed them how to use it. There were only 23 letters, and it seemed easy to use, so they began making words and spelling them out and they got quite used to it. They then were going to decide pronunciation for some words when their mothers opened the door.

Alex quickly ran to the wall and pretended he was playing alone. He said to his mother "Can we play more?" And mumbled. Nobody replied. Then, Wendy, who was holding Alex put him down on his bed and turned on the television to watch a chick-flick, but her husband Liam grabbed the remote and turned on the news. It was about the war that was happening. The reporter said "We are fighting the foxes for our safety and it is very dangerous. We are very amazed that we are having wars with an animal, but foxes appear to be quite clever. They are killing many of our solders and attacking nearby towns."

Meanwhile, John was sitting down in his room. He wanted a break after all that talking and he needed to think about his issues. He still felt weird. He wanted to still know about His birth. He did pretty much know everything though.

He knew he was not born and made, and he knew that his parents did technically not exist, because he was made, but that he was related to Ben and Ron. He still did not get how they both turned into humans. That was something he did not know yet but he was too scared to ask Ben because he knew that even if he tried, he wouldn't tell a soul.

Ron was not really an option either, considering the fact he was opposed to them. He knew there was still one option which was reading the book. John knew he did not read anything like that yet, so he went to the part where he had stopped reading and laid down on the bed beside Ben who was taking a nap after an early dinner.

John turned on the reading light and started to read about the history of the fox world. He read for hours but he could not find it. What John did not know was that it had fallen out of the book when he was in the tunnel and had been discovered by Ron. After a couple hours, John gave up.

THE BIRTH OF A HUMAN

Control Begins

9. Control Begins

At that time Ron was walking in the corridors and thinking about something. He was thinking about teaching the foxes. It seemed to slowly work out, but he needed it to work faster, so he got an idea. He could go to fox tribe in the battlefield and start teaching the solders. He would teach the humans and the foxes and it would be easier since they were already getting used to thinking in the ideal way. Ron was going to make a plan in the glass tunnel, so he went there.

He had arrived at his own glass tunnel. He looked at the tunnel and checked his small vehicle then started to ride along and check the rooms and supplies. But when he went and checked the virus room, he found out that some of the beakers for making new viruses were missing. It was not a very big problem since there was more, but this started to make Ron feel quite weird. He wanted to investigate it more though he knew that he needed to go to the battlefield for his next plan. But he thought that he could investigate this later so he rushed towards the end of the tunnel and headed to fox tribe with his bag that contained the fox suit. When he got out of the tunnel, He looked around. He thought that since it was fox tribe, that it would be way better to look like a fox now so he went back into the tunnel and put his fox suit on.

He then popped his head out of the tunnel and walked out onto the streets and headed to the battlefield. While he walked, Ron thought where he should head first. Thinking, he had already arrived at the human's tent. He removed his suit and put it in the bag. He then thought of a plan. That day, Ron waited until midnight that day when the humans started to guard the tent.

He prepared a small light and went up into a tall tree and waited until the guards started to look at the tree with the gleaming light and made sure he was not seen, and watched the sky until a small bird passed by. He quickly grabbed the bird's leg and linked the light onto its leg, and let it go. The solders gasped. He repeated what he did every day for one week. Soon, the soldiers were horrified.

The next day, he dressed in a black cloak and went to the human tent. The humans looked at him. Hiding his face, Ron said to the solders "Haven't strange things been happening these days?" The solders all agreed. Ron said, "There is a reason. It isn't anything amazing, but it is from what the foxes have done. They will try to conquer us and our world. We need to act back. And I can help you greatly." The soldiers were already used to knowing that the world was unfair and wrong from others since they needed to fight, so they accepted Ron without suspecting him too much. But Ron said that he would come back the next day and left. He was glad that his plan worked out and he was ready for his next plan. He first went into the deep forest and changed into his fox suit, then wore his cloak again.

He then headed to the fox's side very slowly. He entered the tent and sat down. The fox soldiers stared at him with great interest and asked him, "What did you come here for? It's dangerous here. Ron stared at them curiously and said "I have just come here to tell you some news. Just from the other tent. Something seems to be happening there today. So, I thought I could help you by teaching you some things. It's fine if you do not need me to do this. I'm really just giving help, you see………." The soldiers said "You could help us, but how? And what news did you bring?" Ron said "The humans. That's what it's about. They plan to attack. It's not totally their fault though. It's the worlds. Anyway, the humans plan to attack because they envy you. And what I want to teach you is about how to defend them mentally."

The soldiers accepted but still approached carefully since they did not know Ron well yet. They said "Why are you not saying anything? We want to know what you will tell us before the human's attack. This place is not safe for people to come into." Ron said to them "I need to tell you it for a long time. It is not a short story indeed. What if you guys let me stay here? I will teach you three days a week and will stay at a different place for the other four days. I plan to teach you four days later."

Ron then left to the human's tent quietly after taking his fox suit off in the forest. The humans all greeted him. They said "What will you teach us?" Ron said "The foxes will try to conquer us by controlling our minds. So, I will train you so that you can defend yourselves. First, I will give you something." he said and showed them some books that he had made through a printer called **Lesson 1: The rules** and gave them one each. Ron then said "This book is very basic and teaches you skills and ways to defend yourself along with easy ways to identify the world. Could you all please read the first page?"

The first page had a small writing on it that read chapter 1. All of them stared at the page because below it, in small letters, it said that it was all about the incorrect ways. Ron spoke up right away and said "As you can see, it is all about some incorrect things in the world. You may be thinking that this is not related to defending your souls or protecting yourself from the foxes, but is has many relationships. Because their act was caused because of many irresponsible things in the world. There is only one way to stop the foxes. If they are being wrong, we need to do something that is equally incorrect in their way. Or else, the foxes will bother us even more. This is because the foxes think they are the best animals in the world. To prove them wrong and to tell them that we are better and the best, we need to make them be defeated and make them give up. You can see that what I said is mentioned on the next page. So, I want you to just take a moment and flip to the next page which has what I mentioned along with some description."

They all looked at it carefully for they were being more and more convinced. So, they asked Ron "What can we do to make the world better?" Ron then answered them "The world can never be better now! It's like the virus. The virus is very important and is way more dangerous than what all of you think. Anyway, since the world cannot get any better for everyone, we need to make it better for us. And to do that, we need to make the foxes sacrifice. They will never do it voluntarily, so we need to use our strengths and attack with our strong army." Everyone clapped.

Ron then continued his speech. He said to all of them about the importance of strength and told them that it was very natural for better creatures to rule over other creatures. He said that that was the true way to make the world fair and right. Everyone agreed. Ron then looked outside and said, "we need to sleep." The soldiers then told him that it was only 6pm outside but Ron said that they needed to wake up very early and attack. The solders all trusted him so they did as Ron asked them to do. When they started to head to their beds, Ron said that he would not be there the next day until ten.

They all said that they would wait and turned to look at Ron, but Ron was already gone. He had headed to the tunnel to make another plan and find out the culprit that had stolen his virus beakers. He opened the door and rode the vehicle and thought about his plan to save time. He was going to first load food for the humans along with guns secretly from the fox tent.

This was because he wanted the humans to win rather than the foxes so that he could achieve his dream. To rule over everyone. And this was the first step to do so. He put on his fox suit once again and walked out of the tunnel which let directly to fox tribe. He also put on his cape. The foxes greeted him and said "What have you provided for us?" Ron pulled out a book which he used for the humans, but changed a little for the way foxes think and translated in fox. He said to everyone after they read the first couple pages "As you have read, the first chapter is made out of incorrect ways of humans. Have you all read the first couple pages?" the foxes said yes. In the book, each word was convincing and seemed true. And Ron's heavy but mystic voice when the spoke made it even more convincing. Because Ron had that very type of voice.

When he needed to say something against others, his voice and face always both changed. This was a time like that, but the foxes were able to get out of that thought right away because Ron said, "I will be back after about four hours. Until then, you guys need to fight in the battlefield. The humans will probably come out soon." And when he said that he also said, "Can you please give me the key to the storage? I need it for my plan." The foxes said yes. And Ron went to the storage quietly. He opened the door after showing the soldier guarding the storage the key and hid the food, guns and many other tools for the war in his sack secretly.

Then, he went to the deep forest so that nobody would notice and took off his fox suit, then headed towards the human's territory. He waved at the humans and walked towards them. He went in the tent and said to the humans "I have prepared for you, a very special treat." He said as he revealed the sack from behind his back. The solders watched him draw the red lace from the leather sack and open up the bag. And as soon as they saw what was inside the bag, their jaws dropped.

Ron looked at their reaction, then just said "I have brought you various tools and foods." The humans looked at him and said "Where did you get it? The tools look like the ones the foxes used! What kind of food is that?" And many other questions. Ron answered them by saying "The tools are from the fox storage. If they do not have this, they will not be able to do anything. The food is from the fox storage too. Please do not ask any more questions. And do not use the tools on the foxes. Or they will notice. Do you understand?"

The humans all said yes. Ron then said. "Now I need to go. I will come back soon." Ron then changed into his fox suit after getting far away from the tent and went into the storage, got some more things in his sack, and headed to the tunnel.

Meanwhile, in dog tribe, all the dogs that did not go to the humans were calling the dogs in the human world and having a meeting. When everyone arrived, the king of the dogs said "Welcome. I have called you all to ask if we should join the humans in the war. I have thought of this idea because if we join the humans as they go out to war more than what we did before, then the humans will win and the foxes will lose which will mean that we can gain us long-lost freedom once again. And we will rule all the other creatures." The dogs all clapped and said to the king "That's an excellent idea your majesty. But how will we help the humans?" The king said "You can help them however you want. We can attack the foxes from the back. Now go back to your homes before your owners start to search for you!" At that moment, in the hotel, a tremendous thing had also happened.

The babies had started to talk with each other again and were writing letters while their parents were watching the news about the war which they did not know about. They usually did this for three hours and they stopped so the parents would not notice. While they were talking, their brothers and sisters came in. They turned away from each other to explain the situations to their siblings before they saw their friends. Dreamer and Sprout said "Actually, we made friends here. Could you see them?" and turned towards the wall. Autumn said "Gosh...... What is this odd thing?" Aurora yelled "Get that away from me! Whatever that is, take it out of here now!" Midnight and Marina, who had heard about the humans and not about the war that much looked at them with curiosity. Then, Sprout said "Don't worry. `We can speak the same language and they are harmless." Nobody said anything for a short moment. Then Dreamer said "They are totally fine. You don't need to back off." At the same time, Alex and Tablo were introducing the foxes to their siblings who also were greatly surprised.

After they calmed down, Alex and Tablo said not to tell their parents and the foxes did the same. At that point, the fox and human children looked at each other and froze. They were already shocked from seeing the younger kids, and the foxes thought that the humans were getting uglier as they grow up. Before they could run away, their younger siblings said "You need to learn our language now. We are the teachers. Ok?" Both the foxes and humans wanted to run away, but their baby brothers had an eye on them so they could not do so. Also learning the language was like doing homework. But for some reason, after about an hour, they had started to catch on.

The language had a weird spark that attracted them in their mind. They also were now able to concentrate on their work and not the weird other creatures. They still needed their siblings to translate to speak with others though. Because they could not speak comfortably in the human-fox language yet. But then it became time to go to bed for the foxes. And before they said their goodbyes, the kids all told the older ones not to tell their parents. They agreed, but were also worried about what would happen if their parents found out about this. Still, they were more afraid to tell than anything else. Because they did not know what would happen.

But in the human's house, Tablo was thinking about telling his parents all about this language. He did this because he wanted to get some attention from everybody else. He was not particularly playing an important role, or good at something amazingly. But he wanted everyone's attention. And he was making a plan for when to say this.

THE BIRTH OF A HUMAN

Discovery of the Truth

303

10. Discovery of Truth

Meanwhile, John and Ben were sitting down on their beds. They were greatly surprised because of something they heard upstairs. It was not any language of the humans. It was not the language of the foxes. Ben told John about this and said to him "I suddenly thought something weird. That the humans and foxes might be meeting together. I am quite sure that this would be true since we talked about communication between humans and foxes, but still, I also do not want you to think that this is true yet, because there are some things we cannot explain. They are things like how did they meet, how come we do not hear fox and English and something mixed together and many others." John then said "How about we go outside and think about it?"

Ben answered "But the main thing is that we need to investigate. We need to make a plan to look at what is happening. Then, if they are communicating a lot, then we could begin our plan easily and start working with them. Also, we would need to contact many people." John then said "that's not a bad idea, but they might see us when we look at them….and they might not be doing any sort of communicating at all." Ben then said "Still, if we work to make up a good plan, then we could do this without getting caught. Also, we are doing this to check if they are communicating or not." He then said to John "Now, I've made up most of our plan. It will be very easy. First, I found out that the sound is heard from 2 to 4 so we need to go between then." Just then, John said "Quiet! I hear something."

But was just the faraway sound of gunshots and screaming. John said "Sorry. It's just because of the war. Well, if they are communicating, then we sure can stop the war a little bit easier since they would be able to do us some help. Right?" Ben answered "But nobody knows if the war will end. So, for now our goal is just to end it. Not to end it soon. Though this may sound negative, if we do anything wrong, or slip up a little, or miss a little hint about Ron, we are sure to fall in somebody's plan. I mean, it might not be just Ron that we actually need to avoid. Don't you think?" John said to Ben "Well, you are quite correct. Still, at least let's have a hope that it will all be over one day but still be careful. How's that sound like?" Ben answered "But the part that's important is that one small thing done incorrectly can make everything into a big mess. So, you have to be very cautious for this thing." John said "Right."

And they talked over this through the whole night but could not get a definite answer because they were not able to settle on a certain plan. Then, John suggested "Why don't we just sleep and think about it next morning?" Ben agreed on that plan and said "We can think about this more next morning." So, they went to their beds and slept. However, John was not able to fall asleep. He read a book, had some milk, and looked at the sky. He also had a bath with hot water. But he was not able to fall asleep because of the sound of gunshots. He sighed and said "I should take a walk near the battlefield. It is so annoying. Still, I know better than to get to close or I might get hurt."

Meanwhile, Ron was getting ready to go to the battlefield. He was going to meet the foxes on night duty to teach them some extra things and to tell them some wrong plans so that the humans can win the war.

He was holding a pen that he had picked up

from the table but as he walked faster, it slipped out of his hand and rolled backwards. It kept rolling back until it reached an upwards hill.

John spotted the pen and said "Strange. Is there anything written on it?" And looked at the pen, but all that John was able to find was a faint, erased name. It seemed quite odd, so John kept walking towards where the pen came from. And as he walked towards the place, he was able to see someone walking way in front of him. John stared at the dark figure that was walking ahead and ran towards it. But then, he saw that the sun was shining and walked back to the hotel.

Meanwhile, Ron had arrived at the fox's side. Now most soldiers were awake. Ron said to them "I came here to tell you some news. It's about the war. I just found out when the humans are going to attack you. They will attack you tonight at precisely about eight. So, until then, you guys can defend and just rest." Ron still knew that the humans were actually going to attack at eight. It was just to make the foxes follow him. Also, if the foxes win and start to rule a small part of the human's territory, then they would put most of their supplies there. And then when the humans attack, the humans would gain more supplies.

But the foxes did not know anything Ron thought yet, and so they listened to what he said. Still, a plan for a war could not be changed that easily, so the foxes told Ron that even if they changed the plan, they would have to only let some soldiers out at night because the others that were in control would not allow that either.

Ron nodded then said slowly said to the soldiers "Why do you even care so much about other people? You are being controlled by them. Believe me. This is a great chance to win the war. I mean, this is a chance. Well, you don't have to say yes, but I'm just telling you. That's all. Then Ron left as he said "Make sure to study the book!" Ron's next stop was the hotel. He needed to train the foxes more.

Meanwhile, at the time, the young foxes were meeting all together. It was only their second time meeting, but they felt more comfortable already because of all their practice. They were able to speak and write not as easily as in their original language, but still enough to communicate. They started with some simple things. But since the youngest ones could not concentrate, an so they started running all around. Especially Dreamer and Tablo. The same thing had happened today.

Tablo had brought out a bag of chips, and he had hidden it in the corner to eat later. But then, Alex had spotted it and had slowly backed up to the corner. But since their mother did not let him have it, he did not know it's taste so he called Dreamer silently and asked him to taste it. But as a fox, Dreamer had never seen such thing. But when he took a bite, he realized that this was something quite delicious. And when Alex saw the look on Dreamer's face, and knew that it was something good.

He stole the bag of chips from Dreamer quickly, and took a bite. Dreamer started to whine. And he stole the bag of chips from Alex again. And this time, Alex started to cry. This was bad. All of them knew that their mothers could come in at any time. But as if they did not know, Dreamer and Alex kept on crying. Tablo panicked, and threw the bag of chips down the railing. The chips landed on the floor below them.

John and Ben were planning something. They were trying to think of a way to go upstairs and find out about the strange and odd thing that was happening. Just like last time, they were not able to think of anything. Just then, John said "Let's at least take a walk. We can find some ideas." Ben said back "And who knows if we won't get an idea? What would be the true point in a walk like this today?" John looked at Ben and then frowned.

He then said "If you say so, I will just stop near the bakery. I'm planning to buy a cake. I know today is nothing close to special, but the day will become special if we eat something special. And I think you can think better on special days." And with that word, John disappeared into the streets. Leaving Ben to think alone. But John did not have this in mind. He knew that to save some time for brainstorming, he needed to go quickly. He knew that on a foggy day like this, the true point in buying something was not really because you needed it, but because you need to rely on the point of shopping.

And this was such a time like that. When John entered the bakery, it was filled with people sitting there quietly. The store was busy, but not its usual cheerful soul. And someone that John was not expecting was also there. It was Ron. He was with a man all bundled up in scarves and masks and hats. So much that you could not see his face. John forgot about the cake and stared at them as they exited the bakery, and waited until they were not able to be seen. Then, he ran after them. John was hoping that they would go somewhere odd, but they were heading to the hotel.

John was about to turn back to the bakery when suddenly, he saw them going into the zoo. John was surprised, for he knew that the zoo had closed soon after he had left the hotel. John watched them go into one of the cages and hid behind a bush near it. And as soon as the man with Ron took off his hat, John could not believe what he had seen. The man all wrapped in scarves dropped to the ground, and Ron looked at the man calmly. John wanted to burst out, but John knew that he could not do that.

After the man dropped to the ground completely, Ron looked around and started to draw something in the air with a stick from the ground. John knew that it was not a wand but Ron did not seem to care about that at all. When he was finished, blood-red circles appeared. Ron put his mouth there and whispered something. Then, the man stood up.

John followed them as they went into the hotel, and then saw something even more surprising. Before they entered the hotel, Ron removed all of the man's bandages and scarves. The man's face was revealed. Except, he was not really a man. He was a fox. John had read about how somebody hypnotizes another.

THE BIRTH OF A HUMAN

Communication and Disconnection

11. Communication and Disconnection

John was now shaking. He ran away to his own room. He then sat on the bed and said slowly to Ben "I can't believe my own eyes. I know what Ron's doing!" Ben said to John "Didn't we already know?" John said to Ben "No, it's way worse. Ron's plan is to hypnotize the foxes, and I just saw one in the zoo with him."

Ben said "What? Could you repeat that one more time?" John said "Ron is hypnotizing the foxes and I just saw a hypnotized fox walking around the zoo!" Ben tried to keep calm. John said "I think this might have a relationship with the war. If that is true, then Ron may be making up the war situation by hypnotizing. But what I saw was a hypnotized fox going into the fox side of the hotel. So, this might mean that Ron has started to hypnotize the isolating foxes. We need to find out about the sound there right now."

Ben then said "Have you also thought about the possibility of Ron spreading the virus itself? I mean, it's a quite possible situation if you think of it. The virus is the reason for war, the hotel, and everything that Ron is doing. Don't they all fall together like puzzle pieces? But I still feel like I'm trapped in a maze for some reason. What do you think?" John said "Sadly, that seem true........."

Just then, Ben cut in. He said "Let's go investigate upstairs. You can pretend to be staff checking in to make sure they did not escape. John rode the elevator even though it was the next floor. There was one elevator, and they wanted nobody to know what they were doing. As soon as they arrived, John got into his uniform and went to the room exactly above his own and knocked.

Just then, a women came out of the room. She said "Why did you come? Are there any issues?" She asked them. John said "No. We Just need to inspect the rooms today." He said as he walked to the terrace and looked. There were some children, saying something in front of the wall. He quietly looked at the kids and saw who they were talking to. John ran to the couch and said "Everything seems fine, so I think that we can go."

John left the room and ran to Ben. He said with an expression that was delightful, but also very worrisome. He said to Ben "The sound was the kids playing. But it was not just the kids chatting. They were talking to the foxes on the other side with another language! The parents did not seem to know. Perhaps they have formed their own society. I fear this will make the foxes and humans not understand each other if they

319

communicate because they did not look quite cheerful when they were talking, but it is positive for there is communication other than fighting."

Ben said "How could you know they were using another language? Those little kids? Even if they were using another language, they created themselves, there is no point in communication if it is secretive. I think there may be more to fear than to keep watching."

When they got to their room, John suddenly said to Ben "We should call Agatha. She is an expert for these things." Ben moaned, then nodded. John said after a moment "I'm not sure if I can get connected with Agatha. I think she is using her mind-connection with another person. She might call back after she's done." John said this but bit his nails, as if he hadn't been able to contact her for a week.

That night, John was thinking about Agatha. He said to himself that she happened to be busy that day, but his imagination soon took over. He was already thinking about Agatha being trapped, or teaming with Ron, or betraying them. John shook his head, then thought 'I should just go to bed. I can wait until tomorrow.'

John fell asleep, feeling like he was falling into a trance. It seemed as if thousands of ropes were binding into the bed, and he couldn't breathe. The blood-red circles appeared again into his tightly closed eyes. John kicked and tried opening his eyes. John tried to resist and yelled in a muffled voice. Then, he finally felt the overwhelming emotion fading away. He panted and looked at Ben. He was also panting a little bit, so John woke Ben up by shaking him. Ben seemed okay. He said "Why did you wake me up?"

So, John said "Um…. The thing is that I felt too overwhelmed for a moment during my sleep and you did too, so I thought it would be better to wake you up. Ben said "Okay." Then asked if he could go to bed. John agreed but felt like something would happen. He was thinking about the hypnotizing that he saw. John did not sleep a bit that night and looked around with irrational fear. He spent the night biting his nails and looking around. John then looked at the clock. 5:57. He had spent most of the night worrying and thinking. But now he could not go on without sleeping. He also could not do anything but be awake. John felt that there was a curse on him, so he looked at the thick book once again.

He looked at the book, page by page. Nothing was there that he wanted. John felt odd and dropped down to the ground. There he spent the rest of the day. He forgot to even go to work that day and realized what he was doing when

Ben came back from school. Ben looked at his expression and said to him "What is the problem? Why are you sitting here?" John said "I don't know. I feel like I see weird things though. I see someone walking to a forest!" John shrieked.

Ben looked at him in an odd way then said "You have been like this for quite a while. I feel there really is something. We have fallen into a very big trap. We need to do something about it, and I cannot feel it. Let's look at this together. So, first I have a question. What did you see?"

John said in a small voice "Someone is in a forest with another person. They both look quite familiar to me but I cannot recognize them." Ben nodded. John said "Last night I think I saw one of those people too. Well, I did not see him, I just felt him. So, I am not so sure." Ben said "You look frightened. How about a nice cup of tea?" John nodded and took out the teabag and put it in the teapot. He was about to heat it but his hands were trembling and the tea spilled on the floor.

He quickly wiped it up and said "I didn't mean to do that…" He then got another teabag and heated it up. While he was heating up the tea, Ben set the table. There was a moment of silence. John then sat down and asked Ben "Can I continue speaking?" Ben nodded and said "You were also sweating as if you had been influenced by the thing I am talking about. So, I woke you up and you replied as if there was nothing, so I felt weird. Everything seemed to melt in slowly to the dark, so I stood up and looked around. There was nothing." Ben said to John "So it's kind of like an irrational fear that you cannot describe, and you can't control the feeling."

John said "Uh, also um…the thing is that I uh… no, not that. Never mind." Ben poured the tea into the teacup as the lowered it from the stove and looked at John. John could not look at Ben. He wanted to tell him how he feels like there is a relationship with the hypnotization but he could not dare to say it. Something stopped him from saying it, and he felt like saying it was forbidden. He sipped the tea so he could look at something other than Ben. John did not want to break the silence.

Ben wanted information and he wanted to solve the problem quickly. John could feel that. John felt scared and felt like he was a coward. John did not know why he said that, but he looked at Ben and said "I can't think of anything right now." Ben said "That's okay. You must have been scared. Let's rest for today."

So, they walked outside. Just then, they ran into Ron outside. It seemed he was just coming back from somewhere. There was nobody else in the streets, so John knew it was not a good situation. Ron did not seem to say anything, but then whispered something as he walked into the lobby. It seemed like a puff of smoke, or a grey cloud. John felt weird.

Ben kept quiet until Ron disappeared, then said quietly to John, "He knows us, we know him. It's just that we need to keep in a formal relation when with other people. That's pretty clear. Ron's going to do something to us though when we are all alone with him. And tell me. What did Ron whisper to you?"

John said "I don't know what it means. He just said 'You know.' And left. I can't explain why, but he did not mean that. Ron meant something else. And he was wondering if I knew it. Clearly, I don't know the meaning. It is not a nice feeling. Oh, and you're right. He defiantly is going to act quite differently when there are people around and when it's only us. That's what worries me."

Ben said "This is real...And to make this better there is only one way. To work hard and accept reality." John answered "I know that too. We can realize that we aren't it a good situation. Then, you can work for it. Because storms can come at any time. Still, I fall into a feeling where I feel something others don't know. It's scary." Ben said "That may be true, but be careful. You may be pretending to be idealistic when you actually aren't. Don't lie to you. Huh...But if it's scary, we can think of cursed things, but it's not the case, just don't think about it too seriously."

John did not seem very comfortable, and kept glancing at the ground. Ben noticed that, and stopped talking. They then went to their room without a word and slept.

The next thing John knew, it was about four

327

in the morning, and it was Friday. He thought that his phone had an error and reloaded it. Still Friday. John then thought of how he saw Ron hypnotizing. He then thought about Ron making another plan. He then saw images flashing in his head.

Someone was crouching down in the forest and weeping. He could not tell if it was a human or fox. Beside it was another figure bursting out laughter. The scene then changed to a battlefield. John could recognize right away that it was the battlefield he knew. It was just the same. John waved his hands in the air to pull the images that seemed to be floating away. He saw those images melting away. He was once again in the hotel room with Ben, sitting on his bed. John wanted to run away, so he walked out of the hotel in his pajamas.

He did not feel embarrassed at all. He was

full of fear. He hoped that he was dreaming and hit himself to see if he could wake up. Nothing happened. John felt like as if he were living in a nightmare and returned to his room, full of despair. Ben was still sleeping, so John decided not to wake him up. A few minutes later, John fell asleep again. He then woke up and started to shout. He saw someone coming closer to him and trying to do something to him. But he then fell asleep again, and thought that the odd thing he saw was also part of his dream.

At about seven in the morning, Ben woke up. John was already awake and getting ready to start the day. Ben asked John, "What time is it?" John answered "7am, Friday. You missed school and I missed work. I phoned the school and told them you were sick. I think I need to go to work now." Ben said "Okay. I need to head out anyway too. Bye!" Ben said as if he was totally fine, but he thought that it was weird how they could sleep like that. Ben did not feel like he slept well either. John said he saw a man trying to poke him. Ben ignored him and headed out the door.

John started to clean the hall for the day. In his mind, John was still thinking only about the odd dream. Just then, someone came in. It was one of his peer workers, and they were cleaning the hall. John thought that it was very weird, because he had been quiet all the time, so rarely someone spoke to him.

He said to John "How come you were not here yesterday? Did you have a schedule? John thought he would think it would be weird if he said that he was sleeping, so he said "I forgot to tell you guys... Sorry. It was an important family thing." "Oh, really? That must have been really nice to have seen your family, right?" John was offended because he did not have anybody in particular that he could call 'family' but he had to pretend. John said "Yes, I really enjoyed being there, but I am very sorry about not coming here yesterday. You guys must have had a hard time without me."

There was a short pause, then he said "Well, John, I think it was not very busy. We tried out best, and we did not have any problems with running the hotel. In fact, we could run the hotel without you coming here. Our boss was a little bit concerned about you not coming sometimes, but he was quite satisfied with how well we worked without you." John said "Oh, thank you very much for looking after all that. I'll go down to the office and talk about the issue. It's very good to hear you worked well without me."

Then, he left and John was left alone again. He thought it was weird that someone would say that but he knew that he needed to go and see Ron, so he went to Ron's room. John hoped that someone was near because he knew anything could happen when there was just the two of them. John took a deep breath and went to the room. The door was locked.

John thought it was particularly strange, because he had not seen Ron lock the door to his office. What was even stranger was that there was not a sign showing there was a meeting going on, but there was some noise inside the room. John felt a little bit odd but tried to calm himself and thought about the things he could do. He went closer towards the door but then, he heard the sound of chairs moving and windows opening. John was so surprised. Then, it was quiet.

Some people stared at John, but John did not think about that at the moment. He then saw all the other people looking at him and returned to the front desk. That day, it was amazingly busy.

All staff had to be working without any rest, yet everyone was coming to the hotel. John was worried, because this meant that the virus was spreading and more people were going to come to the hotel and possibly be controlled by Ron.

He came back very late that night, at about quarter past ten. Ben looked at him then said, "Why were you so late?" John said "Well, it was a very busy day for the hotel, but that's not the only reason. It's because of something else." Ben said to John "Then what is it?" John sat down and started to think.

He was helping out at the kitchen after someone else came in to help with the front desk. Everyone was preparing the food for the next day and wrapping up the food supplies set to deliver to the families. It was about half past eight at the time when the head chef allowed him to go. When he went outside, he heard a voice loudly booming in his head like a curse. He could not call it a language, nor a sound. It was the dark and attractive feeling itself, molded into a voice.

It then showed him an image of a man storming into the forest. The man arrived at a cave and rolled the stone blocking the entrance. Inside was a bushy figure tied up with a rope. John was about to scream but the image disappeared and all that John saw was the hotel. He then had hysterically stomped into his room.

When Ben heard about all of this, he was oddly calm. Or you could say he looked calm, because he too, was quite dazed with the odd experience. John then said slowly... "Something must be chasing me. I can feel it. Always!" And when he said this, for a second, it seemed there was a small flash in John's eye. Ben could actually kind of understand what John meant, but something else blocked him from completely understanding it in John's position.

Still, Ben tried very hard to look as if he was understanding John's speech. John then noticed Ben was not interested in the subject and quickly finished his sentence. John thought, then said "As I know I will be replaced shortly, I better hurry." "What?" "Better to live in a nightmare than die in a dream."

Meanwhile, somewhere else far away, there was sounds coming from a forest in dog tribe. The dog tribe's dogs had a big problem. Humans were not caring about, or relying on the dogs as much as before. Ironically, this was because of the war. The war made people rely on new owner's love and attention, and many of them had returned from the human world except for a couple dogs which had been sent as war dogs. Another thing was that humans did not know that dogs were also equally as smart and clever as them. That they created the human languages now used, and that it was humans that truly were obsessed with this odd creature.

One of the dogs that came back from the humans' world complained "Except for men working in the castle, we had sent all the dogs out to the human world. Look at this! How's the local gardener going to make food for us? Where are the houses? Anyways, this is a nightmare. If we can do anything to solve this, we have two things we can do. One is to go deeper into the war and try to play a bigger role. Fighting, more military dogs, better idea. We could try getting out of this mess, but it won't work. It can also mean getting attacked by both......The humans AND the foxes." Then suddenly, there was a buzz through the crowd. The speech continued. "Let's decide what to do." Somewhere else near the forest, Ron was watching the speech.

He had been thinking of a way to make this war enough to fool everyone. He thought that using the dogs would be perfect for it. He smiled and kept watching the speech. He was afraid that someone would see him, but he was hiding behind a bush far away, using a telescope to monitor them. He carefully examined the forest and left. He knew it would be no good if he was going to stay there longer and headed towards the battlefield with his cloak and suit. The wind kept on blowing, and he hid behind the bushes and smiled. At that time, far, far beyond the dog's territory, in an unknown place, there was a sound coming. Sort of sounding like something whining. The sound echoed outwards towards the outside of the forest and even near the battlefield, as quiet as a light gust of wind.

At that time, John was walking down to the river near the hotel. He was scared and lone, for now he started to see odd visions of some men, walking in to a forest. They were trying to find something, and were walking back and forth to find it. Then, they crouched down in front of a huge tree somewhat familiar to John. They seemed to think, and think again, but sadly it seemed that they haven't got the result they wanted.

But if that had been the only thing that John had seen, he would not have run all the way here. Because after, he saw someone coming up the stairs holding a tiny key. The man seemed like a shadow, approaching him. But the man then attacked John swiftly and tossed his keys to the ground. Just as he was about to attack back, he awoke from his vision.

Yet still, he saw the keys on the ground with his own eyes. Ben was not there either because Ben happened to be on a field trip. He was alone to deal with his issue. The keys were very old, and was made with brass. John clutched the keys and put it on top of the old book. He then looked at the book and thought that he should try reading it. He flipped the pages to find something helpful, but the book had way more information than what he thought. So, he flipped the pages to the end of the book, but surprisingly, nothing had changed. The book would usually make up thousands of pages in a second, but nothing was happening at the very back page.

He was quite surprised, but he thought he saw wrong so he rubbed his eyes and looked again in to the book closely, but still all that he was able to see were the pages he had seen minutes ago. He shook his head, trying to resist the sequence of odd events like a dream. He then thought of someone who knew about these things very well. John believed Agatha was an expert at things like this. He thought that she knew almost everything about things happening in the fox world, and that was quite right. For in fact, not many people to better than her about that place.

He decided to call Agatha, and picked up his phone. He waited for a moment, then a couple more minutes, but sadly, Agatha was not able to answer. This time, John called her by using magic. But after some time had passed, she still did not pick up. John thought that it was strange that she did not pick up for such a long time, so he decided to go to Agatha.

Meanwhile, Agatha was sitting in her house. She was very confused. John was not able to get her messages. She had tried to contact John, but he did not answer. So, Agatha thought that she should go to John. She did not want others to see her, so she went through the middle of the forest. At that time, John was going to Agatha's house. He went to her house, but she did not happen to be there. John was frightened and stood still.

Agatha also was crawling into the tunnel and found nobody. She was quite confused, and was worried something had happened. John was also worried because he was having bad dreams recently. He crossed back towards the forest, but nobody was there. John thought that something really was wrong and that Agatha was in big trouble. At the same time Agatha was running towards her house. John was so worried and was wondering into the forest. Something was spinning around and around. When he looked again, it had disappeared. Then John headed back to the hotel. He arrived soon and was still very scared about what had happened to Agatha.

At the time, Agatha was trying to call John. She was wondering why John was not answering because he usually would have picked up right away. She was not able to see John at the hotel, and now she was a little bit suspicious about what was happening. It had been such a long time since she was able to get in touch with John, and she was able to find him at the hotel.

Meanwhile, someone was sitting on a chair and busily working on something. Red rays shot out of it, and it was a round shape. It was creeping on the ground and spreading out onto the ground. It looked horrific, yet once you looked at it., it would be very hard to take your eyes off of it.

At that time, Ben had just come back from his field trip. As soon as John saw him, he told Ben about what had happened. Ben was not as surprised as John, but was still quite shocked by this news. Ben then said to John "Do you know if there are any possibilities that she would have gone somewhere else?" but John shook his head.

John mumbled something and said to Ben "Maybe someone took her." Ben said "I mean, that is something that could possibly happen, but Agatha is very powerful. Who could ever do that? I don't think anyone could do something like that even before we noticed. Not that I'm worried. She's a horrid old woman." John ignored him and said "Still, I can't think of any other thing that could have happened.

Ben replied "Well... I think there is only one other thing possible, though it doesn't make much sense. Somebody has to be blocking the connection between us and her." John then quickly said "But then how could we not have seen her?" Ben said again "That's the thing that doesn't make sense. There's barely a chance that you guys could have gone looking for each other at the exact same time, in different paths."

John interrupted and said "I would rather believe that somebody kidnapped her. It's complete nonsense!" Ben then asked John "Both of them seem impossible, yet there has to be the correct answer between them." Just then, they heard a loud sound coming from behind the forest. John said "It must be a hand grenade. I feel so odd that we are trying to stop this thing, but the fact that we are so used to the war is completely ironical." Ben looked at him and sighed. The foggy sky was getting darker and darker as the Sun was setting.

Later that night, they woke up from a colossal sound coming from the forest. John said to Ben "Woah, what's that?" Ben looked at John and said "It's probably not something big." John said "Not big? It's colossal! We're so used to those noises, but we woke up from that!" Ben tried to say something, but John looked at him

344

and pulled him towards the terrace. There were blue sparks coming from near the forest. Ben looked closer and said "Never mind, it's not coming from the forest." John looked at him and said "Then where is it coming from?" Ben held his breath and said "Farther towards fox tribe. John then said "No! It can't be so far! What could possibly be heard from a distance like that? John took a deep breath and then whispered "It's quiet now. Let's go look at what's happening. Ben did not agree with that idea. He thought it would be too dangerous to go near somewhere that could be so threatening.

Eventually, the blue light died down too, and both of them figured that it would be meaningless to go after everything had happened, and it was hard to even tell if they could arrive where the sound came from. So, they went to bed. Shortly after that, Ben fell asleep, but John was not able to get to sleep very easily. He could not stop thinking about what could be happening where the odd thing had happened. So, he crept out of his bed and went towards the terrace to see if he could find the blue light again. of course, he was not able to spot a single thing outside, and everything seemed normal as usual. In fact, it seemed as if nothing had ever even happened before.

Now John was not even so sure if what he and Ben had seen actually existed. He still was quite sure that it existed, but now the thought that was coming to his mind was the question of who had created it. He could not think of anyone who would be able to do something. John first thinks that it was a sound that had been made because of soldiers attacking the village, but John knew it would not make a sound that big and thought that if they had been attacking the village, it would have made more sounds. Plus, it would be terrible if the war had gone that big.

He had already realized that no matter what had happened, it would be something horrible, but now he was more frightened than curious. He then heard a tap from the upper floor and went outside to the terrace. He climbed up, but the iron bars were wet and he looked beneath him. He climbed up and sat on something. It wasn't the floor. There, he found some children looking at him very curiously from under him. He got up, then glanced at them, but didn't dare to speak to them. Lately, there had been so many things that made him hard to trust people, even if that was young children.

After a minute of silence, John realized that the children were not going to speak to him unless he did and thought if he should talk to them. It was hard to avoid people who looked so innocent. Just then, two more children crawled out. Actually, it was hard to call them children.

They were more like toddlers. John thought to himself 'More?', But before he could head back inside, the young child asked him "Who are you?"

John did not want to reply to him at all, but before he could stop himself from doing anything, an answer shot out of his mouth. He introduced himself to those children as if he had meant to do so and thought 'This is totally crazy. What is happening to me right now?', but his mouth even started to ask questions to the children now about who they were. The children smiled and one of them giggled at said "It's a secret!".

John did not want to do anything with them at all, but was also curious of what they were doing. He then thought 'What are these children doing at this time?' and became more concerned than curious. This time, he asked the children "Where are your parents?" but it seemed they did not want to reply. They just looked at each other, and only one mumbled something about them crawling out. John right away noticed that this activity was done secretly and that the children have been observing him.

Now John's feeling changed from concerned to frightened. John did not ever like the feeling of somebody watching him. He quickly dashed in, and locked the window. He flopped into bed and covered himself using the bedsheets on top of the bed. Just then, Ben woke up from the loud sound John had made when closing the door, because John had slammed the door and not closed it. Ben said to John "What's that?" John said right away "There are some kids watching us!"

Ben looked at John and said "That can't possibly be happening. Why would any kids want to watch us? Look, you're just seeing things again, like when you woke me up." John looked at him and said "You'll know when we get out!" And pulled him outside. But when they got to the terrace, nobody was above them. Ben looked at John and said to him "See, there's not a single thing up there. You must have seen another odd thing. Who would want to watch us?" John looked at Ben and said to him "No, I actually saw them, and I even spoke to them. They also asked me questions!" Ben looked at John and said "Are you okay?" John told Ben he was, but Ben was no longer trusting him. John said to Ben "No, let's check again tomorrow. I insure you there was people up there." There was no answer, and they went back to bed.

Meanwhile, Ron was walking towards one of the human's tents. He had not seen the soldiers for a long time and needed to check how they were doing. Though it was night, all the soldiers rose to see him as soon as he went in. Ron grinned and said "How have you been?" One of the soldiers said to him "Not much different. We have been making some plans, studying your book when we have any time leftover, and attacking the foxes. Those creatures are brutal." Ron answered "Sure they are. I am glad to hear that everyone is still doing good. You should know that every one of you are a hero. Eliminating those creatures is an honor." The humans nodded and then said "Recently, the foxes have thrown another bomb towards our side, and they have restored a lot of the land that we had taken from them. We think it will be quite helpful if you could tell us how to win." Ron looked at the soldiers and said "Let the foxes do what they are doing. In the end, not a thing will be left on their side. Just focus on stealing the land that the foxes restored."

The humans nodded and Ron left. He then put on his fox suit and went to the other side, where the foxes were. They also greeted him.

Ron looked at them and said "It sure has been a long time since we have met." The foxes chanted "It sure has been, and it is a pleasure to see you again." Ron asked how they were doing, and the foxes said "We are just fighting, making plans, cleaning our weapons, and reading the books you have given us when we have time." Ron said "That sounds good. You should always have time to read my books. I would like to...."

Just then, one soldier said "We recently took back some land that was stolen too!" Ron looked at him and said "I already knew. Those spots are not very important. Actually, it is not good for you to keep. If the humans had still been owning it, their lands would have already turned to ashes. The land is cursed." The soldiers then said "Then what shall we do? Oh! Tell us the answer!" Ron said "Put some of your food that has been given on every spot that you have taken back. Then, leave it. The humans will take it again, and slowly, doom will come upon them. This I insure you."

The foxes nodded and did as ask. Ron said "Good." And left the place. He took off his suit, and looked at the sky. The sun was rising, and he could hear the soldiers putting their armor on. Ron scoffed and went back to the hotel very slowly while the soldiers fought again. When he arrived at the Hotel, Ron went straight to the fox's side of the hotel and met one of the workers. He asked the worker if 'the plan' was going well the worker nodded. Ron smiled and walked up to the top floor.

He was able to see his plans working marvelously. He looked around the room, but tried not to show himself to the test subjects for 'the plan'. Ron hoped that nobody would have seen him and went to the other side of the building. Ron looked around and went into the office. He there thought of the next plan. Meanwhile, the war had paused for a moment.

The humans had been very confused about what had happened. The land that they had lost hade come back to them, even along with some food. Then, he saw a letter that had been left. It was written on a slim piece of paper, and it only said one thing: 'keep it' the humans thought nothing would go wrong if they took it, so they did.

The foxes saw them building tents there and jumped around, not being able to resist the happy feeling inside their hearts. They would win, and the war would end. The foxes were tired of the war, but were told they had to win. They also did not want to lose. This was their first time participating in the war, and they did not want to fail. The humans were also quite happy. They had got their land back. They were sure this could be the key to winning. They thought now that they had the land, the war would end before they knew it. Then, the war resumed. The humans had gone towards the fox's tents and had started to attack. The foxes attacked back and started to fight. It was like before.

It was raining, and the sky seemed somewhat grey. One human accidentally dropped his bullet, and it rolled into a stream nearby. It hit the bottom, making the stream a muddy colour for a short moment. That didn't matter anyway, because the stream was going to be filled with the blackish red colour soon. The loud sounds that were made from the battlefield were even able to be heard by Ron, who was in his office. He shook his head and thought that these creatures were so foolish to follow his plan, thinking of it as their choice.

He was fascinated by the humans because of

their imperfection and their foolishness. He then started to write some documents for the hotel. He turned on some music and went back to working. He concentrated very hard, and after about three hours, he finished his work. It was now about eleven, and he was a little bit hungry. He went outside and went into a restaurant. He ordered a sandwich and went back to the hotel as soon as he got it.

He looked around the building and checked if everything was going well, including 'the plan', which was the most important thing he had to check. He then went back into his office and decided to write a book for the soldiers, because he knew that most of them have already finished the one that he had given them.

Ron started to type and made a couple chapters in a jiffy. He was very good at writing things in a short time. He checked his grammar and spelling as he wrote, trying to write a perfect book. After all, he was a perfectionist, and he wanted everything to look neat. He kept on writing and checking his mistakes.

Ron knew it would be hard for him to write a book fit for the foxes, but that was also fine because he only had time to visit the humans and tell them his next plan. Ron was very excited because absolutely everything was going his way. When he arrived at the office, he started to write. Writing was something he loved, and it was very useful to be a good writer, especially because his plans needed to have something that could convince creatures when he wasn't there. He typed like mad, and when the sun started to go down slowly and he saw some students returning home, he was finished. He printed it out and made copies of it. He put it in his backpack and wore his cloak.

He smiled and ran to the battlefield. He hid in the forest and looked at the people fighting. The battlefield was turning red, and there were corpses lying around. He waited for a moment, and looked at them. He loved just seeing what people did and tried to choose. After a while, it came to point where everybody was tired and sleepy. This was the exact moment where Ron slid into the human's tent.

Half of the people that he had seen before were gone, but that did not matter very much. He was just sad that he had printed out too many books. He said to them "Well, how have you been? I have something for you!" The humans all told Ron about how they stole the land again from the foxes. Ron nodded and told them to keep the land safe. He then took out his books from his backpack and gave it to them. Then, before the soldiers could say anything, Ron left, telling them to study the book.

They were all very confused, but thought that Ron must be busy and just went back out to fight, since there was not much time to sit around when there was a war going on. They were also worried not enough people were out on the battlefield since they had gone inside the tent.

Meanwhile, outside the tent, people were still fighting. It was starting to get late, but today's battle did not seem to end. The sun was setting, and turned the sky a colour quite similar to the blood lying on the ground. It did not look very pleasant, but everyone was so used to it nobody thought that fighting like this was horrible.

Meanwhile, John sat at the counter at the hotel, going through papers about the customers, which showed which room they booked, what services they needed, and more. He knew all the important things were in the office, but he did not feel the need to look at those. He wasn't going to stay much longer anyway. Today, not many people were coming, and this was because the virus had worsened and not many people were willing to go traveling.

One family came, and John guided them to their room. He then went down and started to mop the corridors. It already looked clean, but someone always pointed out somewhere was not wiped completely now and then. He did not care much, and he just tried to ignore comments like that, or show more effort on it so it would be harder to point that out. When he was done wiping, the mop suddenly snapped in half. John knew for certain that he was in trouble. He hoped nobody saw it and tried to hide it behind the counter, then ran to a store to get one, but they were sold out. Hoping nobody was waiting at the counter, John went around to five different stores, and finally managed to find one. It wasn't cheap, but he was glad to be out of trouble. He ran back, and was relieved to see nobody waiting at the counter. He then went to the kitchen to wash and dry the dishes.

The hotel did not have a dish-washing machine, so the workers had to wash all of the dishes, and there were not many workers. On the board at the front of the building, they did say they were recruiting staff, but nobody volunteered because the wages had gone down awfully. The place was huge, and there was barely anybody there. John was not sure about the other side, but just on this side there was sixty people for the whole place, and most of them worked at the counter or hall, so there were not enough people for the kitchen. He was not a professional cook, so he did not do any of the cooking, but he gave new spoons, forks and knives to rooms, washed dishes, dried dishes, mopped, dusted, wiped, and even swept the hotel. He also worked at the counter, as it was his main job and sometimes went outside to water the gardens.

He was one of the busiest people, but he needed to make a living and he knew that since him and his boss were enemies, he had to be very obedient, at least in his job. He knew Ron was only keeping him to use him as part of his monstrous plans, and he had found out he was slowly being erased.

He then saw another family come in and lead them to a room. He got his basket full of knives and forks, and a meal kit and gave it to them as they went in. They did not complain, and John was very grateful. He liked to see other people feel satisfied, and he loved hearing compliments. He then went back to washing dishes, and thought about Ben.

Ben had not been acting like how he used to. He always ignored what John said, and John tried everything to gain his trust, but it seemed Ben was now also thinking of him as an adversary. He tried coming back early, giving him presents, and cleaning the house, and spoke more about ideas Ben liked when talking about things such as Ron's plans. Despite all that effort, nothing happened. Ben still seemed to hate him. Was he also being erased from Ben? John didn't know.

Something was also not feeling right for Ben. Ben was starting to feel unsafe. He no longer could trust anybody and needed to defend himself on his own. It seemed he was falling into something deeper, and he felt something else awaken in himself sometimes. It made him feel like a different person. This made him even more confused and it seemed like his life itself was a conflict now that there were so much things to worry about in his life.

He did know this was his second life, but he did not think it was worth getting another chance to live at all, because he had tried having it, and it was no use. School was better, but not enough to wash away all of his worries. He was quite a silent boy, and he had not talked to anybody. Nobody talked to him. He had only spoken to his teacher to say answers, he never asked anything else, and he didn't do anything else either. Which was funny, because he used to be very talkative when speaking with John, and even before that, he also was very chatty when he was with Ron. Well, now he just was quiet.

He did do some research on the other side when John was still at work, but he hid it so that John would not see. He was going to keep going against Ron, but it did not quite mean he and John was going to keep working together. Ben thought the risk was too high to work with someone saying odd things, and he had also seen John sometimes wandering out to do things. Ben was not ever told what had happened, and he had never dared to follow because he did not have a plan. Ben did, though ever since he discovered the truth about himself, and according to his plans, he had to leave.

Ben then followed John, who was going on a walk. He wanted to see what John was doing before he made his final decision.

John was just getting ready for bed. He did feel odd when he went to put his mail, but did not think of it as a very big problem, so he was perfectly fine. John also did not notice Ben acting slightly differently either, because John saw those subtle changes as very ordinary things. He also thought they only occurred because of the incident that happened between them recently.

Still, John was wondering about why he felt so weird when he was walking to the mail box. He was just going there to send his letter to fox tribe. His mission was pretty much complete, but since he was staying here, he still had to send letters about how things were going. He did think it might have been Ron, since he had seen Ron follow him when he did this before, but John wasn't sure. The world had already turned against him.

Meanwhile, somebody was typing up a letter. It was Agatha. She had not received a call from John and she was so worried. She was going to send him a letter to see if he replies. She kept on typing, but her children were climbing on top of here and trying to look at what she was writing. It was almost impossible to focus on writing a letter. Soon, one of her children got into one of her work cabinets and spilt all her files. She stopped typing and started to sort them while scolding her children. They went to their rooms and Agatha was able to get some peace. She continued writing.

Once she was done, she walked up to the hotel and put it in the mailbox for John to see. She never trusted other people to carry her letters, so she did it whenever she had the time. She walked back home and went to bed. She then thought "What a tiring day. I went to work, then back home, and to the humans, and back home again. I think I am going to fall asleep!" Then, she fell asleep.

This did not last very long though, because her children woke up from having a nightmare. She thought it was strange for all three of them to have nightmares at the same time, but thought it was quite possible and just put her children back to bed. Now she was wide awake, and couldn't get back to sleep.

Meanwhile, at the hotel, Wendy was washing the dishes when suddenly, her children came to her. Tablo was trying to say something, but Alex was blocking him from saying it. To Wendy, it seemed clear that they were having a fight, and that she needed to stop them. She asked them what the problem was, but Alex ran away, pulling Tablo to the balcony.

He said to Tablo "Be quiet! I told you not to tell her!" But Tablo responded "I want to tell her about it! We need to say it, or it's going to be too late!" Then Alex said, "Let's tell mom next week so that we have more time." They agreed and pretended to fight over their toys as soon as they came out of the balcony. Wendy separated them and took away their toys. Then, her other children came out of their rooms and asked what the problem was, but Wendy was far too tired to answer her children. She panted and sat on her chair.

At the time, Alex was sitting at the balcony and looking in through the window. He was trying to find where Tablo was. Actually, Alex was not able to spot him because Tablo was at the end of the halls, near the elevator. Their mother separated them. Alex didn't have a clue where Tablo was, but needed to talk to Tablo right now. He thought about secretly sneaking out of the balcony and trying to find Tablo, but was afraid that he would get in trouble for doing that from his mother, so Alex decided to tell his mother that he was ready to apologize.

He opened the door, and went straight to their mother. He told his mother that he was ready to apologize, and Wendy brought Tablo into the room and told both of them to apologize. They did, and Wendy told them that they could go play now. Both of the boys ran right out of that room, glad to escape the place.

Then, they called all of their siblings in the balcony. All of them ran to them, and asked what happened. Alex and Tablo called them to the balcony and told them that it was time again. Soon the kids on the other side ran out. They did the usual things, like working on their language, which they were very good at, but the older kids had told them something a couple weeks ago, and they were making a new plan. The humans told the foxes the first plan was completed. The foxes all nodded and said "Well, now let's start our next plan."

THE BIRTH OF A HUMAN

Maximization of Conflict

12. Maximization of Conflict

"I don't want to hear it." Ben said, getting out of his chair. "It's all true though! We need to do something!" "About what?" "There is something to fear, and I can see it." John said. "What if there is? I thought we were trying to stop Ron. Stop the things he's triggered. Now what? Are we running away to save our necks when everything else is in trouble? We already couldn't save anything. Everything. People are being killed because we failed to stop it sooner, and all you're doing is running away!"

John looked at Ben and stared into his eyes. "I'm not running away, though. I'm taking a step back, and a step forward to a different direction." Ben scoffed. "You're crazy." Ben glanced at John and scoffed again, then said "So? I'm fed up. I'd be better off myself, wouldn't I?" "But... We're so close! I saw those kids talking, and I saw someone attacking us somehow, and the kids smiling at me, it just made me realize all we had to do was put the puzzle pieces together. It all fits in perfectly, but I can't do anything alone."

"You need me for everything. Do I have to babysit you forever? I mean, you need to get independent."

That night, both of them didn't talk at all. They didn't even bother to look away. They just ignored the fact that there was another person in the room. John went to bed early.

The war worsened in a terrible manner. The fact that the foxes had more people and an endless supply of weapons were clearly an advantage, but the humans knew how to work the weapons better, in a more efficient way. The fact that they were even meant the war wasn't going to cease anytime soon. People may have grown tired of the occasion, but there really wasn't a reason to stop, either.

John stepped out the hotel doors and walked over to the mailbox. He had been checking every day to see if there was a letter from the foxes- or Agatha. The mailbox had always been empty, so he was surprised when he saw envelope inside the box. John picked it up, and slid it inside his coat pocket, then ran back to the hotel, eager to find out who gave him the letter. As soon as he stepped into his room, he teared opened the envelope and walked into the bathroom. When he turned on the lights, he saw a very familiar signature. Agatha's.

What the letter said explained everything. Agatha couldn't reach him either, both using magic and on the phones. Something had been blocking them. John was more than sure the 'something' was Ron. He just hadn't realized they would also communicate by post. Ron had shown images to John that almost made him think Agatha was trapped while he was sleeping. He was glad to find out everything, but then realized something even more important. This wasn't any help in stopping Ron. Sure, John said he had a plan, but that had just been to convince Ben. Ron had cleverly shown John only things that would not matter he found out about them.

John couldn't sleep. All he knew was that Ron was using his abilities to erase him, and to confuse him. Only if he could listen to the calls Ron was making around the hotel… But then he got a better idea. He wrote a letter to Agatha.

Ron could barely see through the fog that was covering half the forest as he walked towards the hotel. He fought his way through the wispy white air until he saw the dim outline of the building. There, he threw off his cloak and tucked it under his coat. Ron entered the doors that nothing but an empty hall as he whistled a tune from his favorite song while climbing up the stairs.

Room 502 was dark, except for the pale light coming from the bathroom. Ron flashed a grin, then stepped up to the bed, trying to form a purple ball. It was barely visible as always, but it was able to transmit a dull image into John's mind. Ron knew John's human brain was easier to break through than those of the foxes. Ron focused, projecting an image of the forest into John's head, when John woke up. Ron swiftly ducked under the bed, making the purple light vanish with him. John tilted his head to one side, then looked around the room. John got out of bed, and started looking around the room.

John froze when he saw a nice, polished shoe poking out from under his bed and lifted up the long blankets with trembling hands, scared because he knew what it would reveal. Ron. John watched as Ron got to his feet, coming closer. "Get away!" John screamed, hoping someone would hear him. The hotel was silent. John shook Ben to wake him, but Ben was sound asleep. John was sure Ron was going to get him any second, but Ron just laughed.

"So, did you think I'd be foolish enough to let all the others stay awake?" "You hypnotized them. That's why nobody's waking up." "Yes." Ron said, a grin spreading across his face. "I did! Yes, it was a tough job... it took me a week to go around this whole floor." "Why aren't you doing anything to me now? You've been waiting to catch me, haven't you?"

Ron said "I was desperate, but I decided it would be wiser to spare you for a while. You see, I was too foolish. The war continues because of you, and I would hate to stop it now. You see, they've been trying to find you. I hypnotized a few humans to forget your face, and it is convenient that you have such a common name." John took a step back.

Ron looked into John's deep brown eyes, and then closed the door behind him. John was petrified, and didn't know what to do. Ron was only playing with him. John knew that the war, a blazing fire, was using him as fuel to continue. John wanted to run away. But to where? The human world turned against him, and constant danger faced him. The foxes were afraid, and they thought of John as a monster. Something that should never have been made. John went to the balcony, but this time he realized he wasn't alone anymore.

"Hey!" a voice said "You're spying on us again!" John looked around, and saw a few small, chubby faces above him. The children he had seen only days ago were here again. But they weren't just children. John realized it wasn't his second time seeing them. They were the children that created their own language. 'This is the key to resolving the problem.' John thought. Communication! What a wonderful thing this was! Without hesitation, John climbed up and said "We need to talk." The children did nothing but stare.

"You did it. How? You are so young..." "We managed. You see, it's not too complicated for us." John's eyes then darted to the crumbling wall, as he discovered the young foxes that looked at him with interest, though they also looked slightly scared. John talked to them too, and they gave the same answer as the humans. John was surprised that they had managed to creep away from their bedrooms, but these foxes managed to do plenty of impossible things. Now that John knew what these young creatures could do, he needed them to cooperate. But what would he tell them? And how? John didn't know what to say.

Luckily, before John said anything, the young children said "We'll try helping you, but just for a little while. It's kind of obvious that you want our help, so you can ask us to do anything you'd like for the next week." "Really?" John said, thinking it couldn't be this easy, though also slightly disturbed by the thought that the children saw him as a figure desperate for their help. John looked at them and said "How long can we talk?" "Until any boring adults wake up. Until then, we're safe." "All right then." John said. "I need you to explain your language to me."

"Our language?" The kids looked stunned "Why would you want to learn our language? It's just something we made up to talk with our friends." They said, looking at each other.

"Exactly. It can be used as a code, and has good purpose. I need to know." The children hesitated for a moment, then said, "We will." As they showed John the tiny letters that they created.

Meanwhile, Ron was walking into the hotel. He hadn't checked on his program for a while, and was curious if any progress had been made since then. When he changed his clothes and stepped into the fox side of the hotel, he saw that his workers were scurrying about, hoarding the occupants of the hotel into the attic. Ron was very pleased and decided to see the program himself that day. He wanted to start actually making some real progress.

When Ron strode into the attic, he saw that he had arrived before everyone else. The room was empty, and very bare. Ron didn't mind the interior; it helped people get into the right mindset, in his opinion. He looked around and found out there was nothing in the room. He thought to himself that he needed to make some books, then went into the old cupboard that had been occupying the hotel ever since he discovered it. It was the only piece of furniture in the room, and therefore the only thing to hide in. Ron watched all the humans coming through the huge double doors, and pulled out his phone to start recording.

John yawned, climbing down the railing to return to his room. He saw the sun rising, and he was disgusted. The reddish sky reminded him of blood. Blood reminded him of war. The people that were dying. The things he failed to do. John knew he needed to make a move, and he wanted to be prepared for anything. However, he wasn't prepared to see Ben, standing on the balcony, demanding an explanation of why he snuck off in the middle of the night.

"Who did you meet?" Ben asked. "Nobody you'd be interested in. I don't feel like fighting." John said defensively. "Actually, I am interested. Did you climb upstairs to prove your useless theory about those kids?" "It isn't useless. It's true. And you're also a kid." "It's nonsense! You haven't proved that those kids even exist, and yet you say it every time. And don't think I can't see through your foolish tricks, because I know you enough to see what you're trying to do. You're either using this to cover up for some activity you don't want me to know about, or you're out of your mind." John started to get angry at Ben for constantly snapping back, so he went inside the room, hoping Ben was too angry to follow.

Meanwhile, the human children were discussing what to do about the strange relationship they had formed last night with John. They had already told him most things, but Tablo was not happy about forming a relationship with an adult. "When we started this thing, we said adults were not fit for this thing, and now were just letting this guy in when we don't even know who he is?"

Agatha was confused. Nothing made sense. The strange things that had happened in the castle were too much to be merely coincidental, or a little bit of mumbling, but Agatha didn't know what was going on, even after hours of struggle and research in the book. It just didn't help, and she had no idea why this stuck in her mind, other than the queer event that occurred and the odd word. *'Planted'* was a weird word, and had to mean more than what she knew. She decided that she needed help, and picked a leaf from a tree to write John a letter. She was that desperate. Desperate enough to rely on John. This had to do with *'Planted'*. It had to. The words were far too suspicious. Though the word wouldn't have been as weird if the fox that was saying it hadn't been the king of the foxes.

John walked onto the street, looking around as he approached his mailbox. He'd been checking it every other day to see if there was a letter, though there never was. John no longer expected to see an envelope in there, much less a leaf. So, when he saw the leaf bearing Agatha's signature, he was absolutely shocked. He didn't know what to do, for he had no intention of going inside the hotel; Ben was still very angry. John still didn't know what to do, but decided that somewhere private would be best, and found himself going to the forest, dangerously close to the war area.

When he settled near the bank at the entrance of the forest to open his letter, he found a bullet flowing down the stream. 'The soldiers must be near.' He thought as he settled into an especially shadowy corner under the bridge crossing the stream.

The letter read;

Dear John, if you are reading this letter, please read it alone, without anyone that might see it, and once you have read it, please tear it up and throw it away, for what I am about to write could easily be seen as treason. However, I will tell you the good news. The king is better and is slowly recovering, with help from Marvin, one of the king's most beloved courtiers whom I intensely dislike. What really seems odd is that we don't have any ideas of how he healed the king. I think he used the statue to activate something, though it no longer works. However, after the treatment he got, he was blubbering weird words for a while, which were mostly nonsensical and likely side effects but I caught quite an unusual word and (this is the bad news) I have no idea what it means. He said 'planted' in a different voice, and he spoke in a really thin and wispy way.

John was confused. Why would the king do that? Did that word really have a meaning, or was it just side effects of his treatment. John decided he would look into it when he had the time, and slipped the letter into his shirt pocket, forgetting that he was supposed to destroy the letter. After all, he had a lot on his mind. Nothing was suspicious about the foxes, the things from Agatha were mysterious, but impossible to understand, and he didn't know how to connect the children's ideas into a solution. Nothing was any help.

John decided taking a stroll may help him concentrate and returned to the town, out of the forest. He didn't want to go to the hotel because he had a bad relationship with Ben currently, so he just wandered around through foggy streets while the sounds of guns could be heard from far away. John thought about the television in the main hall, and thought the city felt like it came straight out of one of those dystopian movies that he'd seen on that TV, as he headed near the battlefield.

Ben took his things and put them near the door. The arguments they'd been having were pointless, and now he couldn't stand it. If they fought again like this, Ben decided he would leave and build a new residence. He felt a little bit of sadness, but it faded away. After all, this was his original plan, and he wouldn't have to leave if they didn't start another big argument. 'This isn't my fault.' He assured himself as he waited for John to return.

"King's orders!" A messenger hollered trotting towards the fox camp. "Again?" A soldier whispered as he painted his paw towards the messenger. The messenger then gathered all the soldiers with the emergency cry, as he announced the new policies. "Anyone that fails to terminate less than five enemies each day will be sent out of the camp." Some soldiers were angry with the decision. They said "Sent out?" "We'll starve!" "Silence!" The messenger said. "It ought to help if some motivation's added in." The foxes then went away.

John couldn't believe what he just heard. Was it true? Agatha was right. Something was wrong. Planting those things in people's heads... Planted? That was the word Agatha had pointed out. So, someone had planted information in the king's head. Put him in a trance. It had been like a tree, spreading its roots out, in a violent way. Like the life tree. That's when John realized. The king was being controlled.

By *Ron*.

It all made sense. Ron had created the humans by the trees, and was proud of it. He would have needed to get control of the foxes, if he wanted to encourage to fight. Ron probably hated the foxes, so he would have realized getting ahold of the government was key. And Ron had been excellent at hypnotizing people, John had seen it already. But this also made him hopeless. Ron was ahead of him this much already, and John probably didn't know half the things Ron was planning. Communication was needed, more than ever.

John returned to the hotel, very troubled. If Ben hadn't been so mad, he would have asked John what he found out, but right now he didn't feel like asking John anything other than to leave the room, though he didn't say that either. Ben just pretended nobody was there. "We have to talk." John's voice said, ringing through the room.

"Go away." Ben said, resisting the temptation to ask John what happened. "But I know something! The-" John was cut off by Ben's annoyed voice. "I'm not repeating it! Go away!" "I can't, because we need to go see those kids again. Now."

"That's it." Ben said, looking at John, reaching for his things. "Goodbye."

And Ben left the hotel.

John stared blankly at the door that Ben had just left, and started to tremble as he collapsed into a heap on the bed, he tried to stay calm, but he couldn't. Ben was gone. Perhaps they'd never see each other again. Why had he been so stupid? They shouldn't have fussed over the kids... He could have done it himself. John sobbed slightly, and clutched his phone in hope of seeing Ben again. But beside it, he saw Ben's phone. Ben was showing his determination like this.

The next day, John visited Ben's school, and looked at the teenagers pouring out the door. Hundreds of them. And amongst them, Ben wasn't there. John walked back to the hotel, full of despair. It was all done. He was alone, and nobody was standing with him anymore. Why did this have to happen, when he was actually getting an idea of what things were like. Why did he even mention the children to Ben? John regretted everything.

But then, he thought about something. He had to do this alone. He couldn't let this drag him down. He had to do something. John walked back to the hotel, hastily went into his room, and climbed up the rail to find the children. "Hello." John said.

"Hello." The kids said back. "You've learnt our language. Haven't you?" "Listen... I haven't had much spare time lately, and..." "Right. So, you haven't practiced. No excuses. Now, do you remember anything at all?" said a fox who seemed to act as the leader. John pulled a notebook from his pockets where he had written all his notes, and flipped to a black page, demonstrating bits of writing, though the kids weren't very pleased. John did better with speech, however, and therefore continued studying with the children, who taught him as if he were three.

Later that night, John returned to his room, taking a notebook out of his pocket. He flipped to the last twenty pages. John sat down and put the notebook on the desk beside Ben's computer. Ben's computer. It was the only thing Ben had left besides the phone. John's eyes lingered on it for a moment, then he looked at the phone. It was locked. Since when had Ben put a password on his phone? John thought. Ben obviously had not wanted John to look into his phone.

'Concentrate on what you need' said a voice in his head. He just crumpled on the chair.

Ron sat down on his chair and took a sip of his water. He didn't need to bother checking the fox kingdom anymore for a month. A whole month. The king had been hypnotized very well, even better than last time, when Ron made the foxes believe their king had been cured. The foxes didn't know so many things. Ron knew, however and nobody else would ever know. Ron laughed, satisfied, and stood up, then walked out his office to go to the battlefield.

Agatha received a leaf from John that evening, that informed her about John's theories on the king's odd behavior. She read it over and over again, desperate to abandon the information she just saw. The things that had been going on were terrible, but Agatha had never imagined that Ron could have raided the government. How did he even take control?

It made sense, in a way, but Ron, a hypnotist? It seemed unlikely, and even more unlikely that Ron snuck in to the castle and hypnotized the king. You had to hypnotize people often to have them under control. How could Ron do that? John's theory didn't make any sense, and it would be impossible to take control of the king.

Then, an idea came into Agatha's head. What if it was the other way around? John wouldn't need to accuse the king unless he was desperate to blame someone. But Ron would. Perhaps it was John who had been possessed. Yes, this had to be the truth, how else could John have figured out Ron was a hypnotist? How else could he have worked with Ben, the man who hated him most? And she had willingly shared her secrets with him... Agatha dropped the stick she'd been writing with and shuddered. She should have known.

She threw John's leaf on to the ground and stepped away from it, like it was a monster. After she'd seen who John was, she couldn't bear to touch it, or even go near it. What would the king think? After all those years, the human had finally become a threat to the world.

Yes, Agatha knew the day would come, she knew that John wouldn't belong, and that as a creature not fully fox or human, John would be dangerous. But yet she had tried to protect him. And now this. John was the enemy, after all. She wrote to the king first, then wrote to John: 'I know what you are.' That was all she could bear to write.

THE BIRTH OF A HUMAN

The Discovery of a New Power

13. The Discovery of a New Power

After two weeks of overnight sessions taught by overenthusiastic toddlers, John was able to write and speak their language wonderfully, though some thought he had a poor accent. Like all other days, John climbed back down to his room when he saw that the sun was rising. John was quite confident now, and was planning to put the language to use. He sat in front of the computer, to see if he could use it for any of his projects. He wanted to record his plan, but in a more secretive way.

When he turned the computer on, it glitched. John went into files to make his notes, and came across something odd. It was labeled: planting. The file beside it said roots, the next said leaves, and then the great tree. There was also one unnamed file. John thought something about this had to do with Agatha's words, and the king being controlled, so he clicked on the first file. Planting. The same word the king had said. The one thing Agatha tried to say. But how did Ben know and record this? What else did he know? What was the great tree?

Planting was short. It said 'the seventh planting' The first step of the great tree is complete. All are under control; the regulation centre is working well. The battle has been triggered, and the taint is unsuspecting. John looked at this and was confused. Something was under control, there was somewhere called the regulation centre, and Ron had triggered the battle. Somebody was 'the taint'. Likely me, John thought.

He moved on to the next file. 'Roots'. 177-4530- 5641. That was it. What did it mean? He looked at his phone. This was a phone number for something. John moved on to leaves. Redemption island, May 31, 9:00am. This was clear. Redemption island was a place. May 31 was two weeks away. Something was happening there. Then, John noticed that he still had to read the great tree project. John opened it.

The file read:
HELP.

John stared blankly at the screen, and realized somebody was actually screaming for help. Upstairs, someone was in trouble.

John climbed up the balcony railings and opened the door to get inside the room. It was empty. John dashed through the halls and flung open the doors. There was nobody. John dashed down the stairs and got to the first floor. John didn't find anyone in trouble. John went back up to his room and looked out the balcony.

Somebody wearing a brown coat was running away with a few humans and foxes. John gasped and ran back to the door to chase Ron, but he had disappeared into the forest.

John was shaking, but picked up his phone and dialed the number he'd seen in Ben's computer. A familiar voice started to speak. "Hello." "Ben!" John said, but Ben didn't reply. It was a recording. "I don't have much time, but I'll tell you while I can. Ron's a hypnotist. He's angry because you don't seem to fall for his tricks. But I got hypnotized, and I needed to escape the hotel. But I wanted to tell you some things. Ron hypnotized the king by pretending to be one of the courtiers. He seems satisfied because the king got hypnotized really well this time, but Ron accidentally possessed the king, so the king might say some things Ron's saying. The great tree project is the codename for human creation, and the conversion of all creatures into human, using the life tree and its seed. He realized the tree reached out to some kids in the hotel somehow, and tried to give them some sort of temporary shield against Ron, and he's going to kidnap them and their family sometime. I don't know when you'll discover this message, but when you do, you have to go to redemption island. Ron's using its powers to spark and continue the war. The virus isn't a real disease. It's Ron's way of manipulating the society. It's got mild symptoms, but they have effects that help Ron control them. I found the information from..." A buzzing sound came from the phone, and some sound resembling an explosion came from the other side. "From within." Ben coughed. The recording ended.

John would have been shocked, but he wasn't. Ron knew more than him, and had more planned. John knew he couldn't win this game. Why had Ben put so much faith in him? He was the odd one out, the one with all the odd powers and genetics. Just then, something came to John's mind. A crazy idea that he wouldn't have dare used, but he needed to do it now.

John took his things, and put them into his old sack. Then, he opened the last file. It was not written in English, but in the children's language. It said Find my true purpose. Ben and the children were requesting help, and this had it, in the children's language. I'll find it from within, John thought, and ran to the other side of the hotel. To the foxes.

He dashed up the stairway to the top and opened the attic door. He saw foxes chasing him, and ran into the room. Some foxes were staring at him curiously. "Are you the enemy?" One of them said. "It's a human!" Another replied. "We have to destroy the enemy!" John looked at them and said in fox "Stop! I... You need to get out of this! You need to get out of here now!"

Everybody looked blank and emotionless, but then attacked with rage that seemed uncomfortable, almost artificial. John smashed the windows and escaped onto the roof, then took out a hammer he'd packed in his sack, and smashed the roof as hard as he could, until he fell through. He landed right on the stairs, and then ran back upstairs.

If he couldn't get those people out of the trance they were in, then he'd have to at least case commotion enough to get everyone distracted. He smashed open the door, then ran back on to the roof. He repeated this several times, to cause as much damage possible to the hotel. 'This is a prison, not a hotel.' John thought, as he ran through the hall and burst open the doors to each room, trying to see if anyone would escape. "I'm really sorry!" John yelled as he passed a few startled foxes.

He took one last glimpse at the hotel, and then ran away to the forest, for he knew he would never be safe at the hotel ever again.

John turned back, suddenly feeling afraid. The forest was not safe for him, either. If Ron was controlling this war, then walking into the battlefield would be a terrible decision. He dropped down to the ground, and started to quiver. He longed for someone that actually could care. Someone that would help him. "Agatha!" He suddenly said. He rushed out of the forest and ran to the mailbox. He took Agatha's letter, and carried it as if it were a treasure back to the edge of the forest. He opened the letter and read it.

"I know who you are." John said, looking at the green leaf and the carefully written letters that were gleaming in the bright sun. There was someone who actually understood him. Someone wanted to help. He wasn't all alone. Somebody cared. "Oh, Agatha!" He spoke. "I can't believe I didn't run to you right away!" John said. He rolled up the leaf carefully and put it in his pocket, as he walked off to the side of the forest, towards the fox tribe. Towards Agatha.

Agatha ran hastily to the castle. The king had summoned all the courtiers to the castle, and all the people of the tribe were gathered in the courtyard for the announcement taking place. Agatha, like the other courtiers, had fluffed up her fur and had put some berries and leaves around her neck. She walked in through the hole, and into the castle. Most of the others were already there, and were standing solemnly. They were all facing the same way, towards the large hole that served as a gateway. Agatha touched the moss at the gateway, and was strongly reminded of the curtains at the human zoo that covered the windows of the building. The humans she had cared for so dearly had turned against them.

One of the courtiers drew the moss curtains, revealing the crowd standing in the courtyard. The king quivered and stood on top of the high rocks in front of the curtains. "Today," He said, "Marks the start of an entirely new era in our history. It is the end of one story and the start of another. I have decided that we leave our old rules. We, by the humans, have been forced to change and make a new decision. Therefore, I have decided to extend our laws so that we may use fire for our weapons and ordinary life." The crowd gasped, and Agatha started to shake.

The king continued his speech. "Second, I will establish a squad amongst my courtiers to make all governmental decisions with me. The rest of the courtiers will be asked to patrol the streets daily and supervise our citizens. I have a scroll here that have our new laws. You will receive these scrolls and make sure none are breaking these laws. Anyone the patrols have reported breaking my laws or have shown actions that you may suspect a certain connection with the humans will be immediately handed over to the human soldiers." The king then said "I would also like you to welcome the superior commander of my squad, and therefore now the leader of the government, along with me." He pointed his paw towards one of the courtiers, the one that had cured the king of his disease.

The citizens were silent, startled by the new rules and the leaf scrolls being handed to them with more laws than the tribe had ever had. The courtier stepped up to the high rocks and said "Foxes of the tribe, rejoice! From today on, you will be safe and happy in your burrows and holes! All will join our forces to fight against the enemy, and will have the honor of fighting for the king! Male foxes will join the army of resistance and fight for the king. Females and children will learn of greatness and will study the blessed book our soldiers have been able to learn. Be proud, for you are fighting for a new world of beauty and wonder!" Everyone clapped, and tried to conceal their fear for the new things that would come.

The next day, thick books were given to everybody in the tribe, and all male foxes were sent to the battlefield. The king and his chosen one had said it was an honor to study the great law, so the foxes read. The first page of their book was a song of praise for the king and the leader. The second page carried the newly made laws of the tribe.

After that, it was identical to the books the

soldiers had received. To study this book was the greatest thing a fox could do. All the children were sent to live at their schools, replaced their history lessons with the studying of this book, and they learnt songs of the greatness of the king and the leader, and of the terror the enemy would bring, and of the new weapons they had brought into their world. They also got used to the daily patrols, and the plain-clothed ones, hiding among them, to take any foxes breaking the law of speaking ill of the leader to the humans.

Agatha was a patrol, as she had once been a courtier and was not part of the king's squad. She was in charge of bringing the lawbreakers to the borders of the tribe and the battlefield, where she then handed them over to some of the lower squad members that brought them to their doom. She always wondered how everything went nowadays. Everyone was but a small part of the system that had been constructed by 'the leader' that courtier in charge of everything who knew all. Though she was grateful that he cured the king, she still secretly despised him for the laws she was made to keep, and despaired when he banned them to speak ill of him. She was quite sure most of the courtiers felt the same way as her but did not dare to break any laws because of the severe consequences.

She sometimes looked longingly at the castle, the place where she had worked with pleasure, and where she had less worries, because she was confident that all the troubles happening in the world were known by her. Now she knew nothing. The human world became a mystery when John revealed to be a traitor, and the fox territory was now full of secrets. All she knew was the short path between the place where the other patrols gathered the outlaws and the gateway from the fox territory to the battlefield.

She wondered how her husband was doing in the battlefield. 'I should be proud.' Agatha thought, 'because he is fighting for the king.' However, she still wished dearly that she could receive some cards from him. Mail was banned now, and everyone was not allowed to communicate with anyone. She wished she had her children to comfort her, but they were gone. They were at school, where she could never visit them. "So close, and yet so far." Agatha often said as she looked at the tall brambles preventing anyone from getting in the schoolgrounds. The school was twenty strides away from her home that she didn't live in. The patrol's burrow was her home now.

The first day the children were told they had to leave their homes, they thought it was some cruel, grown-up joke that they were too young to understand. School wasn't bad, so when it became reality and they had to pack, they didn't dread it. School was different now. Instead of the tall trees and endless plains, they were surrounded by brambles.

"Do you think this is worse than the 'zoo' mom told us about?" one of them whispered to the other. "It can't be. The zoo was human made, right? We can't be that bad." "Silence! If I hear your voices again, you'll be sent to the humans!" Roared the patrol. "Do you not know it's forbidden to talk to others unless you have a governmental permit?" Now get to sleep!" He snarled again. To most of the cubs here, sleep sounded impossible on top of all these thorns and bushes. They longed for a warm hole with leaves and twigs, like the one at home.

John called out Agatha's name. It echoed desperately around the house. He looked through the sandy banks. It looked like it had been slept

413

in not that long ago. I'll wait. He thought to himself.

The waiting lasted a week, and that was when John saw how much the world had changed. Thorns that stung more than barbed wires. Bushes that hurt like metal bars. The tribe was different. That's when he walked out of the house, hiding from the others, and he saw a sign. John didn't see anything odd about it. A sign, made from fine wood, with nice engravings of laws. John looked at the letters for a moment, then started to feel queasy.

New rules.

John thought. The king had now become Ron's slave. Ron had disguised as 'the leader' now. The rules were wrong. But rules were what determined if something was right or wrong. "Right is wrong." John muttered. "Wrong is right."

"Right is wrong..." He fell to the ground and looked at the sky. He looked at the dirt. There was nowhere to go. He could not rely on anything. "Revolution!" John cried. "Mercy... Mercy..." He mumbled. "I must." "I can't!" John ran back and forth. He at last said "I am." And decided he would devote himself to change. To return everything that was altered.

THE BIRTH OF A HUMAN

Despair and Escape

14. Despair and Escape

He walked, walked, walked, and walked to the castle. It had thorns and thistles around it and was guarded by foxes. John went around to the back side. Only two foxes were there. "Stop!" They cried. "Reveal your identity!" "A human!" John said, throwing back his hood. "Are you scared? Just let me in, if you don't want me to do... Do something to you!" "Did you think we'd be afraid?" Said the foxes. "The king and leader have a great power that shall not be compared to the humans. Now, who are you?" John glared at them and said "The only sane person here, I suppose. If they don't wish to be compared, why are they fighting? You could put your trust in better people."

The foxes picked up the guns. John dodged the bullet swiftly and snatched the gun from the fox. The other fox shot at him. It sped past his ear. John took the gun from him too and put both the guns under his feet, and jumped. The guns smashed into pieces instantly. "There." John said. "If you don't want to be compared to the humans, you might want to lose these." The foxes growled and snapped at him. John growled back and snapped. He went on to all fours, and ran into the castle. The soldiers guarding the gate only saw a brown and red figure dashing inside.

Bullets flew at him from all directions. John tried to clear his mind and get to the main hall. He galloped and sped into a doorway and shut the door behind him. The space was mossy and damp. It smelled odd too. John knew the soldiers would catch up before long, and looked up. There was a crack. John touched the ceiling. It crumbled around him, and made a small hole. John looked at the vines along the walls. He pulled it. The dirt crumbled a bit more. John jumped and hit his head on the ceiling. He continued until the ceiling made a hole big enough to crawl through. He went up it and saw very many things at once.

The first thing he saw was a bullet, flying across the sky. It made an ark across the sky and hit a bird. It dropped on to John's head. 'A dove.' He thought. The thing he saw next was soldiers. Foxes and humans. John thought they looked like toys. John then hoisted himself on to the roof. It was wood, leaves and dirt, the traditional fox style. The roof was quite low. John tried to think of where the king's room would be from there. He thought for a moment, then jumped right in the middle of the roof. He felt himself falling. A rock hit his knee. He started to bleed.

He landed right in front on top of somebody. John looked at his face and saw that he had landed on the king. The king's face seemed lifeless, yet John could see that he was in pain. John heard a voice behind him.

"Do you pity him?" Ron said. John gasped. "It was you. Wasn't it? All the nonsense and laws here... You're the leader, right?" "Yes." Ron said. "You realized." Ron held up a rock and threw it at John. John caught it, but it still cut his hand. "It hurts. Doesn't it?" John just snarled and glared at him. "I'm going to get rid of this. All this nonsense. Rocks will become steel. Branches will be concrete. Leaves will turn into lightbulbs." "No!" John said. "That isn't how it's meant to be."

"It is. But there is a greater plan. All the foxes will become humans." John said "They won't." Quietly. "What?" Ron said, in a mocking tone. "They won't!" "Ooh, and how are you going to do that?" "I'll just do it!" John said. Ron looked around the room and said "How will you do that, when you can't save a single person?" Ron then took the king and walked out.

John chased after him and ran. He suddenly stopped and started to walk. Somehow walking felt so much faster. 'Calm.' John thought. John then saw something. He saw that Ron was creating a trap. John thought about something so wicked, and decided to do it. 'For the greater good.' He thought and dropped to the ground.

"That's crazy." Whispered one of the children. "It isn't!" Said another. "Look. Something IS wrong. All the things that are happening aren't good!" "Then why would they change anything?" "Exactly! We need to escape now. We'll find mom, and get out of here." "And go where? Besides, mom will lose her job." When the other children heard this, they also felt unsure of what they were planning to do.

"But still...," said the other cub. "We can escape to another place though. Cross the sea, or go live in an area where nobody's there to boss us around." "What would we live on? We'll have to hunt everything ourselves, if mom's not going to work, or if we escape alone. And think of the dangers we would face! The guards at school have guns. Just think! We might be sent to the humans." Everyone shuddered.

"We can dig. We're foxes! We'll dig east, towards the beach. Nobody's ever there. We can build a burrow, and wait until it's safe." "Do you think they wouldn't go looking for us? You know they can dig faster too. Right?" The other cub groaned and said "That's exactly why we need to go right now." "Now?" "Yes. Right this moment. Get ready."

They dug silently, stopping each time they saw the others twitch in their sleep. Eventually, the tunnel was deep enough to hide all of them. They went in, and continued to dig, this time ceaselessly. They dug east for a very long time, then dug a tiny hole upwards to see where they were. The sun was rising, and they were on the edge of fox territory and close to the unknown lands. "I'm scared." One of them said. "Why?" Asked another. "This place is way too close to the dungeon." "Then dig! We'll be at the beach in no time."

They dug as fast as they could, for they knew that by dawn, everyone in their burrow would notice their absence, and the sun was already starting to rise. They dug, and occasionally looked outside to see where they were. Then, they finally found themselves near the beach. "Good thing the school was on the edge of the territory." One of them said. They then got out and gathered rocks and thorns and mud and vines, and walked back near the school through the hole, then plugged the hole from there. They then rolled a boulder to cover the hole completely. At last, they were free.

Agatha couldn't believe her eyes. When she had finished her shift, she had wandered into the forest. Somehow, she wound up in the place, as if spellbound. There, she had encountered one of her peers, escorting a criminal to the battlefield. She realized she had travelled to the battlefield, and knew she needed to get back. However, curiosity got the best of her, and she found herself following the human soldier that had taken the fox. The soldier occasionally looked back, but never seemed to spot her, so Agatha carried on.

There, she saw something most peculiar. The human took the fox to a small car. Agatha of course was not familiar with one, and was surprised to see how fast it went. She followed the tracks on the muddy road, and saw that they were near the shore. For a moment, she thought they had returned to the fox kingdom, but then remembered that the beach reached out on to the human lands for millions of bear-strides. The foxes then boarded a motor-boat with one human steering. They would get on, terrified, then would become tiny little dots, and disappear. After following the humans for another day or two, she discovered that this was how they disposed of every fox that came into their territory. But where did they go? Agatha wanted to find out.

"I'm hungry." One of the fox cubs said. The children hadn't eaten for a day. The beach provided no food, and all the bushes there had been ripped out by the roots, supposedly from years ago. No animals went by. The children were starting to get angry. "Why don't we leave?" One of them suggested. "Yeah. We'll starve if we stay here any longer. We need to build a raft and leave the place." A timid one said "I wish we just stayed at school. Then we would at least have had food." "We can't go back now though! We need to leave."

So, they rolled a few logs off the side of the beach and linked them together with vines, and went on. They used a few long sticks as a paddle, and moved towards the sea. Then, it started to float with the waves, and the raft shook. The famished children occasionally dove underwater to search for anything to eat. They never found anything. They eventually got tired and slept, because you were never hungry when you were asleep, and they knew that well. They slept for half the day, and tried to keep sleeping. However, the only reason they woke up again was because they were hungry. The shore was no longer visible, and they were in the middle of nowhere. "I miss mom." One of them suddenly blurted out.

Nobody heard him. They were all asleep again.

At that moment, Agatha was also on a ship. She had been found hiding in the bushes, and the humans thought that she was one of the lawbreakers trying to escape. Now she was on a motor boat, with a human driving it. She felt miserable, and terribly sick. She wished she had never left. She sometimes clawed through the tarp that covered her and peered out the railings of the boat. She then saw logs drifting in the middle of the sea, and wondered where they had come from.

She felt the smooth surface of the boat cutting though the water, and felt fear. The humans were so powerful, that they could do things like this. Was there really any point in fighting, or were the foxes simply walking towards their doom? The other foxes somewhat seemed in a trance already. Agatha felt weaker, and collapsed to the ground. The sun shone. Everything still looked perfect.

John looked up, and was relieved to see that nobody was there, and that he still had his sack. He was alone. However, it was dark, and unlike the king's room, which he had believed he was in. John sat up, and looked around. He was in some sort of hole, covered with sticks. John stood up and carefully lowered a few down and stacked them, and hoisted himself out of the hole. He found himself in the forest, on the edge of the human territory. John walked out of the forest and saw a small restaurant. He was miserably hungry, and so decided to go inside. He pulled money from his sack and sat down. A woman was looking at her phone.

May 9th, the phone said. John looked at the date for a moment then remembered. Redemption Island. John ran to the beach. He desperately looked around, and saw a chained-up motorboat. There was a spot for a few more, but they weren't there. John hit it with his hammer, and started the boat. He never learnt how to drive, he didn't really know where the island was, but he needed to go, so he drove the boat away from the shore, as fast as he could.

The children woke with a start when they felt the cold water of the sea hit their face and sat up. A white motor-boat passed by, speeding away. It was going so fast that the waves made the raft rock from side to side. They had never seen a motor-boat before, and thought that it was a new kind of water-beast that they didn't know of. Then they saw the face of a man and was terrorized. "Humans must know how to charm animals!" one of them shrieked as the waves carried them towards the boat. "What are we to do? We need to get away from here!" another said.

"Let's paddle with are paws." Said one that was still not fully awake. They couldn't think of anything else and so that is what they did. The pushed the raft away from the boat, though they hated that their paws got wet. But one of them that had particularly sharp claws paddled too close to the boat and cut through the vine linking the logs together, and the vine got stuck in one of the small hooks on the outside of the boat as the raft started to come apart. They screamed and grabbed at the logs desperately, but foxes are not water-beasts and don't know how to swim to things, so they ended up grabbing the closest thing to them, the vine.

"Help!" They screamed as the vine pulled them towards the engine of the boat. The vine swung majestically as they tried their hardest not to get pulled in. If they held on, the one in front would be pulled in to the engine. If they let go, they would all drown. Just then, the one that had been at the very back pushed his way into the front, trying to delay the others from getting pulled in to the engine. Just then, the boat stopped moving. Their grip slackened on the vine, and they saw someone stepping out onto the deck of the boat slowly. It was a human.

What's more, it was John. The children had never seen John any more than they had seen a motor-boat, so they were very frightened, for he seemed like a human. John looked at them and helped them up then said to them in fox "Are you all, right? Why are you here? You need to go home. Where are your parents?" "You can speak fox!" they exclaimed. John repeated "Who are you?" "Foxes, of course." They answered.

"What are you?" They then asked him.

"I... I don't know what I am. I'm just John."

John answered.

"John? Like the human?" they said, wide-eyed. "Yes, I'm afraid so. I'm sorry." John sighed, then said "How do you know me?" "Our mother, of course. Who in the tribe wouldn't know Agatha!" John said "Are you, her children?" "Yes. And we know who you are, perhaps even better than you know yourself. Listen. The tribe's in trouble. We escaped, and we want to go somewhere that nobody can find us. We don't know where our mother is." John said "I'm terribly sorry, but I need to go somewhere quick, and I think it's dangerous. If I see an island, I'll drop you off, but you might have to come with me." John said.

They nodded solemnly as a boat sped by them. John looked. The boat was called leaves. Unusual name, John thought. It reminded him of trees. Then John felt a sudden chill go down his spine. Leaves was the title of the file that led him to redemption island. John screamed "Hold on!" and followed the boat as fast as he could.

He saw the other boat speed up, as it zoomed across the ocean. The children held on as tight as they could, and John occasionally slowed the speed so that they could hold the railings. The other boat was going as fast as it could, and the thin tarp that covered the very back of the boat flew away, which left John and the children to see the many foxes on the back of the motor-boat, though they didn't know that one of them was Agatha.

The children yelled "Foxes! On the beast! Why are there foxes riding on that water-beast?" "It's not a water-beast, it's a boat!" John said "And they wouldn't be able to drive the boat themselves. They're getting kidnapped!" "By who?" Said the children. "How should I know?"

Said John, though he felt that this may also be one of Ron's many schemes. It couldn't be a coincidence that all this was happening. He needed to know where the boat was going. He needed to do this.

John forced the boat to move, and chased the other boat. Then, he froze. As he got closer to the foxes in the boat, he was able to distinguish them quite clearly from one another. He thought that one of them looked familiar, though he didn't get to see very well who it was, as he needed to drive extremely fast to catch up to the other boat. But when he caught up, he heard the children shout "Mother! Mother! Look at us!" and realized that it was Agatha whom he had seen on the boat. He was so happy to finally see her, but then realized that she too, was being kidnapped. He instructed the kids to keep quiet and promised to bring them to their mother when they caught up with the boat. John then wondered why Agatha didn't reply to her cubs. This all felt weird. He started to feel very queasy.

THE BIRTH OF A HUMAN

Different Purposes
and the Same Destination

15. Different Purposes
and the Same Destination

"This is a rebellion, a rebellion from the hypocritic government." A fox said quietly. "It is a fight for true rights. A fight for all creatures. A war to restore our rights. To be free. And more people deserve those rights. We have planned this for a long time. If the government is trying to become humans, we will go the opposite way. We will find the place where humans were made. We will find why. We will restore the humans to what they once were." He spoke. "Foxes!" The crowd roared. At least half of it did. The other half was accustomed to something else. They spoke angrily, asking if they were challenging the king. Still, nobody doubted that someone needed to have the power.

The fox continued his speech. "Ever since we

saw the humans challenge us, we formed an underground association. We were hidden from everyone. Nobody knew of us, because our goal was something nobody wanted to hear. It was a truth kept hidden. We, and we alone, deserve to rule. Foxes are superior." The fox paused in his speech. "But! We want everyone to have power. So, we thought about how we could accomplish this. And we found a way. If we can all be foxes, we will all share power. We urge you realize the importance of this. If you truly love our species, and truly love the world, this is the one way to save it. That means we sail, out to the sea, and find our tree from years ago, and we use its power." Here, he lifted up his head and looked at the sun. A fox in the crowd shouted "Do you disapprove of the king?"

"NO!" The fox giving the speech shouted. "Do you know what the king is thinking? The king is a captive, and has sadly been forced to parrot the words of the human spies in our world." "How would you know?" Said the fox that had questioned him. "Do you think the king agrees with the disgusting ways of the humans? Do not question him in such a way!"

"Now, who will travel? Who will have the honor of journeying to the island?" He said, addressing the audience now more than ever. "Who would like to go to the island for our plan?" Nobody spokes. "So- none! Nobody is willing to save our nation! Oh, how tragic, that nobody cares for us as much as their own safety. What a sad fate for the tribe, that endured so much and conquered all! Every time there were dangers, there was always a hero. Now there are none. This must be it. We will be ruled by the cruel and sadistic humans. We will be treated brutally and viciously. We will become slaves. Oh, but you wouldn't care. You seem eager to be the servants of humans, and reverse the laws of nature.

Though humans were creatures that should never have been created, and should have been contained, they wish to dominate the world. But who created them? We did! We are their rightful masters, and are responsible of saving them. And to save them we must return them to what they once were, as I had stated. But if none wish to act………."

Then, his voice became soft and soothing. He spoke with soothing words and wore a smile on his face as he said "Ah, I see you are quite concerned about safety. Do not worry, for we provide. We have taken a human boat to disguise you, and we found soldiers and took them away from war, which seems to me but a play for the triumph of humans that will end with our defeat. We rescued a few, and they will accompany the hero. You will sail, with plenty of good food and tons of fresh water, and when you return, be greeted by all and live for the rest of your life surrounded by delicacies and comforts. Now who wishes to travel?" Almost everyone now asked to go, shouted pleas to the fox giving the speech.

"Well then," He said, looking at the other courtiers, "Pick a few of the strongest and have them go to the boat. You know where it is." He then left, and the other courtiers who had joined in the rebellion started to pick out the people for the journey to redemption island. The foxes that were picked glowed with pride and looked down at the others as if they were slugs, and the ones that had been left out groaned and looked at the chosen ones with envy. "It's not fair... I want a chance to be surrounded by comforts... I'd like to see what it's like to live in a way like that." A fox groaned as she returned home. "Who'd want to pick someone like us anyway? It's always someone else that gets the good things, you know." Another said. "Well, it's too dangerous anyway. Better to see what happens when someone else goes, before you try it for yourself. It's better to just stay home, where you're safe and happy. Isn't it?" Another joined in. They all walked back home gloomily.

The chosen foxes boarded the ship and set off to redemption island, and everyone else watched. They got on to the boat and looked at the driver. The driver was looking slightly jumpy, as if he was also scared of the terrors that awaited them at sea. The soldiers that accompanied the chosen foxes looked slightly more confident than the driver, but were still trembling, knowing that foxes were not sea-animals and that they were meant to stay in the forests. It also turned out that the food and water that would be provided was also very minimal, as the food was a few freshly caught rabbits in a human paint can that had been washed in the sea water, and there were only two paint-cans that contained water. The chosen foxes were now stunned, and wondered how they would survive the journey.

The driver got into an awkward position, as the boat was a motorboat that the rebel organization had stolen from the human harbor and had been clearly intended for human use. The fox ended up attaching an odd wooden stick to all four paws to drive the boat and was driving at top speed, as he had difficulty finding the breaks. Everyone aboard felt odd, as none of them had ever been seasick, and was only beginning to feel more frightened than ever about this journey as the boat approached the human harbor to follow their ships. The foxes were instructed to hide, and only one of the soldiers occasionally lifted his head up to check if a human boat was leaving. As soon as they saw a human boat departing the harbor, they followed them, once again at top speed, thanks to the confused driver. All the foxes now started to vomit, including the driver that was making the once shiny, silver wheel look a greenish brown. The trip had not gotten off to a wonderful start.

They went at top speed without stopping, now ways ahead of the human boat. However, they did not realize this, as they saw another human boat driving well ahead. They thought they were behind, and were devastated as they had been driving at a nauseating speed. Then, the boat turned and they failed to follow it. The driver stopped pressing the accelerator and looked behind him. The soldiers and foxes were still somewhat keen on finding the island and saving the world, but also wished to return home and rest, though they knew they were way too far away to do that.

So, they drove on straight across the sea, that had started to ripple with waves and shake the boat lightly. The driver was still very incapable of controlling the accelerator and continued to drive the boat so it zoomed across the water in an odd fashion. They drove for a while until they spotted an island and decided to spend the night there. A few of them also set off to find the legendary tree, in the hopes that this may be the island they were looking for, though they all doubted this secretly in their heads. They all felt a little bit silly.

John drove towards the other boat, now driving slightly slower. The children, in hopes that their mother would spot them, had stayed up all night, and were now fast asleep, though it was already half past noon. He did not want to disturb them because he saw them call out so many times, trying to talk to their mother through the loud sounds of the motor and the distance of the two boats. John thought they deserved to rest more than he did. However, something was still on his mind.

He was thinking about the children at the hotel, the young but brilliant kids that designed their own, magnificent language, and their family, that had been kidnapped by Ron. John also thought about Ben. John didn't know what he was like, really. Ben was quite mysterious, and it was hard for one to know what he was thinking about at the moment. John was even more unsure as Ben had left him and mistrusted him, but also had left him valuable information. However, John still did not know where Ben was or how he had contacted him, as Ben left his phone with John.

Ron grinned, looking at the sea. He was waiting now. There were no flaws in his perfect plans, no slips, no unexpected events. He knew that more and more foxes would come to his beautiful island, and become what he needed them to be. He knew it was only a matter of time before the newly created creatures, all being educated by him, would become the majority. Not too long after that, he would be able to take control of the world he wanted to rule. He looked at the few hypnotized foxes he had brought to the island, and said "I'm boarding the boat on Friday. We'll come back the day after that."

He wanted perfect control. Perfect control, perfect enough that he knew everything that was happening. He needed to hypnotize the foxes, and have them under perfect control. This was the only way that he could govern the world the way he wanted. Of course, they needed to be changed too. Ron knew that they could not stay foxes for long. Ron thought this was his greatest discovery.

His discovery of the tree led to him creating humans, then becoming one, then making everyone one. He found a way to control the tree, possess the tree, and use it, which was such a simple process that he was ashamed of himself for not discovering it any earlier. A tree possesses no intelligence at all. This tree, though it is the life tree, would of course be the same, only more powerful. Things like this are always the most convenient to use. He said often to himself.

He also often said "I know the war would tire people, tire them out enough that they would want a powerful leader. I could be that leader. The people would want me. The best way to gain control of something with any intelligence is to make it agree with you. War is convenient for another reason. You can wipe out things you don't want without making it look like you intentionally did it. It helps you eliminate people that think. People that think are useless. They are dangerous and harmful. They always disagree with those who have power, and question everything. They question things that need not be questioned. I need people that do not think. People that do without thinking about it. They are the ideal type for society. They are but one of the million building blocks that support their one powerful leader. This, and only this, is who I am actually in need of. Isn't that right, Ben?"

Ben stayed silent at the odd question. He simply stared at the ground, as if he didn't understand a word that Ron was saying. "Well?" Ron asked. Ben still didn't say a word and touched the ground. "You disgust me, Ben." He spoke. "Don't you know how filthy that is? True beauty cannot come naturally. It requires some sort of treatment, and the treatment is needed in everything. That is the beauty of elimination. You don't seem to understand what it truly means though. You disappoint me... I expected much more of you than that... What, indeed has happened to you?"

Ben still didn't reply. "I see you've been with John quite often lately. Why? He is nothing but filth. He is the taint. He is a gruesome mistake. And you know it better than anybody. Why does a man like you wish to spend any time with him? And working on his side... No! Indeed, the only wise choice you have made lately was your choice to join me. And even now, you aren't committed to our plan. You must show that you believe in me more than that. I always trust you, and help you, and care for you. Why don't you do the same for me?"

The water rippled gently as the boat moved across the water. John was getting tired of following the other boat, never-stopping and fast as lightning. John wondered who drove that boat. Surely, nobody could drive a boat like that. At first, this only seemed slightly queer, but John noticed how peculiar this was when the boat didn't even stop in front of the tall waves. John thought the boat acted like it was programmed, though he knew the boat could not act that way. He then started to think about the driver. Who could drive the boat that way? Then he felt a chill down his spine as he realized the only reason, he was following the boat was to get to Ron. Ron was a hypnotist. So, the boat was programmed. Except who was programmed was the person driving it. This had gone way too far, and John felt scared. He couldn't stop thinking about it.

Night came, as always. The sky was lit with stars that moved from side to side. They twinkled softly on the ocean darker than the sky, dancing with the moonlight. John, knew the constellations quite well, being educated with foxes. The constellations were probably different from the human ones, John thought and added, if they even have such things. He felt odd about how little he knew about human's while being one. But was he even a human? John looked up at the sky. Stars were always just stars. They didn't drift around everywhere, like he did. They just swayed from side to side.

John then noticed something. The boat ahead of him stopped. He stopped too. He looked up again. Something was changing. Perhaps he was seeing things... The stars started to drift. They moved. They twisted. They became something. They looked like letters to John. The letters of the children. They looked faint, but then became brilliant and brighter and... John sounded the letters out. What did they mean? He repeated them over, and over, and over again.

"Ah!" he shouted. "How did I forget... It means tree!" He looked up again. He liked the way the word sounded, and the way it looked when it was written down. But the stars were gone. They had disappeared as suddenly as when they had appeared. But it had to mean something. John didn't know how anything could affect the stars, but the message was too clear. The only tree he knew of was still the great tree project though. Nothing else.

No. The life tree. He had nearly forgotten. "Hey!" John said, looking up. "If you're trying to talk to me, just tell me. Can I do this? What am I even supposed to do? I haven't ever tried saving an entire species before. Like, who has? I need more help. I don't have anyone that could help."

Nothing happened. He looked behind him to check if the children were still asleep. One of them were awake. John said "Did you see that?" The cub said "See what? It's a weird night. The stars are so dim, I can barely see them. The moon looks pretty nice though. Do you mean that?" "Er, yeah!" John said. "You can go back to sleep." He nodded and started to snore softly. John then thought, 'What else did I see in that language?' The file. The file called the great tree project. And it wanted to find... It's true purpose? Well, the project is to convert foxes in to humans using the life tree, and... What *is* the life tree's purpose?'

John had never thought about this before, and was surprised that he hadn't. If he had determined the purpose of the tree, he would have known so many things, like whether or not it was evil. But what was evil? Could you sort something merely into good and bad? John started to feel very confused, and wondered whether his creation was against its purposes, or if the tree even had any purposes at all.

He wished the tree would send some kind of message to him. Something helpful, and wiser than the things he'd been hearing of late, spoken by foxes and humans. Not that I am either of them, anyway. John thought, feeling like some sort of disfigured mutant-creature. He wished he would belong to something, in the least. The stars seemed to offer help, but seemed to be the cause of all this confusion at the same time.

But something that could manipulate the stars would have to be powerful, powerful indeed. And it felt like a good force, not something that would harm him. However, John didn't trust his feelings as much as he used to, and was still unsure of the message. Besides, though the message to him was of great importance, there was more he needed to consider than his nerves.

His main concern was of the children (in the island, and on the boat), the clues, Ron, and of course, Ben, who now seemed to John the greatest mystery, above all others. He wondered how he had managed to send a message, and where he was. He thought it would be helpful to consult Agatha too.

John was feeling the absence of her presence ever more and hoped he would be able to ask for her help if they could just reach her. He would have rescued her right away, if it weren't for how risky it would be to climb onto the other boat. John suddenly felt as if he were alone. Then realization dawned upon him that he was. Nobody could help him now.

John's thoughts then turned back to the life tree. He thought about all the things that sprang up from it... John couldn't find anything good about it. Half the terrible things that had happened had seemed to come from it. John also found it somewhat creepy that the tree got revenge by making the king ill after king had ordered it removed from its original place. John felt like the tree was causing the trouble. But why? Surely, it had to have a reason to unleash such terrible and powerful things. Perhaps, John thought, did it have anything to do with it being removed against its wishes? But surely a tree couldn't think about something like that and use its powers. Could it? But if it could, why did it let others use its powers to create a new species? There was no explanation for that except that the tree was evil if you were to say it could think. But how evil are humans? John asked himself.

He thought about the humans he had met while working in the hotel, and of their behavior. John could think of nothing particularly eviler about their behavior than the foxes. But then was it a good thing that the humans have been created? Did the world benefit from them at all? Absolutely not, John thought. So, it wasn't a good thing that they had been created. John decided, though in his head he was still thinking of the human children he had met.

Then he thought of the foxes. Did foxes ever do anything wrong? John thought about this, and an immediate answer suddenly came to his head. The human training centre. Training anything, after the training he saw Ron do, didn't sound so wonderful. John pulled out his book, and opened up the book which had grown so large that John didn't know where to begin. So, he just closed his eyes, and suddenly, his hands seemed to flip the pages until it got to one that just felt different somehow. John didn't know exactly how, but he opened his eyes. And right there, the first thing he saw on the page was The Centre for Human Pollution.

John looked at the words, and read every bit through the long chapter. In fact, even after the other boat left, John drove the boat while still glancing at the book. The book had the information he wanted, but it was much more terrible than he had ever expected. The things that happened that he didn't know were simply stunning, and all his childhood mysteries were being solved. Why he had to go to the castle, why he was the only human in the tribe, why the other humans were in the centre (now the hotel), why he wasn't taught magic, how the foxes thought of him, and how they manipulated him, and how they controlled everything. When he finished the chapter, he didn't know how to feel.

He had always been taught of how wonderful the foxes were and their complete perfectness. John could not consider this perfect. The foxes did everything they had said the humans were doing wrong. Perhaps even worse, John thought. At least the humans knew what was going on. None of the foxes knew anything that had happened. They probably didn't know much about what was going on now either, though. Not that it was their fault. A few people in charge had made it so that they could control everything that was happening in the tribe. Then John realized his dilemma had been pointless. It would be impossible to call anything good in a situation like this. It was pointless to try to find anything perfect anyway.

THE BIRTH OF A HUMAN

Reminiscence

16. Reminiscence

Ben raced through the forest, desperate to run away. The island was completely in Ron's control, and Ben knew there was only one way to end all of this. He had to find *it*. He had to destroy *it*. He didn't know what risks would come with it or what it would also destroy. All he knew was that he had something Ron didn't know of, that just might lead to Ron's downfall...

All of this had started when he had stormed out of the hotel that day. He was completely driven by rage, and uncertain of what to do. He had left John out of pure anger, feeling that their relationship was unfair. He had left all the devices he could possibly contact John with at the hotel, so that it would be impossible for John to contact him in any way.

He walked towards the beach, and sat down on the bench, thinking of what to do next. Ben knew it was very unlike him, but he had never planned on what to do after he had left the hotel. He sat on the bench, thinking about what he could do. He had many dilemmas, but they were all melting in his head like an ice cream cone, swirling around his mind in a somewhat distorted state. He felt like there was a radio buzzing in his head, and had a tremendous headache. This prevented him from thinking about any other matters, but irritated him so much that he was infuriated by anything he thought was even the slightest bit annoying. Ben felt odd, and couldn't think. He then fell asleep.

When he woke the next morning, he felt different. He felt like all his thoughts were clear and his own, and the fury inside him had gone. He felt free. Then, when he tried to think again, he felt odd, and confused about himself. He thought about what he had been doing lately, but thought of them as if they had been another person's actions. They felt unfamiliar. He couldn't understand himself at all. Then, different memories started to flood his brain.

He was in his room, asleep, then Ron came in silently and invaded his mind... Ben remembered everything now. He remembered every single thing that had happened. He had been controlled. Hypnotized. Ron's slave. Nothing like himself. He started to sweat all over, and stood up to return to the hotel, then fell back down. He felt weaker than ever.

Then, somebody came up to him. "Need a hand?" asked Ron. Ben looked at him with confusion, but then got an idea. "Yes." It was nothing like hope, and yet it was the biggest hope that he had. Ron took his hand, and said, "Well, Ben, I'm pleased to see you again, and even more pleased to see you alone. Is someone waiting for you, by any chance?" "Nobody is waiting for me." Ben said. "So, you stopped working with... that, that... I mean, I don't know what you see in him. It's simply atrocious, that someone like you uses your knowledge, and abilities, and ideas for him. You deserve to be with someone worthy. Someone who really knows you, really cares about you. Someone like me. I hope you will join me again." "Yes." Ben said. "I will." "You will! Well, wonderful. But tell me. What happened with you and him?"

Ben grew slightly pale, looking grim, then suddenly changed his expression and began to turn red. He said "Me, work for him? No. He worked for me." "You seemed quite happy." "..." "Did you enjoy having others 'work' for you?" "Well, if your business with him is going well, I believe I may have contributed to that." "No. That was something I achieved purely out of my hard work and determination. However, some things did not go smoothly which I believe you may have had an effect on." Ben said "Do you think I would rather help him than you?" Ron said "I'd be pleased if you'd rather help me, but the circumstances make it hard for me to trust you. But I am a merciful leader. I will not discuss any more of the things of the past. Let us now talk about the future." He then took Ben's hand and said "And there's no better place to do that then Redemption Island."

They walked together to the boat, and boarded it. Ben noticed quickly that the driver looked slightly delirious. He assumed that he would have been hypnotized in some way and glanced at Ron. Ron was looking at the ocean. The boat sped towards the island at a remarkable speed, and Ben couldn't help but look towards the driver, who still looked as though he was about to fall asleep. Ron leaned back, and stared at the driver for a moment. The boat immediately slowed down to a much more comfortable pace. Ben, who was already feeling quite troubled, became queasy and felt slight fear from the fact that Ron was feeling absolute comfort in a situation like this. I *must* carry out my plan, Ben thought. Or else *this* is what the future will look like.

When they reached the island, Ben was able to look around. Ron muttered something to the delirious driver and he sped off. They were now alone. "There aren't any people here." Ben said. "People? Oh, there are some beings, though I wouldn't call them people. However, they are all far away, out of our sight. Don't worry. It just leaves us free to talk. You know, away from all that hustle and bustle, not to mention the impurity." Ron replied.

"Impurity?" Ben asked. "Yes, impurity. You

see, Ben, I have a plan. A plan to improve the world. Right now, I see terrible things. Some people are getting much less than they deserved, while some are getting more than enough. You see... Some beings are very primitive. They have existed for a long time, and are not given a chance to evolve. They simply go on, doing nearly nothing useful. However, some are different. Some beings have been carefully designed, are much newer, and do new things. My goal is to give the beings of the old times a chance to become a being of the new times, so that they can enjoy life like the newer beings. One thing about the newer beings is that they think in a new way. Neither way, you will truly think for yourself, but in the case of the old creatures, they can never give up traditions. Their minds are fixed on it. If you educate the newer beings, you can make them think however you want, regardless of whatever tradition existed in the past. Isn't that amazing?"

Ben did not think so, but nodded. Ron continued to speak. "Now Ben, the old creatures are called foxes. The new ones are the humans, the very creatures we made. But as you know, foxes can become humans, using the life tree. We had only seen the small parts, but in this very island, I found the life tree, and how to manipulate it. I can now change the courses of all life. I'd be pleased if you could help me. It wouldn't be anything dangerous. I care for you. I would not put you in danger. I will not let you use the tree for this reason, or educate the new creatures. All I need you to do is to bring the creatures to become humans. I have already set up all the ships. All you need to do is bring in the people as fast as you can and hand them over. They may put up a fight. Do you understand?"

Ben said "I never agreed." Ron's face forced into a smile. "But Ben, it's such a wonderful opportunity. And don't you see? You're trapped here. You can't get out without me. I can do whatever I want to you here, and nobody would know. If I were you, I wouldn't dare disagree." Ben looked at Ron and said "Under one condition." Ron asked "What is it?"

"Don't hypnotize me while I take care of the boats." Ron gasped. "You knew?" Ben said "Of course I knew. I couldn't even think properly, and I did know bits about what you were doing. I don't mean to criticize you, but it does have its downsides. It would make people do whatever you want, which would be considered very admirable for you, but if that's what you wanted, you could make anyone do it. The only reason you want me is because of my experience of working with you and using the tree. I don't think I'd be able to think like myself if I were hypnotized. Besides, as you said, I'm trapped here. I can't get out without you. What do you have to lose?"

Ron forced his face into a smile once again and said "Sure." Ben said "Then I'll work for you." Ron looked at Ben for a moment and said "Ben, do not make it sound as though you are doing this out of choice. You are not. You were simply privileged enough to be chosen by me. However, I appreciate that you wish to work with me. I will now give you a little thank-you present, by showing you the life tree. Follow me."

Neither of them knew at the moment that Ron would live to regret what he said.

When they reached the place Ron claimed the life tree was situated, Ben was puzzled. He saw nothing at all, until Ron started to mutter something to the tree. One of the tiny stems started to grow, until it became a giant tree, bigger than twenty tall pines stacked on top of each other. It had many colours, but each part seemed full of life, though not all of them very cheerful. It seemed different from the life tree he had seen when he created the humans, which was but a plant. It seemed to attract him, and yet we could feel how dangerous and powerful this was easily. He stared at Ron, who also looked amazed.

"I always feel that this may be the best representation of my power." Ron said. Ben felt that Ron was not fit for such a tree, but just nodded, thinking it was best not to disagree. Ron then looked at Ben and said "Well, you'd better get to work. I need to check on some things. I'll have to leave the island. However, I will know if anything happens." "Nothing will." Ben replied. "Nothing can." Ron said, smiling. He then departed the island.

It would be best to earn his trust first, Ben

thought. I need to prove that I'm worth keeping.

He then looked around, and walked up to the tree. He looked at its seeds, and remembering what it did, he picked one, debating in his head about whether or not he should destroy all of them. But when he looked up, another seed had just grown back, as if nothing had happened. He tried picking another one, and this time heard a small voice say "Ouch!" Ben looked behind him. Nobody was there, but the tree flinched slightly. Ben was startled, but picked a few more seeds, to see if the sound had really been coming from the tree. "Ahh!" It definitely was speaking. Ben felt ridiculous at the idea of apologizing to a plant, but muttered "Sorry." Wondering if the tree could comprehend language at all. The tree did nothing for a moment, then grew smaller, like someone curling up into bed with extreme comfort. The tree and its powers seemed to grow smaller as it felt comfort.

Ben needed to investigate more about this plant's powers, so he kicked the tree so as to make its powers grow. The tree immediately grew, and its bark turned into a frowning face. "Bad!" said Ben to the face and kicked it again. This time, images started to fill his mind. War. Famine. Disharmony. Ben immediately realized why Ron was so fond of the tree. It provided a very simple way to manipulate the world.

"Woah..." Ben mumbled as the emotions retreated from his mind and melted into the world. He couldn't believe it. Such a simple and powerful thing, and yet easy to control. It was perfect. It was also drooping. Ben felt slight compassion for the tree and hugged it. The tree shrunk once again, and became calm once again. 'This thing can do more.' Ben thought. 'But is the only thing it's driven by pain?' Ben decided to experiment, and walked around the island until he found a small pond. He took water from it, and gave it to the tree. The tree swayed from side to side then brushed Ben slightly, pulling him into an entirely different world.

He was in John's hotel room, standing beside John who was staring into space on his bed. "John?" John didn't move. "John? Can you hear me?" Nothing happened, and Ben concluded that he must be looking at John without being there. Just then, he felt something brushing against him again, and he returned to redemption island, where he had just been. Ben wanted to see John again, so he travelled to the pond again and gave the tree water. This time, Ben, instead of moving which seemed impossible imagined himself picking up the phone and tried to dial his number, but then remembered he had left his phone there. Ben sighed.

This was going terribly, and if Ron found out

he had used the tree... The only thing close to useful that he had done so far was finding out how to work the tree, and finding out that the tree somewhat had a mind of its own. This at first seemed like an amazing discovery, but what use could he make of this information? After all, Ron had perfect control of the tree and sneaking into John's world seemed almost pointless. "At least I know something that Ron doesn't." Muttered Ben. "You can control the tree in a positive way too."

But that didn't change the world like negative things did. It only showed you who you desired to see most, and that was it. You couldn't do anything. Ben felt devastated. There had to be something more that he didn't know. There had to be more behind this tree. If only he could know all its secrets... He felt that Ron was right. He wouldn't be able to do anything with the tree. He couldn't escape. He was just trapped, trapped in this horrible island with nobody. Yes, that was all he could look forward to. Ben left the tree, feeling worse than he had ever felt before. He wished he had never followed Ron, or met him. That was how all this had started.

Ben spent four days in nothing but despair akin to this, feeling that he was an idiotic man who had put his faith in the wrong people, creating things he never should have made, and had walked into a trap, thinking that he was clever. Of course, he could never seek redemption. He hated himself for everything. This was also the state that Ron discovered him. Moaning, shaking, and mumbling something to himself on the shores of the island, covered in sand. "Time for work." Said Ron, as Ben slowly got to his feet. Ben, feeling he couldn't do otherwise brought the foxes to Ron and pretended not to know of what would happen to them.

A few days later, a very drowsy-looking man took him to Ron, who said he wanted to chat with him. Ben, growing slightly apprehensive, merely nodded and asked Ron what he wanted to know. "Oh, just things." Said Ron. "You seemed a bit tired these days. Is it uncomfortable for you to work with me?" "No, not at all. I just wish I knew a bit more about what happens around here. I know nothing about this place, and that makes it hard for me to work when I don't understand what I'm doing." "Well, I'm not sure if you'll understand this project, but I will tell you if not knowing this makes it difficult for you to trust me. You see, I'm doing something like a project." "A project?"

"Yes, a project. Its main focus is the foxes, but I plan to extend this project to everyone, so that they can enjoy the happiness that comes from being a truly evolved species. I also wish to teach people about true liberty. Doing whatever you want is not liberty. It is negligence. I plan to teach those who have recently become humans about true liberty." "And what is that?" "Finding a good leader, and obeying him, becoming one with him. You would find much more freedom and joy this way. It would be difficult for me, but I know some sacrifice is needed to create a good world."

"So, then what about the hypnotism? What's with that?" "Oh, that was simply because you were around people clearly unworthy of you. This is all in your best interest and this doesn't work on John much... I just can't believe such a thing is bothering me. If the king hadn't made such a racket about that tree, we wouldn't have even had this monster to deal with. I didn't have a choice. Pretended to be one of the courtiers and-"Ron snapped. "-hypnotized him. The only problem is that he's been possessed now. I had to speed up the whole plan a bit, but it's all right now." "Nice." Said Ben.

"How about the virus isn't that also bothering you? "Oh, that? You think it's real? Ha! It's just a way of controlling the rowdy humans. Works great though. I see John has made you a bit dull though. What really is on my mind's the tree. It's very powerful, but hard to control. I may have to use something else as a device to control it." "Something else?" "It's not really something for you to worry about. You see..."

"The tree must have connected to another person." "Well, you could see it that way, I suppose." "Well, if it was able to contact anyone else that's quite risky. What if they knew someone dangerous? Like... John?" "Yes, they do live somewhat close to him. I may have to just check in..." and as he said this, Ron got up and boarded the boat with its driver, still looking as tired as ever. Ben thought about whether or not these were the children that John had so earnestly tried to introduce to him. 'They were real.' Thought Ben and walked towards the tree absent-mindedly.

He looked at the tree, and watered it slowly. The tree once again swayed gracefully and pulled Ben into John's world. He stared at John, pacing slowly back and forth around his room, still looking somewhat moody. Ben stared at John's phone for a while, then walked up to it. He hoped his new plan would work as he turned on the odd computer John hade made him. He typed in John's phone number and other necessary information, then picked up John's phone and recorded all the information that he knew.

Suddenly, he felt a surge of energy pulling him back as more words appeared on the computer's screen, which faded back into Ron's world and the tree, standing mightily. He was a bit concerned. The time he had set seemed a bit too soon, and the time seemed too exact. Would he be able to finish everything by the time John came to the island? Would John come? More importantly, could he do what he should? What would that do to John? What would it do to him? The world? Ben started to think. The dilemma was not simple, but it was staring at him, waiting to be solved, scribbled over his mind in big, bold letters. It swam around his head, right until the moment that Ron returned the next day.

Ben was never quite delighted to see Ron, but was glad to think of Ron instead of his worries. The dilemma required sacrifice either way, and both ways were bound to destroy everything. He could do it, or he could stop. Ben decided two weeks were enough time to avoid his worries and sedated himself with drugs called busyness and Ron. However, both were inclined to leave the island some time, and this was not something Ben looked forward to, though he secretly hoped to see the tree once more. It was where all his worries stemmed from, and yet it was the one thing he was attracted to. He both loved and hated it; yet he could not resist the urge to go to it the moment he saw Ron leave.

However, the tree had changed. Its differences were so pronounced that Ben even felt troubled. The tree was ugly, and no longer reacted when given water. Instead, it seemed to be filled with a powerful urge to resist and evolve. Yet, the very core of the energy still remained very much the same, full of life that strived to gain more. He tried to decide whether or not the change was a good thing in any way, but then remembered the discussion he had with Ron recently.

"What really is on my mind's the tree. It's

very powerful, but hard to control. I may have to use something else as a device to control it." "Something else?" "It's not really something for you to worry about. You see..." "The tree must have connected to another person." "Well, you could see it that way, I suppose." "Well, if it was able to contact anyone else that's quite risky. What if they knew someone dangerous? Like... John?" "Yes, they do live somewhat close to him. I may have to just check in..."

Ben felt terrible. It had to be. The answer was simply right ahead. The tree's new state was due to something he had refused to believe in. Ben's eyes trembled with the deepest terror, and for the first time ever in his two lives, he felt sorrow. He also felt fear. The future he had been dreading upon was finally here, ready to swallow him up. He placed his hand on the tree, and someone placed his hand on Ben.

"I didn't know you were so interested in my tree, Ben." Whispered Ron with a dangerously friendly tone. "No, I was simply passing by... I'd thought you had left." "You were just passing by and happened to touch the tree while I had left? How curious... That's an incredible coincidence." "I don't see why it's incredible. You're always with that tree while you're here, and you never told me that merely touching the tree was such a terrible thing. Please let me admire its beauty. You know we feel the same way."

"Ben, I can sense it when someone wishes to avoid the truth." "Well, then you'd know I'm telling the truth." Said Ben, trying to look merely amused with the game Ron was playing. "Just because you can't see me doesn't mean I can't see you. I sense you everywhere, and my power goes beyond yours." Ben merely nodded and walked far away, now knowing something he wished he didn't.

The truth was now too clear, and it was all his fault. Yet the only way that he could get out of the situation was to do *that thing*, and that was simply atrocious. How could he… But this was the key to solving every single problem. Ron's 'project', the war, his relationship with Ron could all be solved with *this*. The sacrifice could not be something that stopped him from doing it. 'But then what about the sacrifice itself? What did they do so wrong that justifies me to sentence such a fate upon them?' thought Ben. "And yet I must." He muttered as he began running madly, beginning his journey towards the destruction of the tree.

THE BIRTH OF A HUMAN

The Beginning of Realistic Hope

487

17. The Beginning of Realistic Hope

Warfare had created many societies lately, and one day, it felt obliged to do so again when a few children that occupied the sixth floor of Ron's isolation centre were mysteriously kidnapped. After the children's disappearance, their parents had called the hotel's front desk to ask what had happened that day, only to get an unsatisfactory answer that their children had been kidnapped by the foxes, for the human parents, or humans, for the fox parents. Both sets of parents were desperate for help, but none was offered. In the end, they fell into despair, and spent weeks doing nothing.

Finally, after they accepted that they would have to go on without their children, they went out onto the porch. Wendy started to gather their toys, one by one, and started to find some things that had recently disappeared. Among these items were her notepad and pen. Wendy slowly opened the notepad and found tiny scribbled letters and assumed that the children had practiced writing. She stared to tear up a bit but then calmed herself down, and looked to the other side.

There, she discovered a broken wall, and a large fox that was holding some dried leaves and a stick in its paw. Could the fox have been the one that had kidnapped her children? She stared at the fox, not knowing what to do. "What did you do to our kids?" She asked. The fox yelped, then growled. Wendy fiercely glared at it and said "Answer me!" The fox growled, and Wendy felt a surge of fear, while also wanting to attack the beast.

She held her notebook, still open in her hand and walked towards the fox with it, along with a toy fork that was so blunt that you couldn't have even used it for eating cake. The fox also walked towards her, baring its teeth. Wendy wondered if she'd be any match for the fox but walked forward to show the fox that she was strong. She inched forward slowly, making it look like she was shuffling forwards. The fox suddenly sprang towards her, and she hit it as hard as she could with the plastic fork.

"Liam, Help!" She cried, hoping her husband, still shut up in their faraway bedroom would hear. The fox then suddenly stopped, and grabbed the dry leaves and said something, this time a bit closer to a human's words. Wendy stared for a moment, then looked at her notepad, and realized that beside the scribbles, there were English words and pronunciations. She realized the fox had asked her about what she had done to its children and said in the weird tongue "Don't know them. What you do mine?" "I don't

490

know them." Replied the fox.

The fox then looked at her and asked "What happened to you children?" Wendy said "They take by fox." The fox replied "Me children take by human, weeks in past." Wendy felt odd. This language had a mysterious power that made her start to understand the creature in front of her with less hatred, and before she knew it, Wendy was barely looking into her notebook. "This language, human language?" asked the fox. "No. How do you know how speak so well?" "I do not know. My children notebook in, I looked and read." Sighed the fox. "Same. Your children (she gestured towards the fox) and my children may know same language, I think. Talk though wall hole."

"Then what happen to us children? My children lost in this place. I think your children lost in this place too. Then who take them?

Human take them, or fox take them?" "Don't know. This hotel just bad. Human and fox cannot work together, so they lie." Said Wendy. They lied. "Okay. They lie. Why do they lie?" "Maybe they no want distraction. They will lie to give you and me good thoughts about here." "Why they no want distraction? Maybe they take us children." "No. No reason they take us children. They want us not to know. They on kid take away person side, but they did not take us children."

"So, it no human! It no fox! Then what it is? This hotel owns many secret. They make secret there is human on other side, then now what do? They secret gone children! This one place to cross line to other country, no go middle fight, but I say they cause fight to give hotel lots money." Said the fox, quite triumphantly. "But kidnap children bad thoughts for hotel. Big plan not hotel, big plan not fight. Big plan control. We want out." "I am scared. No safe anymore. No person I can trust." "Then we make trust. Then we have one to trust." "Human and fox? No, we cannot trust ever! I like you, but cannot have fox with human. Human bad to fox, maybe fox bad to human." "But I no bad to you, you no bad to me. And hotel and fight people scary. Very scary. We trust until scary persons gone, or scary people win." The fox wagged her tail. "What that mean?" said Wendy, who was holding out her hand.

"It mean I trust you." "And this-"Wendy shook her paw-"means I trust you." She said and smiled. The fox moved its ears forward. Wendy took it to be the fox's equivalent of a smile and said "See you soon." The fox nodded and walked back to the other side of the wall, leaving Wendy to fully enjoy that odd feeling. She wondered what her husband would think if he knew. Would he be angry? Surprised? Worried? Wendy thought about how surreal the whole event was, then calmed down and walked inside. She looked at Liam and said "I've got news."

"What news?" asked Liam. Wendy gulped. She didn't quite know what to say. "Never mind, we can talk later." She said, as she quickly dashed into one of the empty rooms. Now that it had come down to it, she couldn't say it. She was simply scared of her husband's reactions. This seemed wrong, and it was. She wished it had just been her imagination. There was enough on her plate without having to deal with foxes and a constantly lying hotel. Why did she have to even tell him? Why? It could be a secret. But oh, how could she ever keep a secret for that long? Really... She walked out of the room. 'I am going to have this over with. I'm going to tell him.' She walked up to Liam "Hey... Uh, I, it... Never mind!" she said and ran back.

Five minutes later, she had prepared a script

in her head. She walked out of the room once more. "Liam, I want to talk." "About what?" "Just…You know there's lots of stuff going on and I just… Not that anything's wrong, I mean something is wrong actually, but then again… Argggh! Sorry! Talk later!" Wendy panted and walked back into the room. 'I can't do it.' She thought. 'I'll never do it at this rate. I've got to do something different.'

She grabbed a pen and some paper, then walked to the deck and took the notebook her children had made. She looked at the letters and words, then wrote a letter. It took her two hours, but it was quite a nice letter. She threw the letter onto the other side then returned to her husband, much calmer.

"So, what was it you had to say?" "You need to come to the balcony tomorrow. At noon. With me." "For what?" "The kids… Our kids. Their stuff.

Please." "Oh, that was why... Okay. Tomorrow noon? Why noon?" "I wanted to set a time so it doesn't become one of those 'we'll do it tomorrow' things." Liam nodded.

Wendy walked into her bedroom and panted. She felt dazed in a way, and was surprised she was that successful. She had lied perfectly. It was wonderful to have something else to think about besides her children. Suddenly this thought made her feel an overwhelming surge of guilt.

She justified this by thinking 'but it *is* all for the kids. I'm trying to help.' She felt so horrid, absolutely horrible, but she had started this and she was sure that she couldn't step out of this business. 'But why condemn my husband to the same fate?' she thought. The foxes were clearly dangerous, and yet she had trusted them. Now what could she possibly do? All the guilt inside her was bubbling, and she felt like she was a terrible wife, a terrible mother, and the more she struggled to swim out of her guilt, the more she felt her guilt seizing her, strangling her with her own thoughts, and it tired her so much that she fell asleep that way.

The next day, at noon, Wendy and Liam walked out onto the porch. "There isn't much stuff to clean up." Remarked Liam. "Er, yeah. I actually needed to tell you something." Said Wendy. "Tell me what?" "The kids... The foxes didn't take them." "Well, then who did?" "I don't know. But I'm sure it wasn't them. I think it has something to do with the hotel." "Listen, Wendy, I don't see how you're sure about this but we're at war with them. The hotel's protecting us."

"No, the hotel tricked us. The other side of the hotel's got... Never mind. And fox soldiers wouldn't waste their time on a couple random kids. Think rationally. The hotel's being too vague about everything, and their security is overwhelming. Something's weird." "The hotel's security is because of the foxes! Yes, perhaps the foxes didn't take our kids. But the hotel isn't doing anything wrong." "No! Don't you see, the hotel told us it was foxes that took our kids, so if the foxes didn't take our kids, then they're lying for no reason at all! It is obvious that there is something wrong with this hotel." "Calm down." Said Liam.

"Oh no... It's nearly ten twenty. She's running late. Did she not get the letter?" Wendy mumbled. "Who'd you send the letter to?" Said Liam, looking suspicious. "Here." Wendy said, taking a small notebook out of her pocket. "When I was cleaning our porch, I found this and a pen. Look inside," she said. Liam stared at the notebook.

Wendy continued to speak. "Quite interesting. Right? I remember our dictionary being on the floor a while ago. Don't you see why? They were looking up the alphabet and different words. They barely know how to read, but they must have sounded out the definitions one by one and written the words. This notebook is a dictionary of their own. They made up a new language." Liam looked stunned as he flipped through the notebook, at the somewhat different, somewhat familiar language. "What for?" he said.

At that moment, two foxes came to the broken wall. "Sorry late." Said one to Wendy in the children's language. "It all good." Replied Wendy. Both Liam and the Other Fox looked stunned. "I talk to my children dad and take much." Said the fox again. "My children dad now know speak." She said proudly. "No mine." Said Wendy. "He not know of you." "You come early, but no talk?" Wendy nodded. "What that?" "Yes."

Said Wendy.

"What you and other human call?" "Wendy and Liam." "You Rrriam?" "Wendy." "I Sunshine and he Storm." "Grrr-hiss and Growl-Rawr?" said Wendy. "It mean that." Said Sunshine, pointing at the sun. "I call. He call mean that (she pointed at the clouds)" "Bright! And...(she imitated rain with her fingers)It scare!" Wendy nodded "Scare! Bright!" Liam was still frozen and Storm was still slightly shocked. Wendy said "Now I talk my children dad." "Yes."

Then Wendy looked at Liam and tried to explain what had happened the last time she met the foxes. Liam looked at her with a concerned face and told Wendy that she shouldn't trust the foxes so easily. After all, who knows what they really think, and there was more evidence to support the fact that foxes were not to be trusted. Wendy sighed and tried to explain, but Liam was now sure that his wife had a false fantasy about these foxes claimed the hotel must be on the same side as the foxes. Wendy begged him to at least talk to them, but Liam said that he saw no reason to waste his time on those beasts.

From that day on, Wendy met the foxes every day, and tried to explain to Liam that they couldn't possibly be evil just because they were foxes. She talked of cruel humans and of saintly ones, and tried to explain foxes couldn't all be evil. Maybe she is right, but those foxes look like they support the hotel. He explained this to Wendy, but Wendy wouldn't have any of that. She told him he was just prejudiced and that they must have been trapped here like they were. Liam told her that they must have been trying to cross over to the human's side, and Wendy remarked that they were trying to get to the foxes' territory.

At last, after weeks and weeks of something like this, Liam learnt the children's language and gave up trying to convince Wendy that this was all useless. That was also when he joined those daily meetings of hers with the foxes. He started to feel odd. The new language seemed nearly magical, and he felt himself become one with the language. He could just feel what the words meant, or feel it when he said something wrong after a few weeks.

And the more they talked, the more things seemed weird. The foxes told them of some sort of meeting that was going on at their side, and of how it worked. The humans were greatly confused with this, but soon realized that this may have some connection with the hatred steadfastly growing between the two worlds.

Something was queer about all these events, and they were afraid that they were running from false danger, and that by doing so they would soon enough fall into true danger. They decided they had to keep investigating because they had begun to fear there may be more cases like that of their children. So, they started to plan. It may not have been the direct path to saving their children, but it was the way to spare many others from the same fate. Their plan was simple. They were going to escape.

"How we going to do?" asked Wendy in the middle of their daily meeting at the porch. "We too high up to jump down." She spoke. "We not can walk into the halls and walk out front door." Storm said "At no light (the others took this to mean night) we go. We get what we have, tie and go down." "That not work." Remarked Sunshine. "We too high and we need our thing. We need something people not us become wonder 'what that?'" "A diversion." Muttered Wendy in English. Liam nodded. "Something big."

Continued Sunshine. "Far from us." Everyone fell silent and started to think. Something far from them that could attract lots of attention, enough for them to escape?

There were many suggestions, but none of them seemed good enough until Liam, who had been inattentive until now said "You go to centre and talk with fox who supposed to check you and give paper to do." "Well, they tell us that there threats and not fairness really..." said Sunshine. "That not point." Said Wendy excitedly. "You make something big in centre and run with us." The foxes seemed to understand.

"We use magic. Mother nature power not good like before but still good enough for boom," said Sunshine. They all smiled. "We do boom we get catch," said Storm. "We give boom time," said Sunshine. "Get thing today, plan how do out centre today, get all ready day after today, boom after day after today when sun at sky middle," said Wendy. "Get thing now, come this (he pointed at the ground) when done," said Storm.

They glanced at the others then went into their houses and started to pack everything they thought would be handy outside of the hotel. Somebody insisted on bringing their 571 plants, but Wendy convinced Liam to bring only 250. Liam sighed deeply as he looked at the 321 plants he had to leave behind, but soon recovered after Wendy made him his favorite dish (cream soup, without the vegetables). Wendy ended up packing most of the things herself while her husband devoured the soup, not even once asking her to try some. She eventually got quite angry and Liam, who had been thinking about nothing but his soup was confused when Wendy snatched the plate from him and started to yell at him. 'I guess it's still a regular day then.' He thought.

Meanwhile, the underground fox association was sailing in the sea, the driver turning greener by the second. The foxes were now quite near giving up on the whole idea of finding the island and simply yearned to be back home. They were all silent, and occasionally swung their heads around, only to see nothing but the vast ocean ahead of them. However, a few of them still remembered the promise of wealth and fame when they returned home. They looked at the map, which apparently was supposed to guide them to the island where the tree was, and compared it to where they were. With no particular object that stood out in the huge pool of water, they thought all seemed hopeless. The foxes groaned. They did not have much food left, and were now closer to facing starvation than the riches that had been promised to them.

But just then, the captain stopped the boat

and cried "There!" He started to pant. "The island?" asked a sailor. "No, but it's the very thing we've been looking for. According the map, it's only a few days away from the island and it looks like it's got some trees. Maybe even fruits. I Think this is the first island we've seen in weeks!" cried another sailor, who had been staring into the map the entire trip. They were overjoyed, and once again started to look upon their journey as the journey to a new, fabulous life. Rough seas or wind, even food shortages could no longer trouble them. They would be at the island before they knew it, and then they'd be home where they would be welcomed as heroes.

Meanwhile, John was driving the boat, thinking about the tree. He wanted to get to the island as soon as possible, but he began to fall behind. He was the sole driver of this boat, and the boat that he had been following didn't even stop. He was just as tired as the kids were, and was seriously doubting that this boat would lead them to where they desired to go. Near dusk, it slowed down a bit, and they sped up to get a closer look. They started to see familiar shapes and even familiar faces. John gasped and the kids rubbed their eyes. They all simply stared at one of the figures until the youngest cub cried "Mom! It's her! Mom, can you hear us? What happened?"

The oldest immediately blocked his mouth and whispered "SHHH! She's trapped! They must be taking her somewhere!" "What about the other foxes?" "They must have been caught too." Answered the oldest cub. "What for?" asked another fox in the loudest whisper possible. "We don't know." Mumbled John. "You're gonna follow her, aren't you?" said the youngest. "Of course, he is! What else could he do! He'll bring us right to her, and set everything right. That's the whole reason he followed the boat!" said the oldest cub.

John was silent. He had to get the boat to redemption island. He had to save Agatha. He doubted that redemption island was her destination. He needed to choose, and the answer had to be trying to find redemption island before it was too late. But the children... They needed a parent to help. Agatha was the most important person in his life besides... Ben. He was at redemption island, probably. "Come on, let's go!" Said the youngest cub. John, without thinking about it, followed the boat, wondering what would come next.

This 'something' came much quicker than he had expected it to come. Jest as soon as he started to chase the boat, the waves of the sea formed an odd shape that said in the children's language 'cooperation, help'. Who could have been sending those queer messages? What did they mean? John thought. 'Does this mean I need to turn back?' he thought. 'But I've come to far. Cooperation probably means cooperation with the children. But there's Ben... But is there even a better way I'd find if I didn't follow the boat?" he paused, then looked at Agatha's children and said suddenly, without thinking about what he was actually saying.

"Hey guys, I need to tell you something. I'm on a sort of a mission. I've got to go to an island to do some things. I'll try to save your mother, of course, but I'm going to have to make that island my priority. I'll follow the boat, but if I see the island we will have to stop for a little bit. I'm really sorry, but it's about something that's equally important to me. But... Oh, I'm so sorry!" "It's fine." Said the youngest cub.

"As long as you can save her." "Huh?" said John "You're fine with that?" "You're the boss on this boat. What could we do?" said the oldest, slightly grumbling. "Whatever's so 'equally important' that you need to do, if it beats saving someone like mom, I'd hope it's something." John was very confused. Were they being sarcastic? "The youngest one said "You seem nice. If you saved us, you're going to save her. But if you leave her when those people hurt her, I'm never going to forgive you." The youngest one said. "Yeah, we'll never forgive you." "Totally." "No way!" added the others

"But..." said the oldest "We'll trust you now." John smiled. It was something like happiness, the first he'd really felt in ages. Then, the boat ahead of then stopped. A silhouette that looked somewhat like the driver turned around, then started to spin around for four days, until the driver began to drive again at top speed. John had a feeling that he knew they were following them.

THE BIRTH OF A HUMAN

The Miracle

18. The Miracle

Just before these four days, the humans and foxes on the fifth floor had escaped from the hotel. The 'bang' was more than enough to distract everyone else, and Everyone remembered it like it happened yesterday for the rest for their lives. When Storm or Sunshine told other people, the story would always start in the halls of the fox centre.

Storm and Sunshine were walking up to the attic, both thinking about how well everything would really work. When they got to the doorway, they gently knocked on it, and heard a grumbly voice saying "There's a session in progress." They waited for the grumbly fox to start talking to Mr. Whoever-was-inside, then muttered something while touching the walls, and opened the window.

This is where Wendy and Liam's story would usually start. Right outside the window, on the roof of the fox centre. They saw Sunshine and Storm give them the OK sign, and they walked slowly across the roof. "AAH! Liam, this must be the highest I've ever been in my life! I'm going to fall... I know it..." "Calm down." "How DID we climb up here? It's so scary... I can't go down without anything on!"

Liam sighed, then held her hand. They walked to the other side and towards their own side again, then double checked that all the curtains were closed. "Liam, we could have waited in the room until the curtains closed... Why did they have to lock all the doors and windows? It really is atrocious..." "If somebody walked out, we'd be caught! Now come on down! Please! "Gaah!" Wendy yelled as she jumped on to the porch.

"And you're alive too." Remarked Liam, handing her a tarp that he had been holding. "Swing it over the railings and hold both sides that hang down. Once you get down, pass it to me, I mean, if you're still alive." "Wendy flushed red and muttered something that sounded like 'could do better' as they continued to climb down the railing. When they finally got to the fifth floor. They gathered all their things and pushed them on to the other side of the wall. They waited there, Not even daring to make a sound, until they heard a scream coming from somewhere far above them.

"They did it." Said Wendy. "I never thought it would work." Muttered Liam as he watched the top of the hotel smashing into pieces. Right then, they heard a knock and crawled through the hole to open the door on the fox side. "We Do!" said Sunshine in the children's language. "Fast! Come!" They gathered their things and ran down the hall.

"So," said Liam, "You do. How?" Sunshine smiled, then began to tell the story excitedly.

"We had be in hall, call nature and magic. We knock door, until they say 'come' and curtains close. They notice not, so we walk in and they talk. We keep pretend scared, say met another fox, they scary, try do something. Then, when session finish, we run to room, timer for bang almost wrong, we also take much time, hotel fox chatty man. I say fox still think it next person in room though." As they said this, they reached the hotel doors, stormed out, and ran immediately to Wendy and Liam's house, which was only a twenty-minute walk from the hotel.

They sat there, and planned out what to do next. Wendy turned on her phone and said "I be doing something before. This human talking thing, we talk far away and still see and hear. There something call internet too, and it..." "ING-

RRAGH-HET?" asked the foxes.

"Yes. You give picture or word, you put it, millions see it. I take picture of hotel, document, and put it there. I also put up advertisements, they like internet posting but you no get choice to see. It maybe helps. Hotel wrong. We need help, so other not have us problem. You go to fox land, see what happen, then do what want. Try find where your children are. Tell us if you do. We try too, but we no think it works. We just work so this no happen again. Now, you no need trust, but we will trust you."

"Come back soon." Said Liam. "With the kids." Sunshine stepped up and shook Wendy's hand with her paw. "It mean I trust you," she said. "And this-" Wendy folded her ear with her hand and said "Means I trust you." Then she looked at her and waved. "This means goodbye," Sunshine lifted her paw. "But it's also hello. I hope I'll get to use this again." Sunshine waved. "I think we might." She said, as she walked out the door.

They walked through the town, to the forest, once again smelt the flowers, bushes, looked at the great trees, felt the rich soil under their feet, The growing grass, and ran though the tallgrass. They avoided the war area, and were soon able to get to the other side. Their side. The Fox Tribe. However, in the place where another great tree used to stand, there was a large wooden sign with new rules on it. New rules, which shocked them more than the war itself. How much the tribe had changed in the short time was unbelievable.

"Well, Sunshine." Storm said. "I think I know what we need to do." "Everything?" Sunshine said. "No. They've trapped all the kids in schools. They might have taken ours, and even if not, we can't just let the children stay there. Who knows what happens to them there? We can't afford to have more families like us, can we?"

"Then let's do it. We'll do it somehow, we always do." Said Sunshine. "We can start with finding all the schools in the area." Muttered Storm. "Are you blind?" said Sunshine. "They've written out all the schools names," she said. "The closest one's over there." Liam said, pointing over the hills. "Then we're going there tonight." "How? Guns are legal, the security's probably going to be crazy, right? All males are obliged to join the army." Storm said, reading the sign. "How are we going to do this without getting caught?" "Somehow." Mumbled Sunshine. "We always do it somehow, right?" "You've already said that twice." Groaned Storm. "I know we're going to do it, Storm." Said Sunshine. "We can't afford to have more families like us, can we?" she said, repeating what Storm had just said.

Storm pretended not to have heard, and walked towards the forest again, motioning for Wendy to follow. "Where are we going?" Sunshine asked. "We're building a house on the edge of the forest. It won't take too long. Just a tiny little hole. We'll be quick, then plan out how to get to the school without anyone finding us. Then it's going to be night, and we'll go to the school over the hills. If we come back safely-" "Of course we will." Said Sunshine. "-then we'll build holes for the kids we rescued to live in." "That should keep us fairly busy." Said Sunshine. "This would be the perfect spot for a couple holes." Storm said, suddenly stopping. He began to dig, and with Wendy helping, the hole was finished in only thirty minutes.

They then began to plan, thinking about how they would rescue the kids. They argued until it was late enough that all the foxes would be fast asleep. They ran out, still unsure of what to do, and stood in front of a huge wall made of bushes. Storm peeked in and saw a few foxes holding guns that were as big as themselves and told Sunshine how serious the situation was. Sunshine sighed and said "They're awake, right?" "I... I'm not sure." Replied Storm. "Look again. Are you really sure that they are awake?" "Um... Some of them are." Is there anyone awake near us?" "No."

"Take one of their guns, and shoot it in the air after you find a good hiding spot nearby for us. Oh, like that bush!" "Right. You get in there first. I'll take the gun from the guy's hand, then run to the bush, just in case the guy wakes up when I take the gun. He'll still only find me." Storm replied as he pulled the gun out from under the bush wall. He crept to the bush, then pulled the trigger after a couple tries. "Stay here!" Sunshine cried in a whisper as she took the gun, sprinted behind dozens of bushes that looked like they could barely hide a squirrel. She then ducked behind a tree as dozens of armed foxes came out, shooting their guns everywhere. They missed both her and Storm by half an inch, making them shudder.

Then, when they began to move forwards, Sunshine sprinted to the bush, used the back end of the gun and her teeth to rip open the bushes, and grabbed the closest three cubs. She covered their mouths, and motioned for Storm to run with her, this time to their newly created home on the edge of the forest. When they were absolutely sure it was just them and the children, Sunshine took her paws off their mouths and told them not to be scared. She told them what they were doing, and they soon calmed down, though still slightly apprehensive. Storm caught a few rabbits, gave the cubs a bit, and at last asked them if they knew any of their kids. They told them they'd never heard of any of their names, and asked them where they used to live.

"A bit east to the forest. Opposite side of where we are." Storm said. "They wouldn't go anywhere near here. We might know a few schools that they might be in, though." They said and told them about a few of the schools near their house. Wendy and Liam nodded, and told them they would be gone every night, and that they had to stay safely hidden during that time, not going a step outside their holes. The children nodded, and they went to sleep looking at the full moon. More children joined every day.

Meanwhile, Wendy and Liam were outside, trying to see what they could do. They had managed to print anything that could help that they'd handed out to people on the streets, but they weren't sure it was really working. Everyone seemed to want to turn away from the cold, hard, truth, and make everything normal. They walked to the town square, and saw someone giving a speech. It seemed to be a speech about war. They started to listen.

"We must fight. The foxes are taking our most important things. But we will fight. We will try to defend our race against the violence we now face. We must not make the world a place where we must cower in fear of war. Victory is the only way to peace against this outrageous evil." "Is he even in his right mind?" whispered Wendy. "Practically everybody thinks like that. It's how everything looks like, right? We can't do anything about that. Everyone hates the foxes because they broke peace."

"But we invaded first, didn't we?" Wendy said. "Right, because the foxes were becoming aggressive and we had to 'get a head start'? Do you think people know what's really going on? I mean... People believe what they want to believe, don't they?" "So, they only trust those people up on the high platform giving important speeches? Not the people who actually know what's going on?" "Pretty much." Wendy looked at Liam and said "Let's go home." "We don't have to give up!"

Wendy walked back, and quietly started to collect the cardboard boxes around the house and put them together with tape. She took the cardboard platform and told Liam to follow her. Liam understood what she was doing and smiled. Wendy ran all the way to the middle of the town and stood up on the pile of cardboard boxes. Some people stared at her.

"...The foxes will take all from us. Our dignity, our peace, they will ruin our lives. We need more fighters, more people to join us in our fight for peace." "Peace?" Wendy said, slightly louder than usual. "Is war ever for the sake of peace, is hatred something that can be justified by calling it a struggle for liberty? If we do that, how different are we from our enemies?" Someone started to video her with a phone.

"There are people like us everywhere. Not entirely without faults, but still yearning peace. That includes the kingdom of foxes. We can't consider everyone who we fight against evil. We need to stop; we need to ask for peace instead of fighting in the name of peace. Someone has to realize why this is wrong, why it's so important that we know just how much power we have. If you believe we can stop this, we can. We don't need to rule others, and we don't need to be dominated either. Let's show how truly mighty we are by asking for peace!" Wendy said, not entirely sure of what she was really saying.

She just took the box with her and walked back, trying not to listen to the man begging for war. She tried not to listen to the people that laughed, the people pointing, the people saying she was wrong. She walked back with Liam, and they didn't say anything for the rest of the day.

They just despaired, realizing that the world would never truly understand them. They didn't sleep a wink, and they spent the night up reading, trying to absorb themselves in an entirely different world. They were desperate to escape the world they were in, just like everyone else. What could they do for their children, what could they do for anyone if they were just like everybody else? Were they, after all, nothing at all? Helping as much as the people encouraging them to fight? Unrealistically optimistic?

The next day, Wendy turned on her phone and tried to search up some calming music to get her mind off of everything that had just happened. Suddenly, she froze. "Liam, look." "At what?" "Trending videos." "What's the next reason we've got to go to war?" "No, not that." She showed him her phone. "You... You're kidding me! We didn't even take any videos..." Liam said in almost a scream. "Someone else must have! Yesterday, the speech, We're all over the internet!" Wendy said. "I think we did it." Liam said, looking from the screen to Wendy in disbelief.

Meanwhile, Ben was still struggling to cut down the tree. He had waited until it shrunk, sharpened a rock, then had attempted to cut the roots. It simply curled up, as if it were protecting something precious. Ben hacked at the roots, kicked the tree, tried to cut it down, but not even a dent was made. He felt a sudden surge of guilt as he thrust the rock-knife into the tree's roots and trembled.

He had to choose between evil and evil, and he was devastated. Whether he chose to do nothing, or whether he chose to do something, it could to something horrible to the world. He plunged the knife into the tree as if it were pudding, but when he pulled it back, it was just the same. Was this perhaps a message, a message for him to stop? He stopped for a moment and looked around. He heard something buzzing, something splashing, though he wasn't entirely sure what it was. He thought that it might have been the tree for a moment, but the tree never made sounds like that. The sound irritated him, and sounded familiar, in a way.

Ben looked towards the ocean, and saw a boat, coming closer. "Ron." He muttered as the boat came to a stop and the passenger, a tall man with a sly expression, stepped out of the boat. He did not seem to notice that Ben was there. In fact, he seemed only vaguely aware that the island was there, or that he was there himself. His eyes were glued on the tree, and the tree seemed to be the only thing he sought, even in its shrunken and somewhat miserable state. When Ron came closer, he seemed to notice Ben, beside the tree, with the stone knife in his bloody hands and said in a sort of a whisper "I thought I'd warned you."

"About not doing anything?" Ben said, in an oddly calm voice. "I have told you I am watching." "And yet not stopping me?" "Oh, but what have you done that could harm me, or even the tree?" "Is it invincible?" "Yes." "I was able to use it." Ben said. When Ron heard this, he gave Ben a slightly perplexed look and said "In what manner? You had irritated the tree, obviously, but perhaps you were too foolish to realize that it benefited me, and me only." "I gave the tree water." "And it did nothing." Ron said. Ben was puzzled. He knew quite well that the tree had helped him somewhat when he gave it water. Was Ron unable to understand this? Ben forced a smile.

"Indeed, Ben, your presence has benefitted me in many ways. You were useful, and foolish. You showed me that you cannot be trusted and that you wish to betray me-" "What if I never trusted you?" "Oh, you trusted me. You followed me to ensure your safety, and when it seemed hard to trust my power, you switched to someone else." "Perhaps better than who I originally followed?" Ron scoffed.

"You are no longer useful to me. Perhaps, after my triumph, I could have kept you if you were trustworthy enough, but you proved you do not deserve mercy. However, if you show you will serve me now that the tide has turned, you may be spared from the fate others meet." "Others?" "People who, well, choose someone besides me. People like-" Vroom! The loud roar of a boat engine made it impossible to hear the last bit of Ron's sentence.

A few foxes got off the boat and faced Ron. They said "Vile humans." Not even bothering to lower their voice and was surprised when Ron seemed to understand fox. Ron then said in fox "What have you come for?" "The tree. Give us our rightful property, if you don't want to hurt yourself." The foxes answered. "Rightful property?" "It was once the kingdom's," they said. "Yes, and they abandoned it. You do not know of its powers. Leave it alone, or you'll be the ones getting hurt." "Ha! We can use both guns and magic. You are unarmed. Hand over the tree for our king." "Why should I care about your king?" Ron said as he twisted one of the branches. The tree twitched, then began to spew blasts of water. "My ships will be coming soon." Ron continued. "Flee while you can." The soldiers backed away as another boat approached the island. "You choose to stay?" Ron said, like a curious child. The soldiers trembled.

Another boat approached the island, and Ron pointed towards it as he began to count down with his fingers. "Ten, nine, eight, Seven! Six. Five, four, three, two. One." The foxes stayed, trembling. The boat stopped, and a human, along with a few foxes, descended the boat. "What an incredible army you have, John!" Ron said sarcastically. "It's better than you think." John snapped back, glancing at the foxes that were still trembling.

His gaze then rested on Ben, and he looked worried for a second about something. Ben stared into his eyes, blood still trickling from his hands. Ron did not even look remotely surprised at this unexpected event, and smiled. John then rushed towards the tree stumbling over a few roots. "More thieves!" Ron exclaimed. "But only one can own the tree." He said in a whisper as John stroked the roots of the tree.

Moments later, a few scruffy kids, almost unrecognizable because of the mud all over them, crawled out of the ground. They instantly recognized John. "How..." John said, in the children's language. "Roots!" they said in unison. John started to laugh. "You did all of it? The stars, the waves, the computer..." "The computer?" They said, looking puzzled. "I thought you said roots."

Ron glared at John for a second, but John didn't step back. Ben still looked simply stunned, and he inched away from the tree. "We never really told you..." The children said. "Was it you, maybe?" Dreamer said to the tree. "It was." Dreamer said after a moment's pause. "Not us, though." John looked at them. "You guys can talk to the tree?" "Yep." "How?"

"This is the language of trees! The tree sent

us a sort of a signal, I guess." "Wow. I had no idea. What happened? Really, I feel like I know nothing at all." "Well, it's a long story." Alex said. "Yeah, a really long story!" Tablo said. "It would take us ages to explain, and we aren't too good at explaining stuff." Sprout added. "But…" John immediately understood what they meant.

He looked at the tree, and noticed it looked different from before. Now that the children were no longer physically a part of it, it had changed into something completely new. It seemed like it had a dangerous, powerful energy in a way, and yet seemed soothing. It was graceful, majestic, and beautiful, however, it seemed slightly pained, in a way too. John wondered what story the tree would tell him. He was bursting with questions, and the tree could possibly have the answers to all of them. He took a deep breath, then asked, "What happened?"

"Everything." John felt something tell him. "I couldn't do much alone, I'm just the equivalent of everybody, and it's easy to use me in any way. Even for the worst things imaginable. It was hard having to do the exact opposite of what I was meant to do. You know, my true purpose. What I am. That's why I asked for help. Then they answered."

"The kids?" John asked. "And you, too. You've done a lot for me too." "What... Are you?" John said. "Everything, I guess. It's hard to say exactly what I am. There's nothing I'm not though." "Is there something you think you are?" "Growth." "Growth?" John was confused. "Yeah." "Was it you that sent the messages on the computer?" "Some. Not just me though." "What?" "Someone was trying to help you besides the kids, obviously." "Who?"

The tree seemed to think John knew very

536

well. His mind was still trying to comprehend all this new information, but his heart gave him the answer. He then asked "The kids… What happened?" "They came here because they knew how to communicate with me. They were trapped, but they realized they could communicate with me and asked me to do some things. They seemed to want to tell somebody something dearly. They're amazing. They've been talking about some plan, perhaps how to get you here."

"Don't you know everything?" "Perhaps I do, but maybe I know nothing. I'm just everything. Every word you say, everything you see, it's just all me." "This is hard to understand." "Well, it always is." "Maybe you could tell me something I want to know though." "Tell me."

"I want to know what my true purpose is. I don't know what I am. I don't know what I'm meant for. Everyone knows what they are though.

Why can't I know?" "I think you know what you are. Sometimes I feel like you're one of the few people who know what they are." "But I'm just unknown. There isn't anything like me."

"Exactly. You're like a variable. Question marks. You're new, weird, and you're the question people keep asking to realize something they don't know yet. You're special, because you're unknown. That's what you are. That's your limit, and that's your purpose. That's everything you were meant to be. Everything." "But now what can I do? The war, the foxes, the virus, Agatha, everything that's become all messed up. I can't do that." John said desperately, looking around.

"Not alone. Everyone's changing the world, without knowing it. It doesn't have to be just you facing the harder things." "Well, then... What do you want to do? What are you going to do?" John said. "Me? I want to go back. Return to where I was. I'm going to have to leave again one day, but everyone always has to go back home." "Home?" "Yeah!" "I can take you" John said. "I have a boat, it isn't mine, but you can come on. I've got to return it." The tree didn't seem to see why they had to get on John's boat. "It's all right." The tree said. "*You* can come on."

This time. The tree said as it became a majestic boat, and Ron looked seriously alarmed now. Ben seemed to shake slightly, and the children were gaping, their mouths wide open. John was the only one who really understood, and he didn't expect anything the tree did could possibly surprise him. He grinned and helped the children on the boat as he walked on. The children said "This is the coolest thing ever." In unison, then giggled.

John looked at Ben, who avoided his gaze.

"I'm sorry." Ben said. "I didn't have much of a choice, but I didn't want to wait." He added as he inched away from John, who was knee-deep in water. "Yeah." John said, pulling Ben in so that he was standing in the point that divided the sea and shore. "I don't know your whole story, just like you don't know mine. That's another thing we're going to have to do. We'll have to do lots together, and you're going to have to work pretty hard." "I... But I can't. People like- people like you can work miracles, but I'll just get in your way. Just like I did this time. I don't know how to make the right choice. I can't do this." Ben said. "You're so selfish." John said.

"Just because you messed up once, you're going to quit? You don't want to undo what you've done? You can't be scared. We'll do this together, and we'll make it work. I know you were trying to help." "I... I don't deserve to-" "To give up." John finished. "But you know what I did.

I don't deserve to use that boat. You have to realize I'll just be an obstacle, in your way, and you-" "Who made me come here? What would have happened if I didn't know? Redemption Island would have meant nothing to me if-"

"If it weren't for the fact that I named it that." Snarled Ron. "Do you know why this place is called *Redemption* Island?" John shrugged "Because you should start seeking some now?" Ron didn't laugh, or even smile. "*My* redemption is erasing you," he said. Ron looked at the foxes. "I'll spare your lives if you help me get rid of this." He said pointing at John. "You too, Ben." Ben stepped up and walked towards John. Ron smiled. Ben then faced Ron, and stood between him and John.

"Get on." He whispered to John. "I can take care of the rest." John turned towards the boat, and suddenly, the waves began to rise. The boat was pushed towards the foxes, and a wall made of water stood directly between the boat and Ron. John, who had stepped on to the boat reached out a hand for Ben to grab. "Together," he said.

Ron looked at them and said "Everyone's still under my influence. I can get out of the Island. Nothing matters, and you have not changed anything." John didn't say anything, but merely smiled. "I think we'll manage to do it, together." "Together, with who? Who is really on your side, when you are neither fox nor human? What are you? Who are you?" "Me." John said as the wall of water slowly fell, and they were pushed apart.

They had walked out of Ron's world. "Let's go home!" John said. "Where's your home?" Alex asked. "Right here." John said. "Where you can be the most you is home. Right now, this moment is home." "I thought home was a place?" "Everywhere." John replied. "Welcome home."

Dreamer said, giggling. "Is that where everyone here's going?" "Yeah. We'll try to have everyone find home." "Where's our parents?" Someone said. John couldn't really tell who. Ben silently went to the mast of the boat and John saw multiple images flashing before his eyes.

*

Agatha, gloomily sitting on the boat,

A fox couple, running through the forest carrying children,

and a human couple, standing with many others,

holding up a sign saying peace,

in spite of the gunshots, they could hear in the forest which they were facing.

*

"When everything's still about to hurt us,

where's home?"

"How-how are we going to do this?" The children asked.

"Together." John said, looking determined. "And we will do it. We *will*."

Editor's Words

Saerom Lee

I remember the first time I met Susie.

"There's a student you should meet~!"

When I got married, I moved from Seoul to Busan, and at that time, I was mainly tutoring writing for students in Busan. One of the parents suggested that I meet an 8-year-old girl who came to Korea for a short time during the school holidays. Since she moved to Canada when she was 3 years old, she didn't have a chance to learn Korean systematically, but her linguistic sense was so good that she taught herself both Korean and English. The parents, whose best friend was Susie's mother, thought the synergy effect would be awesome if I met her, so she arranged a meeting as a special event.

Then I opened the door, my eyes met Susie, who was thinner and smaller than I expected. She was dressed in a chic black leather jacket. We stared at each other as if we were exploring each other, introduced ourselves somewhat awkwardly, and began to chat. "I want to write a novel," she said. I asked her if she had anything in mind. She said she had a verse in mind. 'A suspicious employee, John.'

A suspicious employee, John?

"Where does the suspicious employee John work?"

"At a hotel."

"At a hotel?"

"Yes, at the Fox Hotel"

"Why the Fox Hotel?"

Susie answered a barrage of questions, taking a break to let her imagination run wild, calmly drawing up a story on the spot. The more I immersed myself in the story, the harder it was for me to believe that such a vast world could be hidden in such a cute fairy-like body. I asked and asked, and I listened and listened.... The bright window had suddenly become dark, and Susie, who had been sitting a little wary, was walking up and down the room.

More than three hours passed in a flash, and to my surprise, the main plot of the story was all decided on the first day, except for the conclusion! Can you imagine how excited we were? It was as if the story had flowed between the two of us, rushing in waves. I just knocked, but this story flooded through the crack in the door!

Before she met me, she had only written once. And that one experience was so desperate that she had nearly decided to end her writing career forever. I almost laughed, but Susie was quite serious. "What was it?" She said that her school gave her homework to write a one-page fairy tale. Susie wrote five pages. She didn't get the good reviews she was expecting, and her teacher told her it wasn't the right style. There should have been a dragon or a prince or a princess, but Susie's novel had a huge black hole.

Beyond that lay a different world, and it was the story of the protagonist returning home after fighting villains for a weekend. In real life, no one knows the protagonist's secret. When Susie asked if she would write again, her teacher said she didn't need to, which made young Susie want to give up writing for the rest of her life. Then she met me.

After a few encounters in Busan, Susie returned to Cranbrook, Canada, and our creative work continued. Communication was less natural than when we talked through direct eye contact, but whether the connection was good or bad, we kept in touch with each other through FaceTalk to complete the novel. At first, Susie would hold a pencil and write crooked words in her clumsy handwriting, and Susie's parents would take a picture and send it to me. I deciphered and typed Susie's elaborate lines every week, and told her my impressions. When she got stuck, she wrote and erased endlessly, arguing fiercely with me. There were times when she wanted to hang up the phone and write immediately, but there were also times when she wept and wailed, and didn't even want to look at her writing.

Sometimes I coaxed her to write it down, and sometimes she just took a break for a while.

Even though she lived in Canada, she loved to read, so I made her read a lot of classic Korean novels and classic essays instead of writing. Once Susie learned how to use Word programs with the Eagle Stroke, my job became much easier. As the world sank into the virus crisis, we became more immersed in the story and found our own solace in it.

The most dizzying moment for me was when Susie became a bit older and was no longer interested in novels. She wanted to know what was going on in the real world, and was more interested in politics and history. Once, her imagination was so full that she would have a lot to say about it day after day, and then she hardly ever wanted to talk about it anymore. No matter how hard I tried, she couldn't find anything to write about. I regretted that I hadn't pushed her to finish the novel. Childhood is too short!

In addition, Susie, an intermediate elementary school student, was ready to read every book in the world, and now her standards were so high that she was hardly satisfied with reading classics. Her second-grade novel seemed far too childish and uninteresting. Sometimes, she didn't like anything she wrote, so she wrote it and erased it without any regrets. It was a heart-wrenching moment for me. Finally, after a bitter conversation, we agreed to keep the original.

New ideas came and went in Susie's mind several times, but unfortunately it ended up as something little but an idea and lost its luster because she was concentrating on Fox Hotel. It took a long time for the novel that had already been written in her head for years to come out.

Especially since Susie was working hard in school, the more assignments she had, the less time she had to devote to writing the novel. Still, Susie was writing steadily at 35 lines a week, and in this regard, I have come to have great respect for her on a human-to-human basis.

In the process of sluggishness, there was an opportunity for both of us to make the final spurt, and that was the [2023 Korea Story Contest]. Susie's family had to come to Korea for a while, and those few weeks were just the time to apply for the contest. It was a great time to meet face-to-face, and I wondered how I could use it in a precious way, and it was the perfect opportunity for Susie. A 70-page manuscript and a 30-page treatment were required. For the original 70 pages, I decided to translate what Susie had already written in English, and Susie were to write planning intentions, character introductions, and 30 pages of Korean treatments, for three weeks. As she came to Korea after a long time, she was busy going to math school, hanging around with friends and relatives in Korea. Even though she was very busy, Susie always took time to write every night. Next to her parents who were sleeping soundly, Susie sat motionless for hours, concentrating on completing the treatment in Korean.

Writing a long essay with a deadline, and even then, writing it in a language other than the one you're most comfortable with (of course, thanks to her parents' concern and her own efforts, Susie was able to speak and read Korean as if she grew up in Korea) is not an easy task even for adults. Susie endured all the pressure alone. In particular, a few days before the deadline, Susie experienced a surge of dopamine, serotonin, and norepinephrine, a real sense of immersion, and she was amazed. Based on the completed treatment, she was able to return to Canada and comfortably complete the novel in about four years.

It wasn't a contest for elementary school students, and we didn't have high expectations, but out of more than 2,000 adult entrants who said they could write well, Susie made it to the top 12 percent and made it through the preliminary round. This was more exciting for me and Susie's mother than for Susie. I was so emotionally attached to Susie that I might not be able to look at the article objectively, but the result can be an objective indicator to some extent. And now the pressure has shifted to me. With the promise that her first book set to publish with me, could I be able to connect this gemstone to the right readers? With such worries, I took more than half a year to revise and translate the article that Susie had already completed.

It was too wordy, but there was so much to this story that I wanted to share the behind story with anyone who was interested in reading it. It may not be formally sophisticated, but it may be more meaningful because it is the first time in her life that she has been able to listen to her inner voices with the direction the writing wants to go, even though she never learned it from anyone. It contains the process of a child's growth and raw worries, and I feel like there are more people waiting in the world to sympathize with it.

The protagonist, John, who is closer to a human than a fox in the world of foxes, and who is closer to fox than a human in the human world, may represent the confusing identity of Susie, who has moved to Canada and lives as a Korean, and who sometimes feels more like a Canadian when she comes to Korea. Not only does she explore the essence of what life is, but she also reflects on the uncomfortable position of human beings, which can be a stain on nature. It was perhaps a shock to me that it delved into the sentiment of a point where even adults who have lived for a long time and are somewhat tired of living in the world can truly relate to it, rather than just a bright conclusion that is considered childish. One day, Susie looked me in the eye and said, "Your eyes are very antique. It's like a very old soul." It was a strange consolation, but maybe Susie is a being with an older, more mature soul.

Have you ever felt hopeless in your life, as if God had turned away from our creation? Could it be that God made us "wrong"? Isn't it just a 'blot'? And one day, out of nowhere, the God who created us will appear and say that he has been wrongly buttoned from the beginning, and that he will get rid of you. Although we have never spoken about it, Susie is able to bring out the vague fear that existed somewhere deep in our heart. And in that situation, Susie is coming up with a solution that is unapologetic. Regardless of the beginning, we are searching for meaning in the process itself, oscillating between the qualities of the protagonist and the villain in the midst of various complex entanglements, and embodying something "together." Life is just "everything" that exists, and it makes no sense to exclude something that is defined as "evil" from "everything." We are part of that "everything," and even though we feel exhausted and isolated at times, we are able to somehow recognize each other, see a little hope, and do what we can, little by little.

In the meantime, Susie moved to middle school and moved from Cranbrook to Vancouver. Now she is writing a new novel that is more profound and aesthetic. I always wonder what kind of story will unfold, and now I want to share this feeling with other readers. I would like to thank the readers who took the precious time to be with us until the end. I sincerely hope that the seeds of life that Susie sprouted will sprout also in your heart, and that you will always be connected to them in any desperate and lonely situation. "We will make it 'together'."

serenabooks@naver.com